SPARKS FLY IN FEATHERWOOD FALLS

FEATHERWOOD FALLS SERIES

HEATHER REYBURN

For my Readers
Without you, my books would not exist. Thank you for
reading them.

1

*A*shleigh Paton's glance rose from the shimmering, heat-soaked bitumen to the cloudless blue sky above, and she sent silent thanks to the pimple-faced mechanic who, two days earlier, had repaired the air conditioning in her aging car.

As she sped down the hill leading to the tiny town of Featherwood Falls, the butterflies in her stomach somersaulted wildly. Was it anticipation? Or terror? Had she made the right decision? Three months ago, teaching in a country school had not featured on her agenda. Much easier to remain in the exclusive city faculty where the children were from supportive families, the class numbers small, and the pupils under her guidance were all the same age. If it hadn't been for that hoity-toity new principal hauling her over the coals in front of the entire staff, she might not have lost her temper and stormed out, spitting her venom—and resignation—at the woman as she stomped past. Okay, she probably shouldn't have used the principal's niece as an example of a bully. But ... how was she to know they were related? Ashleigh's only regret in resigning was leaving her class in the hands of another teacher three weeks before the Christmas holidays.

Too late now. I'm here.

Lost in thought, she failed to notice the kangaroo bound from the bush until the last second. Wrenching the wheel with a jerk, she swerved, narrowly missing an oncoming four-wheel-drive utility as her car slid into the grassy table drain. She switched the ignition off, thankful that at least she hadn't hit the animal, and watched it leap away.

Peering into the rear-vision mirror, surprise replaced her relief. The opposing vehicle had stopped, and the driver's door was partially open.

'Darn. I hope it's not a cop. Suppose I'd better apologise,' she muttered to herself and climbed out before closing the door firmly behind her. Turning, she jumped with shock and pressed her back against her car. The thunderous face of the ute driver stood a bare metre away.

'What the bloody hell were you thinking? Don't you know you should never swerve for wildlife—especially when there's oncoming traffic? You could have killed us both!' he ranted.

Ashleigh's initial thoughts of saying sorry vanished in an instant as she met his flashing green eyes. The dark beard and surprisingly good-looking face failed to hide a mutinous glare. Drawing her five-foot-nothing frame to its fullest, she shouted back, feeling her cheeks burn and not only from the hot afternoon sun. 'What ... and hit that creature? It was the size of my car.'

'Don't exaggerate. It was a male eastern grey, and you wouldn't have hit it,' he snapped. 'If you'd kept your speed down, it would have either turned away or got out of your path.' He pointed to the road sign behind her. 'Can't you read? This is a sixty zone, and you were doing at least ninety.'

She stiffened. 'Don't yell at me!'

'I'm not yelling at you. I'm pointing out the need for you to be wildlife aware.'

'I am ...' she began before reconsidering and closing her mouth. It had been a while since she'd checked her speed and she hadn't even noticed the sign.

Meeting his eyes in a frozen stare, she tipped her chin, clamping her lips tightly, silently daring him to continue his tirade.

His jaw moved as though he was about to say more, but instead, he ducked his head. 'Right. Well ... if you're going to be travelling around this area, I suggest you take notice of your surroundings. There's a lot of bush and good farmland—a haven for wildlife.' Then he gave the slightest nod, turned on his heel, and strode to his vehicle.

Her gaze followed the stiff, broad back and the ragged brown curls touching the collar of his khaki shirt. A tree graphic decorated the driver's door with print beneath it. Ashleigh squinted at the writing, able only to make out the word *Forestry* before the vehicle drove away.

Sliding into her little car, she glanced down, astonished her hand was quivering on the steering wheel. She huffed out an annoyed breath.

So much for my resolution to control my temper. Not exactly a good start.

Her shoulders slumped for a moment before she switched on the ignition. Arching a brow, she swung her gaze around her surroundings, absorbing the peaceful, seemingly lifeless scenery. The rugged, tanned face of the only person she had met flashed through her mind.

At least there's one person out here—even if I didn't get his name.

AFTER THUMPING the vehicle into reverse, she shot backwards onto the bitumen. Then, squaring her shoulders, she changed gear and calmly continued into town.

A quaint general store greeted her, its archaic fuel bowser perched on the road edge of the footpath a bare two metres from the bullnose roof of the shop's veranda. She slowed, studying the pretty building. An ancient blue heeler dog lay sprawled across the doormat and to the casual observer the animal may have appeared dead—but Ashleigh presumed if that was the case, someone would have removed it.

Opposite the store, tennis courts and a freshly painted pavilion filled the space between two small paddocks—one containing a few cows and the other, long grass with heavy golden seed heads drooping in the breeze. She wrinkled her nose. *Cows in the middle of town?*

As she lowered her speed to a crawl, her gaze shifted to the police sign outside the cream-painted building beside the empty paddock, a clearly marked police vehicle squatting in the driveway. *Another sign of life.* Shady trees stood tall on either side of the road and pots of petunias decorated the footpath outside the tumble-down pub that crept into view.

A sign indicating children crossing was planted firmly in the grass verge opposite the pub. At the further promise of life, she blew out a relieved breath, her hopes rising. She braked abruptly and turned onto a wide bitumen strip running parallel with the road before parking in front of the sturdy chain-wire fence. Sitting for a moment, she gazed at the house in the corner of the school grounds before scanning the area for a second dwelling—the one she would call home. There was no sign of a cottage. Only a white steel-clad shed at the rear of the field.

Her stomach plummeted once again.

What on earth have I done?

2

_D_amian Cartwright plodded through the forest, marking the trees to be logged the following week. It wasn't the most rewarding job he'd ever had, but it provided a good income and he could return home each night to be with Charlie and Dot. The best part was not having to talk to people all day. His team met every Monday, put plans in place and, unless a large plantation or logging job was in full swing, he mostly acted alone.

As he worked, a vision of a fiery redhead flashed through his mind. The woman he had berated earlier. He chuckled quietly to himself. She'd looked young—early twenties, he estimated, and from the appearance of her upmarket dress and flimsy sandals, she wasn't a local girl. Not that he was an expert, but the women he'd met since he'd been in Featherwood Falls—young mums he'd run into at the store, and the lady who helped Ned in the pub—lived in jeans and sneakers or boots.

Probably not a good idea to have been so terse—not that it seemed to have upset her. He chuckled again as he recalled their conversation. She hadn't hesitated in firing back at him, and he admired strong women. *I wonder if she stopped in Featherwood Falls. Nah—probably on the wrong road, given a bum steer by one of those stupid GPS things that don't factor dirt roads or closed bridges into their directions.*

As he tied the fluorescent pink tape around the rough pine bark, he dragged his mind away from the event and mentally ticked off his recent purchases. Yesterday's trip to Stanthorpe had equipped Charlie with uniforms, shoes, a backpack, and the books and pencils from the list handed to him at the end of the previous year by Emma, the quiet and efficient teacher's aide. An ache caught in his chest as he worked. It had never been his intention to keep Charlie so isolated, but they'd moved in with Damian's great-aunt, Dot Collins, after she'd had a fall only weeks before COVID-19 had hit Australia. Somehow, the simple, peaceful life Dot led had helped him heal while aiding Charlie's growth into becoming an interested and contented little boy. The only problem was, their lifestyle had become habit, and even after state borders had opened and social mixing was permitted once again, Charlie rarely saw other children. Damian had been busy with his work, and Dot had not been off her bush-clad farm in decades.

'I'm sorry, little mate. Have I been selfish?' he breathed as Charlie's face hovered in his mind. How would he cope with school? Would the other children accept his funny ways? His behaviour was good, and he was as bright as a button, but he'd never watched television or played on a computer—or done any of the new-age things most kids did these days. He had no cousins to play with and no close neighbours except grumpy old Bob, who lived on the farm next door and was almost as old as Dot's ninety-three years.

Bob disliked children and wasn't afraid to show it. Consequently, Charlie was content to keep well away when the old man dropped off the occasional box of groceries and newspapers and sat with Dot for half an hour, drinking coffee and whinging about the world. Damian wasn't sure how the man kept driving his rusty old Toyota and wouldn't be surprised if Bob ran the ute off the cliff edge while negotiating the track up to his shack.

While Damian reflected on Charlie—his knowledge of birds, insects, and other creatures that frequented their home, in addition to his love of books and jigsaw puzzles—he hoped those attributes would be enough for his son to cope with his first weeks of school life.

Most of all, he prayed the teacher and other staff understood Charlie—and that Charlie never had to go through what Damien had endured twenty-five years earlier. His own parents had spent most of his childhood overseas where his father's diplomatic status and the social life it afforded them were apparently not suited to a child, especially an only child. Then they had been killed in an air crash and those long terms in the strict, city boarding school had been hell for an introverted boy from the bush. His only remembered joy was staying with Dot and her husband, Thomas, here in Featherwood Falls.

His mind flashed back to the redhead again, and he snorted. Clearly a city woman, who he doubted would understand life in the country. She'd probably never experienced hardship or loss, either.

At least Charlie wouldn't have to deal with city slickers like that. His teacher was really likeable. Although they hadn't formed a close friendship, Quinn had always been welcoming and chatty when their visits to the pub occasionally coincided. *Yep, Quinn Alderton is a good bloke.*

He finished the last tree, loaded his equipment into the vehicle, and spoke to the cheeky magpie sitting on the bull-bar.

'I reckon Charlie will be okay.'

3

A woman stepped out of a colourful perennial flower bed in front of the standard government-style house Ashleigh presumed to be the principal's residence. The woman's petite figure and floral shirt blended with the foliage and a wide-brimmed hat shaded her face. She lifted an arm and waved at Ashleigh before stripping off her gloves and striding towards her.

Extending her hand, she beamed, flashing a row of straight, white teeth. 'You must be Ashleigh.'

Nodding, Ashleigh gripped the tiny woman's hand before shaking it briefly. 'I am.'

'Joanne Alderton. I'm Quinn's wife.' She waved an arm loosely toward the house. 'This is our place—well, the principal's residence, I mean.' She giggled. 'Come and meet Quinn. He's in the office catching up on paperwork.' Turning toward the school, she beckoned Ashleigh to follow.

Ashleigh trudged along the path toward the old building, a sinking feeling intensifying as the paint-peeled timber boards and iron roof drew closer. The scruffy building bore no resemblance to the neat brick structures of her previous school.

As they approached the wooden steps leading onto a veranda, she paused to glance around. Bursts of colour filled every corner, highlighting the rich green of freshly mowed lawns and further emphasising the shabbiness of the buildings.

'Nice gardens,' she said.

Joanne snatched off her hat and turned her head, stopping abruptly. Ashleigh grabbed the handrail in an attempt not to bump into her.

'Sorry.' Joanne waved a hand vaguely as the smile in her cheery, round face grew even wider. 'I love gardening and we've been working hard throughout these past couple of rather tough years, trying to get the place looking as nice as possible. The students and their families needed hope, and with the restrictions we had to enforce, it was hard on many of them. They're mostly country people and are used to spending a good bit of their day outdoors. Of course, they missed socialising too,' she prattled on. 'So, by keeping our distances and allowing them to help here, we have avoided many of the issues city dwellers experienced—and, of course, we've ended up with this lovely environment.'

Ashleigh met the grey-blue eyes with a small smile. She pointed to the building. 'Who's responsible for painting?'

'That would be the government. As you know, this is a public school, so all maintenance is their responsibility. We're on the list for a repaint soon—we just don't know when.' She laughed, as though the thought was a pipedream. 'Look over there.' She pointed to the white hut-like building in the corner of the school grounds. 'That's your house.'

Ashleigh sucked in a breath, her jaw dropping. When Quinn had phoned the previous week advising the government had delivered her new home, she had envisaged a cottage or one of those smart demountable houses that outback properties often installed when they were unable to attract a builder to an isolated spot. This steel-coated hut, little more than a shipping container with a door and a few windows, was not what she had expected.

'Oh.' Her voice was barely a whisper.

Joanne appeared not to have noticed Ashleigh's dismay as she chatted on. 'It's very cute. Air-conditioned and a nice little bathroom at one end. You'll have all the privacy you want.' She turned back to the building and walked across the veranda, meeting a slight man with a thatch of black curls standing in the doorway.

'Ashleigh! How lovely to meet you.' He grasped her hand and shook it enthusiastically, his piercing blue eyes drilling into hers. 'How was the drive?'

'Okay,' she replied.

'Good, good. Right.' He glanced at his watch before shooting Joanne a smile. 'How about I give Ashleigh a quick tour of the school while you make afternoon tea?' He turned back to Ashleigh. 'I know it's getting late in the day, but I'm sure you're ready for a cuppa. Tea, coffee, or a cold drink?'

She nodded. 'Yes please. Tea would be lovely.' Her stomach growled at the suggestion, reminding her it had been several hours since she had last eaten— except for the chocolate bar and bottle of water she'd consumed while driving.

Self-consciously, she ran a hand over her hip. Unlike her willowy sister, Henrietta—who everyone called Netty—Ashleigh had taken after her mother: short, fair-skinned, and prone to gaining weight at the mere smell of food. She hated that Netty could eat whatever she liked, had straight, blonde hair that required nothing more than a wash and brush, and never had to fetch the stepladder to reach a single thing in the cupboards. Instead, Ashleigh wrestled with her copper-coloured curls, firing up the hair straightener each morning and cursing the time it took to tame her mane. She bemoaned the tempting slices and cakes her sister baked when she was bored—and insisted on sharing—despite Ashleigh's protests.

Observing the slight, effervescent couple in front of her now, a sliver of hope warmed her. Perhaps here, without being exposed to Netty's temptations, she might have a chance to lose those extra kilos that insisted on hanging around. After all, there had to be something positive about living in a backwater.

HALF AN HOUR LATER, Ashleigh raised an eyebrow as she stood inside her new living quarters. *Not as bad as I expected.* The dwelling was small, but well organised with a tiny kitchen, table, and bench seat in the middle, a bedroom with a double bed and wardrobe at one end, and a shower, toilet, and handbasin at the other. Rather like a good-sized caravan or accommodation provided on mine sites, she thought.

She returned to her car to move it next to her little house, her previous observations of village life blurring as two young boys flew past on their bikes, shrieking with delight. Perhaps the absence of people buzzing around was normal in the country. A trickle of satisfaction ran through her. Having anonymity would be a pleasant change. Not that she disliked people. She loved them. But being a politician's daughter had constantly plonked her in the limelight—leaving her feeling watched and criticised. She grimaced. Her own feisty temper probably hadn't helped either.

The evening light was fading, and the warm, pink glow of sunset filtered over the lawn. A young couple strolled past, holding hands, and waved to her. She smiled and waved back.

After unpacking her car, she stowed her clothes in the wardrobe and the groceries she had stopped to buy in Warwick as she came through the town in the cupboard. Most importantly, she carefully placed the container of chocolate brownies Netty had made on the bench's corner. With a pint-sized oven and only two gas rings or a tiny microwave to cook her food, it looked as though Netty's brownies might be the last treat for a while. Her mind flashed to the principal's house where she had enjoyed crackers and cheese with her English Breakfast tea while something fragrant wafted from the oven. Tonight she was expected to dine with Quinn and Joanne, then tomorrow she and Quinn would set up the classrooms and plan the program for the first term. Except for a regular Saturday-night barbeque at the tennis club, to which she was invited, she would be on her own.

The memory of her encounter with the forestry man returned, and she huffed. *Will he be at these barbeques?* She hoped so. After all, she was determined to make this year a success, and the last thing she needed was a random stranger with the wrong impression of her sticking it to her in public.

4

*A*shleigh narrowed her eyes, her organised brain working overtime. The room was small. The entire school was small. But in its past, many more pupils than the current twenty-nine had managed. The problem was, generations earlier, it had been one large room. Now it was divided into two, with an office and kitchen tacked on either end of the back veranda. The room in which she was to teach the thirteen youngest children had been a library, also used for student support. Bookshelves, bean bags, and two small tables with matching chairs filled the space.

'How are you getting on?' Quinn popped his head around the classroom door, and she jumped.

'Okay, thanks. I think we can make this work.'

He nodded enthusiastically and grasped one end of

a bookcase. 'Lucky these are on wheels. I reckon we'll have this sorted in no time.'

They spent the morning arranging the two class-rooms while discussing the curriculum and lesson planning for the term. The corrugated-iron roof crackled overhead as the sun crept higher, and by late morning, Quinn had shut the doors and windows and switched on the newly installed air-conditioning system.

'Isn't it fabulous!' he enthused. 'Not that we need it as much as some places. But hopefully it will keep us all more comfortable during these hot months.'

Ashleigh nodded in agreement despite not finding the day particularly hot compared to the humid heat of Brisbane.

'You'll probably find it chilly here in the winter,' Quinn added, pointing to the bar heaters that ran along each wall. 'In the colder months, we have these running most of the time, so it's quite cosy.' Without waiting for her to answer, he continued, 'Let's have a lunch break now. Emma's coming in this afternoon to meet you so we can go over the daily routine, duties, and we can answer anything else you need to know. Maria, our admin assistant, comes on Tuesdays and Thursdays, so you'll meet her then. Oh, and on a Wednesday, I spend the day in the office while Lyle, a relief teacher, takes my students.'

Ashleigh nodded, picked up her water bottle, and

followed him to the kitchen. 'Thanks, Quinn. Gosh, that's quite a few staff for a small school.'

'Not really. Things have moved on in the last couple of decades, and we have a lot of support. Once the kids are here, you, Emma, and I will take turns on playground and bus duty, and of course when Lyle is here, he helps too.' He studied her for a moment as though contemplating whether he should ask. 'What made you apply for this position?'

What should she say? That she'd overheard her mother discussing an acquaintance's change of heart about accepting the position in a small country school. That Ashleigh's eavesdropping had been a stroke of sheer luck—especially remembering her mother's exclamation of, "I've never heard of Featherwood Falls". Those words had triggered an unexpected desire to escape all she knew and make the change she'd been hankering for. Her spur-of-the-moment application—apparently the only application—had been perfectly timed.

She shrugged and instead, said, 'It's something I've always wanted to do. Move to the country, I mean. And when this came up, I decided the time was right.'

He beamed at her.

Relief washed over Ashleigh. While neither the school or accommodation were what she had been expecting, at least her welcome and inclusion had got off to a good start.

BUTTERFLIES SWIRLED in her stomach as Ashleigh brushed her hands over her hips and waited.

Quinn and Emma stood at the road gate, welcoming children as they jumped off the bus and hurried into the school grounds.

She'd taken an instant liking to Emma—a woman she guessed to be a similar age to Quinn and Joanne—fortyish. She was immaculately dressed in a smart black skirt and a pale blue blouse with the school emblem embossed on it, and her soft, calm voice held a reassurance that put Ashleigh at ease. While discussing duties in their meeting a couple of days earlier, Ashleigh had quickly realised that Emma was much more than the teacher's aide. She was also the first-aider, librarian—and a friend to everyone in town. Ashleigh was yet to meet Maria, but it hadn't taken Ashleigh long to form a picture of the woman from both the school photos on the wall and the occasional comment made by Quinn. Although middle-aged and apparently from a large family, Maria sounded outspoken and controlling, monopolising as much of Quinn's time as she could. Ashleigh prayed her assumptions would be wrong.

A couple of cars arrived, one behind the other, and mothers were dragging backpacks out while children bounced around chatting excitedly, their high-pitched voices carrying in the fresh morning breeze. Crisp, oversized uniforms announced the new students, while bigger siblings guided the little ones through the gate and up the path toward Ashleigh.

'Hello.' Ashleigh welcomed each child as they entered the school building, relieved at their friendly responses.

Two boys dropped their bags at the foot of the stairs and raced straight to the playground, ignoring everyone around them.

For the next half hour, children trickled in, some on bicycles, some on foot, and some dropped off by mud-splattered four-wheeled-drive vehicles. Apparently, the school bus didn't bother about day one of the year. Ashleigh didn't ask why, assuming parents preferred to ensure their children arrived without separation dramas on the first school day of school.

A small child interrupted her assumptions. The child was sobbing as a tall, gangly girl dragged her along by the hand, appearing totally unconcerned. The two of them stopped in front of Ashleigh.

Squatting as the older girl shook off the little hand, Ashleigh nodded a quick hello to the tall girl before she shot up the stairs. The younger girl's face was wet and blotchy, as though this bout of crying wasn't a new thing.

Ashleigh held out her hand. 'Would you like to

come with me, and we'll find somewhere to put your bag? I'm Ms Ashleigh. What's your name?'

The girl hiccupped silently as she fiddled with a long, brown plait that hung over her shoulder. A frazzled-looking mother rushed up, grasping a toddler by the hand and with a baby on one hip, her hair in a similar style to that of the little girl. 'Sorry,' she said. 'We discussed this, and she was fine until we got in the car.'

Ashleigh stood and smiled at the mother reassuringly. 'It's okay and quite normal. I'm Ashleigh Paton, the new junior teacher.'

'Oh. Nice to meet you. I'm Michelle Marsh.' She nodded toward the little girl. 'That's Jessie, my eldest.'

Ashleigh glanced toward the racks along the veranda where the older girl had dumped her bag and was now talking animatedly to a similar-aged student.

'She's not your daughter, then?'

Michelle followed her gaze and laughed. 'No. that's Lucy and her buddy, Kate. Lucy and her family live on the farm next to ours and she promised to help Jessie settle in.' She raised her eyebrows. 'Not sure about that, though.'

'Don't worry. I'll look after her for you.'

Michelle bent and dropped a kiss on her daughter's head. 'Mum's gotta go now and feed the calves. Ms Ashleigh will look after you and I'll see you this afternoon.' Then she turned abruptly, shot Ashleigh an anxious grin, and fled toward the car park.

Ashleigh grasped Jessie's hand before the little girl could dissolve into tears again and smiled at her. 'Come on. Let's go and meet some of the other children.'

Soon after, the bell rang and the clatter of shoes on timber steps mixed with children's voices as they poured inside.

About to close the door behind them, Ashleigh narrowed her eyes at the ute pulling into the car park. Quinn was only a couple of metres away, but she had to raise her voice over the racket. 'I think there's a late arrival.'

Quinn stepped outside and briefly followed her gaze. 'Looks like it. I'll get this lot sorted if you'd like to meet them.'

Ashleigh nodded and hurried toward the gate. Both driver and passenger doors were now open, and her breath hitched at the familiar broad shoulders and khaki shirt. She slowed her stride, incredulity forcing heat up her neck. Putting a hand to her face, she drew a deep breath and focused on the small boy standing beside the vehicle. His shorts and shirt swam on his small, thin body, and the wide-brimmed hat planted firmly on his head shadowed his face.

She reached the gate at the same time as the man, meeting his astonished glare.

'You!' he said.

Her cheeks flushed bright pink as indignation rose. Ignoring him, she glanced down at the boy. 'Hello. I'm Ms Ashleigh. What's your name?'

He lifted his face to meet hers, and she gazed into the deepest blue eyes she'd ever seen.

'I'm Charlie,' he said solemnly.

'Nice to meet you, Charlie. I'm going to be your teacher. Would you like to come with me?'

He turned his face upwards. 'Dad? Come too.'

Ashleigh looked at the man and cleared her throat. 'I'm guessing you're Charlie's father?'

'Damian Cartwright.' He paused, his voice rising with disbelief. 'You're going to teach my son?'

Ashleigh clenched her teeth, forcing a stiff smile to her lips. 'Correct.' Turning abruptly, she began walking toward the school before glancing behind her to check she was being followed.

Damian caught her glance. 'I hope your driving has improved?'

Determined to contain the urge to be churlish, she replied tartly, 'You'll be pleased to hear I haven't been anywhere since my arrival.' Swallowing hard, she swung her gaze from Damian's distractingly attractive face and smiled at the child. It wasn't the boy's fault his father was a pain in the backside.

Damian held his son's hand, his stride slow, in keeping with Charlie's.

Ashleigh marched to the foot of the stairs, desperately trying to regain her concentration while she felt the formidable man's stare burning her back. Perspiration beaded on her forehead.

'Would you like to come with me now, Charlie? We'll put your hat and bag away, and you can say goodbye to your dad. I'm sure you'd like to meet the other children.'

Damian gave Charlie a quick hug and waved as he headed back to the car.

Charlie's lip quivered, and Ashleigh took him by the hand. 'It's okay. We'll have a lovely time.'

By the time they entered her classroom, Emma had most of the children sitting down and relatively quiet. There were five new children in the prep class and only one student had moved on to high school at the end of the previous year—generating the catalyst for the school to become a two-teacher facility as it grew to more than twenty-five pupils. Now, with two new families moving to the district, each with more than one school-aged child, the school was finally growing again after years of having the threat of closure hanging over its head.

The morning flew and Ashleigh was both relieved and surprised when the sound of feet clattering from the room across the hallway announced the lunch break.

Outdoor play followed the enforced sitting-and-eating time and Ashleigh was pleased to see Jessie and Charlie playing happily alongside one another in the sandpit, even if not actually communicating. Although there were three other prep students, all had older siblings and were familiar with school and all it entailed. Two grade-one boys hovered near the sandpit. Ashleigh was distracted for a moment by a child hanging upside down on the climbing equipment.

A heartbreaking cry filled the air, its tones of devastation suggesting murder at the very least.

Ashleigh's attention had been with the upturned child for merely seconds but it was enough time to have missed the drama. She spun around, locating the cry. A group of children surrounded the sandpit.

She ran, almost colliding with two of the older students as they reached the group.

'What's happened?' Ashleigh had to shout above the ruckus.

Charlie tipped his stricken face to her and pointed to an older boy. 'He killed Millie!' Pale with shock, a tear slid down one cheek.

Confused, Ashleigh studied the sand in the box, unable to locate the deceased. 'Who is Millie?'

'My millipede. Diplopoda. I've had her for ages—and now she's dead!'

'How did she die?' Ashleigh frowned at the grade-one boy attempting to hide behind another student.

There was not a sound as the children studied her. 'Did you stand on her?' she asked in a firm, quiet voice.

'They're dangerous. We don't need them,' the child retorted indignantly.

'What's your name?' Ashleigh asked the older boy.

Dropping his head, he muttered, 'Michael.'

Ashleigh turned to Charlie. 'How did you bring Millie to school? And why?'

He pointed to the small jar partially buried in the sand. 'In her house. And they're not dangerous. Sometimes they squeeze out watery stuff if they get frightened—to protect themselves—but that's all. I didn't want her to be lonely while I'm at school. Anyway, Dad told me about "show and tell" and I wanted to show her to everyone when it's my turn.'

Ashleigh's heart squeezed at the little boy's devastation. 'I understand, Charlie.' She drew a deep breath and spoke firmly. 'You can all go back to playing now, except you, Michael, while Charlie and I sort this out.'

The other students drifted away while Ashleigh knelt beside Charlie, and Michael shuffled his feet in the sand.

'Perhaps it's not such a good idea to bring a live creature to school without checking with Mr Alderton or me first.' She hid a grimace. 'Let's scoop Millie up now and pop her back into her jar. You might like to bury her when you get home?'

'I want to go home now,' he cried mutinously.

Ashleigh swung around helplessly before her gaze met Michael's. 'Would you mind fetching Mr Alderton, please?'

Michael sped away without answering while Ashleigh helped shovel the millipede back in the jar with a broken twig.

She took Charlie's hand and pulled him to his feet. 'Come now, I'm sure you'll find another Millie and perhaps when you do, you could make a tiny house for her at home where your mum could mind her. I don't think this Millie enjoyed her school visit.'

Charlie stared at her, his blue eyes glittering pools as tears threatened again. 'I haven't got a mum. She's dead.'

Horror filled Ashleigh at his indignant tone. 'Oh, Charlie, I'm so sorry. I shouldn't have said that.'

He shrugged. 'Now Millie can talk to her in heaven.'

Astonished at the little boy's acceptance, she nodded as Quinn approached with a sheepish Michael trailing behind him.

'What's the matter?' he asked kindly as he squatted down in front of Charlie. 'You're Charlie Cartwright, aren't you? I'm sorry we didn't get to talk when you arrived this morning. What's the problem?'

Charlie stared at him before lowering his eyes to the jar in his hand. 'He squashed my Millie and killed her. He shouldn't have done that. She wasn't hurting anyone.'

Quinn looked up at Ashleigh, quiet sympathy stilling his usually animated face. 'I understand, Charlie. It wasn't right—or a kind thing that Michael did. It's important that we're kind, not just to each other, but to all creatures, too. Thank you for reminding me —and Michael.' He stood again and reached for Charlie's hand. 'Apologise to Charlie please, Michael.'

Michael scuffed his shiny black shoes on the concrete edge of the sandpit and mumbled, 'I'm sorry, Charlie.'

'Right. It's time to go back inside now,' Quinn said firmly. 'Ring the bell please, Michael.'

The little boy walked beside Quinn in silence, and Ashleigh followed helplessly. *Not exactly a good start for me.*

Her mind flashed to the child's father. Charlie may not have a mother, but someone had taught that little boy about love and kindness. She would remember that.

5

*D*amian had to wait until they were almost home before Charlie finally poured his heart out about Millie's death. He had been solemn, silent, and although he answered Damian's questions politely—*Did you have a good day? Yes. Did you make any friends? Yes. What were their names? Jessie. Any other friends. No, just Jessie. Did you eat your lunch? Yes*—there was none of the excitement in his voice that usually followed an outing or a change in his life. Damian had known it would come, though—in Charlie's own time. Nothing would make the child talk before he was ready.

Charlie had only been eight months old when Laura died, and although Damian had done every-thing a parent could do in the circumstances, he battled with his own grief constantly. Eighteen months later, his Aunt Dot had a fall and her neighbour had telephoned him, being her only living relative. After reassuring Damian Dot was not badly injured, Bob had admitted she refused to accept his or anyone else's help. Damian had thought about the situation for mere seconds before agreeing to come and sort things out. With his own sick and long-service leave rapidly running out, and his exasperated boss resenting Damian's juggle of day-care drop-offs and pickups, Damian had handed in his resignation. His plan had been that once Dot recovered her independence, he would decide on his next move. He'd packed enough to get himself and toddler Charlie through a few weeks to begin with, locked his townhouse, and headed west to the depths of Queensland's granite country—where pockets of rich farming land mingled with thousands of hectares of native bush. A month had turned into two as he nursed his aging aunt. He and Dot had never really discussed him staying indefinitely but were both surprised by their natural connections as family. Years of spending his childhood school holidays on the farm with Dot and her late husband had generated a whole lot of instinctive love and intuition between him and the old woman. So Damian and Charlie had stayed.

'Can we bury her next to Fluffy?'

Damian glanced at his son with raised eyebrows.

'Who?' He chided himself for letting his thoughts drift when, clearly, Charlie's focus remained on Millie. 'Oh sorry, you mean your millipede.'

'Of course.' Charlie's puzzled expression drove a pang of love straight through Damian's heart.

'Sure. She won't need a huge grave, and I'm sure Fluffy will look after her.' Fluffy had been Charlie's pet silkie bantam and had died weeks earlier. The hint of a smile touched Damian's lips. He wouldn't remind Charlie that insects and creatures that inhabited the soil had provided much of a chicken's diet. Much better to picture her soft, feathery wing over the top of the tiny millipede.

The ute bounced through the rocky waterway as they climbed higher into the hills. Dot's property suited her reclusive lifestyle. It encompassed several hundred hectares—mostly native bush interspersed with grazing land for her herd of cattle, which provided her with the little income she needed to make ends meet. She had refused to register with Centrelink, so received no pension or help from anyone—except Damian and her slightly less reclusive neighbour, Bob. The dwelling would not have passed a building inspection, and it was only that she had been there so long that the local council turned a blind eye. However, for Dot, Damian, and Charlie, it was home.

There was no electricity, and a gas fridge and large

pantry lined with slabs of granite kept most items cool year-round. A wood stove provided a source for both home-cooked meals and heating in the cold winters that settled over the area from April until October. A composting toilet that had cost Damian a good chunk of his wages had recently replaced the previously oper-ated earth-pit one. With creeks running in several places throughout the property, water had never been a problem, even in drought. They now even had a primitive but effective shower with its own gas water heater, so lugging buckets from the tap outside to fill the ancient fire-generated "donkey" tank was a thing of the past.

When he and Charlie had arrived, books lined every available wall in the one-room cottage. With Dot's encouragement, Damian had built a shelving unit that divided the dwelling into two rooms—one as a bedroom for Damian and Charlie to share, and the other the living and kitchen area with Dot's narrow bed pushed against the wall. A small but beautifully hand-constructed kitchen dresser held all the crockery and utensils they required. The square table, chest of drawers for Dot's personal items, and three mis-matched chairs completed the living room furniture. When the COVID-19 limitations had lifted on travel-ling, Damian had picked up a second-hand bureau that served as storage for his and Charlie's clothes on one of his occasional forays into town.

Damian eased the ute into the shed beside the house and stepped onto the dirt floor before helping Charlie with his bag and pile of colouring- thin that had apparently filled his first day of school.

'Hello!' Dot's battered cloth hat rose from behind the wire enclosure surrounding the vegetable garden. With feral cats, possums, and bandicoots in abundance, growing fresh vegetables was no mean feat, and one of Damian's first jobs had been securing the rickety structure and replacing the wire netting that had served Dot for the previous thirty years. The chicken coop had also required heavy fortification to protect their precious flock from foxes and quolls.

The old woman strode toward them, oddly dressed in a pair of men's trousers and shirt that came to her knees with a thick, full-sized butcher's apron over the top of everything. A black and white border collie bounded past her and raced to Charlie before sitting and whining quietly as if to say, *Please pat me?*

Charlie bent over the dog and squeezed it in his arms, rubbing his face in the dog's coat. 'I'm home, Lass.'

After waiting for Charlie to release the dog, Dot handed the basket of freshly cut vegetables to Damian and reached out to hug Charlie. Her gnarled hands were striped with raised, blue veins, red scratches, and calluses.

The little boy wrapped his arms around the frail

woman and squeezed her before turning toward the house.

'Come and tell me all about it,' she said. Under the shelter of the back veranda, they removed their boots and hats, and the dog slumped in a heap on the floorboards. Dot ran a hand over the wisps of white hair that had escaped the bun at the nape of her neck.

Inside, Damian filled the kettle and placed it on the hob before opening the firebox and poking the timber within.

'I've made a cake to celebrate your big day,' Dot said. She removed the muslin cloth from the top of a chocolate cake, and Charlie beamed at her.

A familiar warmth ran through Damian's veins as his gaze rested on the two people he loved most. While the cottage bore no resemblance to the immaculate townhouse where Charlie had spent his first couple of years, it was filled with a love and happiness that, even now, brought a lump to Damian's throat.

'Dotty. We have to have another funeral,' Charlie announced.

'Oh?' She had nestled into the hard-backed chair with a threadbare cushion under her. Her forehead wrinkled with concern.

'Yes. I took Millie to school so she wouldn't miss me, and I was giving her some exercise and fresh air in the sandpit.' He paused and took a large bite out of the piece of cake Damian had handed him, chewing for a moment before resting it back on the plate.

'What happened?' Dot prompted.

'A horrible boy stomped on her and ... well, she couldn't move anymore.' His voice quavered slightly.

'Oh, dear. That wasn't very kind, was it?'

'No. So Ms Ashleigh had a talk to us all about being kind and, do you know what?' He waited for a moment, ensuring he had the full attention of his audience. 'She gave us all a present.'

'That's nice. What was it?' Dot asked.

Charlie slipped off his chair and hurried to his bag before extracting a sheet of paper with a small, plastic package stapled to the bottom. Inside the wrap was a tiny, padded heart, made of felt and stitched neatly by hand around the edges. Dot cast her eye over the written message and nodded softly before passing it to Damian.

He swiftly read the personal introduction from Ms Ashleigh. *On your desk is a love heart that you can put in your pocket or your bag to remind you that you are never alone in this class. I have also made you a bookmark to use when you are reading at home or at school. I hope you are as excited for the year ahead as I am. Going into the new year, remember to* **always treat people with kindness!**

Damian stared at the last five bolded words for a few moments.

Really? This! From that fiery redhead? It didn't seem possible. Although ... from the way Charlie had described her handling of Millie's death, perhaps Damian had misjudged her. He huffed, and a little of the angst he still felt toward her melted.

Time will tell!

6

*T*he rest of the week passed in relative harmony with no more deaths and none of the playground friction Ashleigh had become accustomed to in the city. By Friday evening, she was exhausted.

Despite her fatigue, the invitation to join the following afternoon's tennis, followed by a community barbeque, sent her stomach fluttering. It took her a long time to get to sleep.

She stretched and glanced at her watch on Saturday morning, astounded it was after eight already. Apart from the occasional car passing the school, bird calls were the only sounds drifting through her open window. No roaring of motorbikes or trucks. No lawn mowers deafening the start of the weekend. And none of the constant phone calls that plagued her father throughout every day and often the night.

After showering, she made herself a pot of tea and searched the fridge and cupboard for something tasty for breakfast.

'Hmm. I reckon weight loss is going to be easier than I thought,' she said aloud.

Grinning, she slid the final crust of bread into the toaster and reached for the peanut butter. While she waited for the toast to brown, she jotted down a list of requirements before gathering her washing and shoving it into a large plastic bag. With little choice, she had accepted Joanne's offer of using their washing machine, conveniently located under the high-set principal's residence.

An hour later, with her laundry flapping in the breeze, she rustled around in her car and found two sturdy shopping bags. She slipped her wallet inside one, lathered sunscreen on her arms and face, pulled her wide-brimmed sun hat on, and wandered up the main street to the general store.

The dog was lying beside the worn timber step out the front. A sign that read "I'm Boris" leaned against the window. She studied the animal to ensure he was breathing before treading carefully around him. A bell jangled as she pushed the door open and stepped inside. The air-conditioning unit blew a cool breeze on the back of her neck, and the delicious fragrance of coffee and pastries wafted around her.

Behind the counter, a short, well-rounded woman looked up at her, a smile widening on her flushed face. Strands of wavy grey hair brushed her cheeks, and she flicked her head to blow them away, her heavy earrings swinging wildly. They reminded Ashleigh of liquorice allsorts on tiny, silver chains.

'Hello, love. You must be Ashleigh.'

Ashleigh nodded at the welcome. Although she didn't know many locals yet, they all knew who she was.

The woman dried her hands on a tea towel and flipped it over her shoulder before reaching a hand across the counter. 'I'm Lola. Me and Frank run the store and post office. So anything you need, you just sing out and I'm sure we'll be able to help.'

Ashleigh returned her smile. 'Thank you. Something smells nice.'

'That'll be this morning's pies. I make them every day except Sunday, and we do lamingtons on a Tuesday. Other than that, it's school tuck-shop on Fridays and what's up there.' She pointed to the chalkboard above the counter where bold, elegant script in coloured chalk formed a list of assorted sandwiches, burgers, and salads. 'And in winter there's soup too.'

'Gosh. That sounds lovely. I didn't realise there was tuck-shop yesterday?'

'Oh, there wasn't. We start next Friday. It takes a few days after everyone gets back into the routine to work out the roster. Never know who's about and who's too busy with fruit-picking and haymaking and stuff until after school starts.'

'Oh.' Ashleigh had never given farm life a thought. Did that mean the women all worked on the farms, too? She supposed it must.

'So, what can I get you, love?'

'Um. I'd love a coffee. And I need some food for this coming week. Stuff for breakfast and lunch—and do you have any of those frozen meals I can just microwave for dinner?'

'Of course. Come and have a look here.' Lola lifted the partition on the counter and slipped through the space, beckoning Ashleigh to follow her to the shelves on one side of the shop. 'Here's all your pantry staples. The cold stuff and fresh fruit and veggies are over here —and this is the freezer for anything else you need.' She waved her arms as she spoke, and Ashleigh had to step back for fear of being hit. 'The truck comes Mondays, Wednesdays, and Fridays from town. So if you're looking for fresh bread or anything else, let me know and I'll put it on the order for you.'

Lola laid a hand on Ashleigh's arm. 'Now, what sort of coffee would you like? The coffee machine's new, so I'm still learning how to drive it.' She let out a hoot of laughter. 'Haven't had too many rejects, though.'

Ashleigh grinned. 'A skinny flat white, please.'

'Righto. Coming up.'

It was a full hour before Ashleigh returned to her little home laden with food and satiated by the delicious coffee and enough information about the town's residents to make her head spin. She looked down at the heavy bags and grinned.

So much for losing weight. It's going to be harder than I thought.

GRATEFUL FOR QUINN and Joanne's company, Ashleigh slid into the back seat of their car. Although the tennis courts were only a short distance away, it seemed Joanne was one of the main organisers and purchased the regular food for the barbeque, requiring a vehicle to transfer it all to the venue. One esky in the back was filled with steakettes, sausages, and a large potato salad while the other contained cold drinks from the fridge under their house.

It had taken all Ashleigh's willpower to resist more than one pikelet, scone, or a small piece of whatever slice Joanne had brought to school for morning tea. Her first week, on three occasions, a generous plateful of treats had appeared on the kitchen bench. Ashleigh was astounded that both Quinn and Joanne were so slim what with Joanne enjoying baking so much, but perhaps it was because neither of them seemed to rest for a moment. She'd already become accustomed to giving them a wave as they jogged past her on the couple of occasions she had woken early enough to go for a walk. In the hour before darkness fell, they played tennis against each other on the school's uneven court that must have been there for decades.

They pulled up behind a light-blue Subaru and climbed out. Lugging the esky of food between them, Ashleigh and Joanne approached the shelter. A tall, lithe-looking woman was attempting to open the shutters at the front of the pavilion while an even taller, thinner man was cleaning a gigantic barbeque on the concrete slab beside the hut. Joanne dropped her side of the esky, wrenching Ashleigh's arm as the container lowered rapidly onto the floor, and stepped forward to help with the shutters.

Ashleigh rubbed her shoulder. *Good thing it's not my racket arm.* She met the woman's worried face and grinned.

'Are you okay?' she asked.

'Yes, of course.' Ashleigh stepped forward and extended her hand. 'Ashleigh Paton.'

'Hi. Lovely to meet you. We've heard all about you —of course.' She laughed. 'This is a small town and news travels fast. I'm Claire Shepherd.' As she spoke, Quinn and the thin man entered the building. 'And this is Rhys Morton, our local cop.' Claire greeted Rhys with a kiss.

Ahh—and a bit more than just a tennis companion.

They chatted for a few minutes before Joanne interrupted. 'Come on. Let's get the nets up so we can be on the court first. Not sure how many players we'll have tonight, but hopefully enough to have a couple of doubles games. How's your tennis, Ashleigh?'

Ashleigh grimaced as she recalled her expensive private-school education and the tennis lessons her parents had insisted she endure—along with music and swimming lessons. While Netty had excelled at all sports, Ashleigh was the opposite. Although tennis had been her favourite. 'Not the best, but I'll have a crack at it. I haven't played since leaving school.'

Claire smiled. 'You'll be fine. We're not exactly in Roger Federer's league either. Although ...' She turned toward Quinn and Rhys. 'These two love thrashing it out and winning at all costs, so it's good to have one of them on your team when we play doubles.'

'Is your mum coming?' Joanne asked Claire.

'Yes. She and Kirk will both be here later. We got the last of the hay in yesterday so we could have a weekend to catch up with everyone.'

The women bantered back and forth. It seemed half the town came whether or not tennis was their forte. This was a fortnightly event that, after the restrictions of the past three years, flushed everyone from their homes to enjoy the company of others, no matter the reason.

DESPITE HER EARLIER TREPIDATIONS, Ashleigh enjoyed the afternoon's activity. She was delighted to discover that playing tennis was not unlike riding a bike—requiring only a refresher and a good dose of patience from her opponent.

She and Claire paired to play against Joanne and Catherine, another woman who had gone to great lengths to explain she was also a recent arrival in Featherwood Falls and was newly married to the son of a local farmer.

Ashleigh was happy to let her chatter. Anything to prevent the personal interrogation she had become accustomed to—and hated.

By five o'clock, more families had arrived, and the adults laughed and chatted, sparring over who would play against who. An old concrete court spread along the far end of the two resurfaced courts. The children banded together and were racing back and forth on scooters, skateboards and—for the little ones—an assortment of trikes and bicycles. They shouted excited encouragement to each other, their form of entertainment clearly preferable to tennis.

Their cheery calls touched Ashleigh, and she

responded with a smile and a few friendly words. It seemed that in Featherwood Falls, socialising with her students outside school hours was a good thing. In her previous position, the staff had been discouraged from interacting with their students outside the official school day, except for sanctioned, school-related events and competitions. Apparently, it wasn't deemed "professional". Here, everyone was a friend—no matter the age.

Quinn fooled around with one of the older boys on a skateboard and Ashleigh grinned. He really was like a big kid himself.

She released a slow breath and allowed the fence she'd built around her long ago to weaken. Her mother, the principal of one of Brisbane's prestigious schools, wasn't here to remind her she must set a good example. Nor was her father within cooee in this part of the country. His political career had always meant Ashleigh and Netty were included in the limelight, whether or not they liked it. It hadn't bothered Netty. She was a true conformist who never did the wrong thing. It was Ashleigh who let her parents down at every turn.

An ache deep inside her smouldered into the familiar flame of rebellion. She grabbed her water bottle and gulped a few mouthfuls before turning away from the courts, seeking a private spot in which to cool down. After walking around the side of the building where the shade was spreading its umbrella, she faced a gigantic, bearded man with a heavy-looking gas bottle in his arms.

Ashleigh startled, almost dropping her water bottle.

'Hello. You're a new face.' The man smiled as he spoke, lowering the gas bottle to the ground and holding out his hand in greeting.

'H-hi.' She tentatively reached for his massive paw, bracing herself for a bone-crushing handshake. He took her palm and gave it a gentle squeeze, surprising Ashleigh. 'I'm Ashleigh, the new schoolteacher.'

'Lovely to meet you—and welcome to Featherwood Falls.' His smile widened, displaying a row of sparkling white teeth. 'I'm Kirk Meyer.'

'Hello.' An older woman appeared from behind Kirk. Wavy, brown hair hung on her shoulders and grey eyes displayed a warm, friendly sparkle. She rested a hand on Kirk's shoulder. 'I see you've met my better half.' She took Ashleigh's hand and cradled it between both of hers for a moment. 'I'm Ginny Shepherd, and I'm delighted to have you join our community.' She pointed to Claire and Rhys, who were talking to another couple. 'You've met Claire?'

Ashleigh nodded. 'Yes, we've just had a couple of games together.'

'She's my daughter,' Ginny said. 'You'll have to come to our place for dinner one evening. Or better still, come for lunch—tomorrow if you like? Bring your swimsuit and Claire can take you up to the falls for a dip.'

Taken aback by this enthusiastic welcome, Ashleigh smiled hesitantly and paused before answering, 'Umm ... thank you. That would be lovely.'

Ginny dismissed Ashleigh's timidity with a smile that lit up her kind face. 'Wonderful. Now then, Kirk, are we going to have a hit first or get started on cooking the meat?'

He put his arm around Ginny's shoulder and shot Ashleigh a cheeky wink. 'I reckon we thrash these youngsters in a game of doubles first ... and then we eat.'

HOURS LATER, Ashleigh fell wearily onto her bed. She had a blister on her heel from her old runners, and she ached all over. But ... she'd had the best afternoon and evening in years, and it was just the beginning. Tomorrow she was going to Featherwood Station for lunch and a chance to explore outside the town.

Her eyes closed and then opened again with startling realisation. Not all the town's residents had been there tonight. She had missed the two people who'd already left an imprint on her feelings—Charlie and his dad.

7

On the dot of twelve the following day, Ashleigh parked outside the picket gate, facing the beautiful stone and timber house. As she stepped out of the car, a cacophony of excited barking greeted her. She froze for a moment, praying she wasn't about to be mobbed by a pack of dogs.

A familiar voice yelled out, 'That'll do!' before Claire threw open the gate and smiled. She followed Ashleigh's anxious gaze toward the dog kennels. 'Don't worry about them. You're quite safe. Come in.'

Ashleigh hurried through the gate, relief flooding her at Claire's reassurance. She liked dogs. Especially Scamp—the cavalier King Charles spaniel she'd had as a child. But these days, many city dwellers had dogs that were inappropriate for both the owners and envi-ronment. Most dogs appeared oblivious to commands, and she knew of more than one friend who had paid the price for assuming a dog was friendly. 'What sort of dogs do you have?' Ashleigh asked.

'Kelpies. We've got a team of five and wouldn't be without them, especially for working the sheep. Both Mum and Dad have always spent a lot of time training the dogs and have taught Briony and me to do the same.' She led Ashleigh up the steps onto the veranda while continuing, 'Mum loves music, so they all have musical names and collectively she calls them her orchestra.'

Ashleigh smiled. 'Your dad?'

Claire hesitated, her voice softening. 'It's a long story. I'll tell you later ... when we go to the falls.'

Ashleigh had no time to answer before Ginny appeared, carrying a tray of cold drinks. 'Hi, Ashleigh.' She placed the tray on the table. 'Help yourselves. I thought we'd eat out here. It's such a gorgeous day.'

'Thank you.' Ashleigh plonked herself next to Claire, her back to the house wall and facing the garden. Amongst the large, freshly mown lawn, shrubs dotted the yard while a round centre garden of roses filled the air with a sweet fragrance. It seemed more like a park than a home garden to her and she drank in its beauty, her face softening. 'What a gorgeous view.'

Beyond the house garden, paddocks rolled down the slope toward the village, with a winding row of trees suggesting a stream flowing at their feet. On the other side of the valley, behind Featherwood Falls, the land rose again toward the east, depicting patches of cleared, green land amongst vast swathes of bush.

'We love it,' Claire said. 'I've only been home for about a year after working in Sydney. It's funny how you don't appreciate what you have sometimes until you've been away and then return. That was the case for me, anyway. Came home for Christmas and didn't go back.'

'I can understand why,' Ashleigh replied. 'I've lived in Brisbane my whole life. And with my parents' careers being what they are, I'm embarrassed to admit I haven't seen a lot of Australia either. We mostly went overseas for family holidays. I think Mum and Dad wanted to get as far away as possible when they could.'

Ginny had pulled up a chair at the end of the table and was listening to the conversation. 'Sounds intriguing, Ashleigh. What business are your parents in?'

Ashleigh frowned. 'Mum's a school principal and Dad's ... umm.' She screwed up her face. 'He's a politician.'

Ginny's eyes widened, and she gave a small laugh. 'Oh. A good one, I hope?'

Ashleigh shrugged. 'I avoid telling people usually, 'cause I'm not a big fan.'

'What. Of your father? Or politicians.'

'Politicians.' She huffed. 'I know it's an important job, and there are both good and bad politicians, but when you grow up with one as a parent ... Let's just say you're always being watched—and that is not something I enjoy.'

'Hmm,' Ginny responded, slapping a hand gently on the table. 'Well, it's good to know how you feel and I promise you now, you won't get questioned by us.' She grinned and pushed her chair back. 'Kirk should be here any minute, so I'll get the food out, shall I?'

As she disappeared into the house, the front gate creaked, and heavy footsteps sounded as Kirk appeared. 'Hello, ladies. This looks a pleasant spot to while away some time.'

'It's the best.' Claire turned to Ashleigh. 'Come and I'll give you a quick tour of the house, so you know where the bathroom is. Then we can tuck in.'

The spread of cold meat, salads, and home-baked bread kept them occupied for almost an hour while they talked about the farm, the village and, lastly, the events that had unfolded the previous year. Ashleigh's eyes widened as they regaled the details of the drug operation that had been going on next door, and the shock that rocked the community when it was uncovered.

'And you guys had no idea?' she asked with incredulity.

They all shook their heads. 'Nope,' Claire answered. 'We knew the guy managing the property was ... um, different. But we never expected them to find what they did.'

'Oh.' She breathed out with a whoosh, absorbing the peaceful vista in front of her. 'And here's me thinking that I've come to the quietest, most innocent place in the country.'

Kirk and Ginny burst into laughter while Claire rolled her eyes. 'That's only scratching the surface. After you've settled in, I'll take you hiking up the back of the property. There's a lot of history up there—with more secrets than you could imagine.'

While Ashleigh digested this information, Ginny returned to the kitchen and reappeared a few minutes later with a pot of tea in one hand and a plate of peanut brownies in the other. 'Let's have a cuppa, then you two can head for the hills and Kirk and I will clean up—and put our feet up in front of a movie,' Ginny said.

Half an hour later, Ashleigh returned to her car to collect the bag stuffed with togs, a towel, her water bottle, and sunscreen. She slipped off her sandals and shoved her feet into the runners she'd worn the previous evening, ensuring the Band-Aid was still in place over her blister.

Slamming the car door as Claire arrived beside her with two kelpies milling around their heels, Ashleigh shot her friend an anxious smile.

'Sit down, you two, and mind your manners.' Both

dogs dropped, their bellies resting on the gravel. One was red, while the other, black and tan. Claire pointed to the black-and-tan dog first. 'This is Drum. He was Dad's offsider and now Dad's not here, he's chosen me as his best friend.' She smiled before indicating the rust-coloured kelpie. 'And this is Chime. She's the matriarch of our pack and is a beautiful nature. She's also fantastic at working for anyone.'

Ashleigh bent to let them smell her hand before giving them both a hesitant pat, taking it slowly. Neither jumped up nor showed anything more than a polite interest as she stroked their heads gently. She stood, blinking. 'Wow. They're well behaved.'

Claire shrugged. 'When you've got more than one dog, they must know the rules or they're trouble. Here on the land, everyone who uses dogs for stock work spends time getting it right. The last thing we need is for the uncontrolled killing of newborn lambs or the dogs tormenting young calves. It's bad enough having wild dogs to contend with,' she finished sadly. Beckoning Ashleigh to follow, she strode toward the wide gate leading into the paddock beside the house. 'Come on. We can talk as we walk.'

The climb up the narrow track took all Ashleigh's energy. She silently resolved she would work on her fitness—starting tomorrow.

After what seemed like a half-day hike to Ashleigh —but was actually less than half an hour—they reached a small rise. On the other side, the land sloped down to a clump of native rainforest and although there was a distance of a hundred metres or more to go, the sound of water tumbling over rocks reached her.

They drew nearer, and she stopped dead. To her left, a waterfall cascaded from a rock ledge before plunging into the pool below. On the lower side, a man-made dam had been constructed with dozens of granite slabs and boulders, allowing a perfect but natural-looking pond that, although not huge, provided a magical place to cool off. 'Wow! This is gorgeous.'

Claire beamed. 'Isn't it?' She stripped off her shirt and unbuckled her jeans, revealing an electric-blue bikini. 'Let's jump in first and then we can sit on the rocks and talk.'

Ashleigh glanced at Claire's pale body. Thin and well-muscled, her limbs resembled those of a gymnast.

'I'll just pop behind those bushes and change,' she said. After hurrying to a clump of tea tree nearby, she self-consciously removed her trousers and knickers before stepping into the plain, black one-piece swimsuit that mostly lived at the bottom of her underwear drawer. After whipping off her shirt and bra, she hauled the straps over her shoulders and grimaced at her solid, white legs. *Thank goodness it's private here.*

The cold water took her breath away as she

stepped carefully onto the shallow rocks under the surface.

'As soon as the water reaches your knees, you're safe to launch in. It's not deep, and there's nothing underneath to hurt you,' Claire called.

Ashleigh followed Claire's instructions, striking out with clean, practised strokes. While Netty was the water-lover in their family, having spent hours in the backyard swimming pool, Ashleigh had swum regularly on the very hottest of days, but never when any of Netty's boyfriends were visiting. No, she had heard enough comments regarding the differences between her and her little sister to know when advertising the facts was unnecessary.

Chime leapt into the water and was swimming in circles, her pink tongue lolling and a canine smile on her face. Drum stood at the water's edge, his lemon-coloured eyebrows accentuating the anxious look on his face.

'Doesn't he like the water?' Ashleigh asked.

Claire hesitated, grabbing Ashleigh's startled attention, then drew a deep breath and murmured, 'We think he witnessed my dad's death.'

A stab of empathy shot through Ashleigh. 'Your dad's death?'

'Yes. They found Dad face down in the creek. Higher up than here. Mum had gone looking for him when he didn't come home as expected. Long story short, but an autopsy proved he didn't drown, but died because of a whack to the head. It turned out our neighbour lost his temper when Dad refused to sell him some of our land. He threw a rock at Dad and … well, it killed him.'

'Oh, my goodness.' Ashleigh touched Claire's arm. 'You poor thing. And your mum. It must have devastated her.'

'It did. It was good to find out what really happened. Nigel's in jail now—they charged him with manslaughter.'

'This is not the same neighbour who owns the property next door … is it?'

Claire nodded silently.

'The one where the drug cartel was working from?' Ashleigh's eyes widened further at the increasingly incredulous story.

Claire huffed a long breath of resignation. 'Yep. The very same.'

The girls remained quiet for a few moments. Ashleigh shivered, rubbing her hands over the goosebumps on her upper arms. 'And you believe Drum witnessed the whole thing?'

'Yes. I've been working with him for more than a year now. I think he believes the water is responsible for Dad not being here now. He's much better than he was and will come in swimming with me when we're alone up here. I think he prefers to be the lifeguard, though.' She released a quiet chuckle. 'Dogs. I wish I knew what they really thought.'

Dried and dressed again, the girls gathered their gear and ambled slowly back toward the house. They talked as they walked, exchanging work and boyfriend experiences, favourite books and movies. Feeling increasingly more relaxed in Claire's company, Ashleigh shared more about her life than she had ever done.

'I'm hearing you,' Claire said. 'I'd hate to have parents who're always on show. It was hard enough when the court case was happening with Nigel. And that only made the local papers and news. You guys must have felt you were being stalked half the time.'

Ashleigh snorted. 'And the rest.'

'Hey. Do you ride?' Claire asked.

'Horses, do you mean?'

'Yeah. We've got a couple of lovely horses and I thought perhaps we could go riding together.'

'Sorry. I've never sat on a horse in my life—although I wouldn't mind trying the experience.'

'Okay. Well, perhaps we could go hiking together. Rhys comes with me when he's off duty. But he works pretty long hours, so that's not as often as we'd like. I could take you up to see the old mining site where Kirk goes fossicking.'

'Sounds great. I'll need to get myself a new pair of hiking boots, though.'

They both glanced at Ashleigh's sneakers, now covered in dust and grass seeds.

Bursting into laughter, Claire linked her arm through Ashleigh's. 'Good idea. Thanks, Ashleigh. It's going to be lovely having a friend of my age around here.'

A warmth spread through Ashleigh that had nothing to do with the weather. She'd had the best weekend in years—and this tiny town and those who lived in it bore full responsibility for her happiness.

8

*W*ith renewed enthusiasm, Ashleigh bounced out of bed early the following morning. After replacing the plasters on her heels and pulling on a thick pair of socks to protect her feet, she marched out of the school gates, following the main road until turning onto the dirt shoulder of a side lane. Having walked for fifteen minutes before turning back, she increased her stride. If she could manage this walk every morning, she would expand on the distance and her pace each week. She was determined that by the end of the term she would be able to charge up the hills as effortlessly as Claire.

The sun was rising, spreading a glow of pink and lavender across the eastern sky. Birds ducked and dived around her—tiny birds that she vaguely recognised but couldn't name, bigger birds with speckled bellies, a crow and a hawk.

She reflected on the previous week, relieved that at this stage, anyway, all her students seemed well behaved. Tom, a boy in his second school year, appeared to struggle with reading and writing, but both Quinn and Emma were aware of it and Emma was already spending one-on-one time with him for part of each day. And then there was Charlie.

An ache caught deep inside her. It had been Friday when she'd noticed him staring out of the window—again. Something had distracted him on and off all week, although he was advanced in every other way. It was as though he had an older child's head on a small, five-year-old body. She'd asked if everything was alright and what he was watching.

'The birds, Ms Ashleigh,' he'd answered.

'What birds?'

'All of them. This morning I've seen an eastern spinebill, a spangled drongo, and lots of ravens. Yesterday there was a channel bill cuckoo in the tree behind the sandpit and ...' His blue eyes burned brightly, filled with wonder. 'Did you know there's a satin bower bird living in the bushes beside the garden shed?'

'Really?' Ashleigh's jaw had dropped, dumbfounded. Not at Charlie's observations, but at the knowledge that was stored inside him. How did he know all this?

Emma had whispered, "Not all children have television" when Ashleigh asked the students about their favourite program. It had taken Ashleigh a minute or two to realise who Emma was referring to. When, later in the day, she'd asked Emma more, she'd burned with shame as the older woman divulged the little she knew of Charlie's home life. It seemed old Bob had shared the information at the wake following Emma's mother's funeral. If Charlie didn't have television—or electricity, according to Emma—he must be gathering this information from books, or his father?

While thoughts tumbled in her head, she barely noticed the vehicle until it spun out of a side road right in front of her. She leapt into the table drain, her heart pounding. The chunky vehicle was travelling too fast for the conditions, and the engine roared in protest while she squinted to catch a glimpse of the occupants before they thundered past. Out here, drivers mostly acknowledged every vehicle or person they met with a brief wave or a lift of the index finger from the steering wheel at the very least. This driver did neither, a cap pulled low over the dark scowl etched into the creases of his face. His passenger was female. And she appeared to have spent days in the bush without a hairbrush or a wash.

She frowned. The old vehicle was not one she

recognised—not that she was an expert. But it was noticeable in its difference to the usual four-wheeled drives about town. If asked, she could only have described the colour as camouflage. *Perhaps they're grey nomads who've bought an old army vehicle.* They didn't look like the usual retired couple enjoying their twilight years as they circumnavigated Australia, though. No, from her brief glance, the man appeared older than her parents, but clearly strong enough to manage the chunky vehicle.

Glancing at her watch again, she dismissed the encounter and lengthened her stride. It was the start of the week, and at the previous week's staff meeting it had been decided they'd allow students to bring in living creatures that may interest other pupils on a Monday. The child would talk about their choice in "show and tell", then the creature would feature again in the science lesson that afternoon.

Ashleigh had been astounded. Featherwood Falls was home to a whole gamut of budding naturalists, biologists, and potential veterinary surgeons.

The variety of interests amongst her thirteen pupils differed dramatically—with one little girl being obsessed with ballet while two more talked of nothing but their ponies. However, across the school, topics of discussion ranged from the capabilities of a John Deere harvester to codling moth in apple crops and what the best recipe for colostrum for abandoned newborn lambs was—none of which had ever featured in Brisbane classrooms. Charlie had surprised them all with his knowledge of birds. The level of understanding he had of all creatures was overwhelming— and far beyond the interest of his fellow students.

Ashleigh straightened her shoulders, dismissed her scrambled thoughts, and swinging her arms, marched along the road before turning into the school's front gate. Remembering she still needed to iron her slacks, she hurried to her tiny house and slammed the door behind her before preparing for her day.

HER SECOND WEEK in Featherwood Falls began the most enjoyable term Ashleigh had experienced.

As she eased into the school routine, her contentment grew while time flew by. With fortnightly tennis gatherings and regular visits to Featherwood Station— which mostly included a walk and a swim—her social life became more active than it had ever been in Brisbane.

Her favourite clothes were a little loose, despite the delicious baking both Joanne and Lola insisted on sharing, giving Ashleigh the boost she had hoped for. She made plans to head home for a couple of days over the upcoming Easter break. In addition to purchasing a new pair of runners and her first ever hiking boots, she would clean out her old wardrobe and bring back some of the garments she'd used on family holidays prior to the pandemic. She might even visit the horse supply shop she'd passed when visiting Maeve's house and try on some of those stretchy pants that Claire wore. Her first riding lesson was coming up and, although she could borrow a helmet and the well-worn boots Briony had left in the cupboard, there was no way she would fit Claire's jodhpurs.

A small grin formed on her face. She and Netty exchanged regular texts and Maeve, her closest friend from her school days, had rung a few times—both women had radiated surprise at how much Ashleigh was enjoying country life. Calls to her parents were more erratic as both seemed to be constantly rushing either to meetings or to address other things that required their urgent attention.

No matter how busy they all were, she hoped they'd find time to sit and talk over Easter—like Ginny and Kirk did when Ashleigh visited the farm.

Most Mondays, Charlie's "show and tell" was a revelation—not only for Ashleigh. Each week, he brought in a tiny beetle or caterpillar and proceeded to describe it and share its purpose in life. But one Monday, he turned up with what looked like a soil sample.

'What can you tell us about it, Charlie?' Ashleigh prompted.

Focusing on the dirt, he launched into the need for microbes in soil to provide all the requirements for healthy plants to grow. Ashleigh's eyebrows rose. Glancing around the students' faces, quizzical expressions and a fascination seemed to have reduced every child to silence. Perhaps it was the information Charlie was regaling them with or simple awe of his knowledge of a subject no one else had considered.

'That's wonderful, Charlie. I think it would be a good idea to have a closer look at the soil through a microscope in our science lesson this afternoon. Then everyone will see what lives in the dirt.' She smiled at him, and he nodded furiously, a wide grin spreading across his little face.

Joanne will be over for morning tea.

As a keen gardener, the principal's wife understood the requirements of soil and would be interested in joining their science lesson. Not only that, but admiration for Charlie's knowledge had also piqued Joanne's interest—and she was determined to have both Charlie and his father join the school's monthly gardening club.

On the final Sunday of each month, parents and students arrived at two in the afternoon laden with garden forks, gloves, and wearing wide-brimmed hats and boots. However, no matter how often the weekly newsletter reminded families of the event, neither Charlie nor his father turned up.

When Joanne had asked the little boy specifically if his father would bring him some time, he'd simply shaken his head and said nothing.

IT WAS during the second-last week of term that Ashleigh noticed the change in Charlie. He was always quiet, but this Wednesday morning he seemed consumed with sadness. It was etched on his face, dulling his eyes, and his usually lightly tanned skin was pale. She didn't want to single him out in class, so she left it alone.

It wasn't until the lunch break that Ashleigh missed him from his usual play areas—the sandpit or the climbing frame and swing complex in front of the amenity block. She scanned the playground and paced around the buildings, certain he would pop up any minute. He didn't, and Ashleigh's pulsed raced.

She spotted Jessie and Libby putting their lunch-boxes away. She hurried over to them. 'Hi, girls. Do you know where Charlie is?'

Jessie looked at her with big, round eyes. She brushed the lock of hair from her face with a sticky hand. 'No.'

'Okay, thanks. Perhaps you'd like to wash your hands before you go off to play.' She smiled, and the girls smiled back.

Ashleigh dashed upstairs, where Quinn and Maria were sorting through a pile of papers in the office. The middle-aged woman scowled. Recognising her expression—and her possessiveness of Quinn—as concern, not annoyance, Ashleigh drew a deep breath and smiled. She spoke more calmly than she felt. 'I've lost sight of Charlie. Would you mind popping into the boy's toilets to see if he's there, please?'

A flash of concern darted across Quinn's face. He gave Maria a brief nod as he headed for the door. 'Sure.'

Ashleigh followed him, casually leaning on the frame of the climbing equipment. While displaying an interest in the capabilities of the children wildly swinging from above, she had a clear view of the entry to the amenity building and was relieved when Quinn reappeared with Charlie's hand in his.

Quinn beckoned to her. Shooting the gymnasts a congratulatory smile, she walked to where Quinn and Charlie were standing and met Quinn's concerned face.

He gave her a subtle nod and dropped Charlie's hand. 'Why don't you sit and talk to Ms Ashleigh for a while, Charlie?' He took a step toward Ashleigh, whispering, 'I'll keep my eye on the other children.'

Strolling across the grassed area to the oval, Ashleigh slowed her steps to match his. 'Would you like to tell me what's worrying you, Charlie?'

'It's the eggs,' he said.

She looked at him, wrinkling her brow in confusion. 'What eggs?'

'The eastern rosellas.'

She blinked, trying to comprehend what he was saying. 'Can you tell me more?'

'They've been nesting. In a tree hollow near the firebreak on Dotty's place.' He stopped.

Ashleigh bit her lip, determined to keep a patient and understanding ear, even if it was proving difficult. Who was Dotty? 'And?'

'Well, they're not there anymore. I've been checking nearly every day while I wait for Dad to collect me from the bus. The chicks still have a whole week before they're due to hatch.'

'Perhaps a goanna has raided the nest. Or another bigger bird has eaten them.'

'But the entrance is so small, I can only peep inside. I wouldn't put my hand in, but if I did, it might get stuck.'

'I see,' Ashleigh said, although she didn't see at all. Wishing she had more knowledge, her thoughts flicked to Damian. 'Does your dad know?'

Charlie nodded. 'I told him, but he said it's nature's way. Not all eggs hatch and no one knows why. He said a snake might have taken them.'

'I'm so sorry, Charlie. I know how much you love

the birds. Why don't we go to the library and find a nice bird story to read after the bell rings?'

He brightened slightly, the flicker of a smile touching his face. 'I know. *Hooray for Birds!* I can read it myself, but it'd be nicer if you'd read it to me.'

'Of course.' They shared a smile, and she squeezed his hand. The bell rang as they approached the main building.

As the children clattered up the steps, Ashleigh breathed a sigh of relief that Charlie's issue wasn't serious. Thoughts of a child in her care going missing brought a wave of horror to her. It didn't bear thinking about. Tearing her memory back to the kangaroo encounter on the day of her arrival in town, she let a tiny smile creep around her lips.

An evening spent researching predators responsible for eggs disappearing from nests—and other potential reasons for them going missing—could make for a good use of her evening. Especially as there was little else to do. Even if it didn't help Charlie, she might at least learn more about her environment.

Damian might think I'm a city slicker with no knowledge of the bush or wildlife, but I'll prove him wrong.

9

*D*amian tapped his fingers on the steering wheel as he waited. The bus pickup routine had forced a change in his workday but, except for when they were felling trees, the adjustment was trouble-free. It didn't matter to his peers. If the bus was on time, Damian could collect Charlie, drop him home, and be back to the logging site before the guys finished their afternoon tea break. The morning was more difficult, however, and Damian cringed with guilt at the number of times he'd had to leave Charlie and Dot at the end of their track, knowing the old woman had to make the kilometre trek back home alone. She wouldn't appear in public—her scars were too deep for that. But as soon as the rumble of the bus sounded, Charlie had told him she would kiss him goodbye and duck behind the trees, watching silently until he was safely onboard. It seemed Charlie accepted her actions without questioning why.

The familiar sound reached his ears, and he breathed a sigh of relief. Glancing at his watch, he calculated the trip up the hill to the shack and back to where he and his team were working would take at least twenty minutes. If anything went wrong while he was away, it would be on his head, not the team's. He would not allow that to happen.

Charlie stepped off the bus, his backpack appearing almost as big as his tiny frame. Damian's heart leapt. His son was the image of Laura—thankfully in appearance only. Today instead of the wide grin that usually greeted Damian, Charlie's face wore a solemn, almost tragic expression.

He threw the passenger door open and grabbed Charlie's bag from him. 'Hey, mate. How was your day?'

The little boy climbed into the cab and slammed the door. Damian waited, struggling to contain his impatience as Charlie slowly reached for his seatbelt and locked it into place.

'Okay,' Charlie muttered.

After first checking the belt was firmly in place, Damian then started the engine, his brow furrowing. 'Only okay? Not great like every other day?'

Charlie remained silent while Damian negotiated the washout on the dirt track. The previous week's downpour had created a flush of green throughout the valley, but its fury had left the road potholed and rough.

'What's the matter, mate? Is something worrying you?' Damian asked.

'I told Ms Ashleigh about the bird's eggs.'

Damian raised one eyebrow. 'Okay,' he drawled. 'Do you mean the missing bird's eggs?'

Charlie nodded, and Damian flashed him a glance, relinquishing his attention from the road for a split second. The ute dropped into a pothole before leaping out of it with such force that Charlie's lightweight frame left the seat, slewing him sideways against the door.

'Ouch. That hurt,' he cried.

'Sorry, mate. We're nearly there.' He paused for a minute, concentrating on the road ahead. 'Don't worry about the eggs. The season has been a good one, so they'll probably lay another clutch.'

He pulled up outside the cottage and turned to Charlie's disbelieving gaze. He reached out to him and squeezed his hand. 'They'll be okay. I promise. It's nature, and many things happen in nature that are for the best—in the long run. I thought you understood how it works?'

'I do. But the rosellas aren't the only ones. Remember the little friar bird nest we found when we went to check the cattle last week?'

Damian grabbed Charlie's bag while the child scrambled out, his concern growing with the length of time he'd been off-site. 'Hurry, Charlie. I've got to get back to work. What about the little friar bird?'

'Well. I went to have a look while Dotty was having a sleep. You know, when you went to Stanthorpe for your meeting—and they're gone too!'

Frowning again, Damian slammed the ute door. The meeting Charlie referred to had been ten days earlier. Had he been stewing over the issue since then? He looked at his watch again and ruffled Charlie's hair as Dot appeared on the veranda, her crumpled face beaming. 'I've gotta go. In the middle of a job. See you later,' he called by explanation. Then he leapt back into the driver's seat and roared off.

His headlights assaulted the peaceful scene as Damian drove into the shed that night. He killed the engine and sat for a moment, his eyes adjusting to the sooty blackness that enveloped him. Lass appeared at the ute, whining softly with pleasure. He stepped out and ran a weary hand over her soft head as an owl hooted from a tree nearby. Something scurried along the side of the shed. A bandicoot? Or a rat? Damian frowned. He hoped it wasn't a rat. Trapping the cunning rodents had proven difficult—the options were bait or predators. Neither were appropriate here in the bush. Cats only exacerbated the problem, and baiting was against Damian's principles.

He shook his head, dismissing the thought, and strolled toward the cottage. A dim light flickered near the kitchen window and a faint grin stretched his lips. He had bought several LED camping lamps to replace the old kerosene version that Dot had used for years. The trouble was, she loved that smelly old thing and insisted on using it when he wasn't there. She treated it like it was an old friend who'd supported her through her troubled past, and she was not prepared to say goodbye.

After pushing the door open, he turned to give Lass a last pat before she scrambled onto her veranda bed.

'Hello, I'm home.' Over the years, his regular announcement had become a standing joke. In the tiny shack—barely six-metres squared, excluding the veranda—it was impossible not to hear him arrive. With no television and a battery radio used only for the morning news and for Dot to listen to the country hour, sounds of the bush filtered in twenty-four-seven. The bird calls, the screech of the occasional fox, and the chattering of bats during the summer when they frequented the old fig tree in the garden's corner had become the sounds of a peaceful home life for both Damian and Charlie.

As soon as time allowed, Damian's next project was

to install the solar panels and battery-charging system. At least then he could upgrade the two-way communication unit, allowing better contact with the outside world. Perhaps, he could allay some of the guilt in keeping Charlie in such an isolated home, despite Dot's protests that modern conveniences were unnecessary.

One of the LED lamps burned brightly beside Dot's bed where she and Charlie lay. She lowered the book she was reading to him. 'Big day?'

'Yeah. We had a breakdown with one of the trucks, so I had to hang around while they fixed it and then it took longer than we expected to load.'

'Your meal is in the warming tray,' she said.

'Dad. Dotty's reading *The 13-Storey Treehouse* to me.' Charlie's piping voice, filled with delight, lifted Damian's spirits.

'Sounds interesting. Where did the book come from?'

'Bob dropped a bag full in today,' Dot answered. 'Apparently Lola gave them to him when he popped into the store this morning. She said they'd been left in the book exchange box that's in the post office now. It was kind of her to think of Charlie.'

'It was.' Damian slid his hand into the pot mitt and pulled a covered plate from the shelf above the oven in the wood stove. The aroma of steak-and-kidney pie hit his nostrils, detracting him momentarily from the conversation. Baked potatoes, pumpkin, and broccoli filled the plate, and his stomach rumbled. He carried his plate to the table where cutlery and a tall glass indicated his usual dinner-time absence. 'Carry on reading, Dot. I'm happy to listen.' He smiled and tucked into his meal.

An hour later, with Charlie asleep, he and Dot shared a pot of tea while sitting at the table.

'I've been thinking,' Damian said softly. 'The school term finishes next week, and I haven't been able to spend as much time with Charlie as we'd both like. You look tired too.' He gazed into his great-aunt's faded grey eyes, worry darkening his own. 'I thought I might take Charlie camping for a couple of nights. Let you have some quiet time, and I'll do some things with Charlie.'

She nodded slowly. 'Don't worry about me. The boy is no trouble ... Actually, I miss him during the day. But you're probably right. A couple of days with no thought of work or school might be good for you both.' She chuckled. 'If you want to do something Charlie really enjoys, you might as well stay on the property. Perhaps you could buy a tent and pitch it up the back near the spring. If it's warm, you can both cool off in the pool—if you don't mind sharing with the cows and wildlife, that is. There's plenty to look at and now he's bigger, you could search for the old plane wreck. That's the sort of thing you loved doing when you were young.'

Damian grunted thoughtfully. Taking Charlie to the beach or Brisbane for a couple of days had run through his mind, but he knew his son well enough to agree with Dot. Charlie wasn't like most kids. His happy place was amongst nature and living creatures. While a trip to the beach would entertain him for a short while, it was a busy time to even attempt the excursion. Being the last school holiday break before winter set in, Damian was sure every man and his dog would want to visit the beach —and crowds did nothing for either him or his son.

'The water in the donkey should be hot enough for you,' Dot said.

'Thanks.' The primitive boiler system nicknamed "the donkey" had served Dot for decades, and Damian had replaced it with a gas water heater for both safety and reduction of workload. But no matter how much time had passed since the upgrade, Dot still referred to the shower as "the donkey".

Damian shot her a smile, scrubbed his plate in the bowl of soapy water, then sluiced it with the remaining hot water from the kettle. Leaving it to drain, he meandered onto the veranda and followed it around the side of the cottage to the lean-to that served as their bathroom. He switched on the lamp and glanced appreciatively at the slate-tiled floor, proud of his achievement.

Having insisted on lining the walls with sheets of waterproof panelling, he had also fitted a small vanity unit in the opposite corner from the composting toilet. Beside the shower wall, a series of hooks provided hanging space—one in the middle up high for his towel and the other two low enough for both Charlie and Dot to reach without effort.

A shower curtain hung from a rod fastened to the ceiling and he pushed it aside, stripped off his filthy clothes, and stepped underneath the old-fashioned showerhead. Gasping as the cold water hit before the heat filtered through, he then shampooed his hair and beard, revelling in the warmth. After turning off the water, he stepped out, startling a large green tree frog hopping across the floor. He opened the door and poked it with his toe, urging it outside.

A little while later, he stood on the veranda and breathed in the cool evening air. The nights were drawing in and the temperatures dropping rapidly.

He nodded to himself. *Yes, I'll take Charlie camping for a couple of days before winter arrives. It'll be good to be just the two of us again. Before then, we'll nip into town and pick up a tent and a few necessities.*

He wasn't sure why, but the picture of an auburn-haired woman with a wide smile and flashing brown eyes tormented him. He had been so sure she would be everything Charlie did not need as a teacher—a city girl with grand ideas that opposed their simple lifestyle. But from what he'd gleaned from Charlie, she had been anything but. It seemed she was understanding of his son's passion for creatures and hadn't asked him once about his mother—or even questioned who "Dotty" was.

There was no doubt she wasn't afraid to speak her mind, but ... there was something genuine about her.

Damn the woman. She rattles me.

He gnawed his bottom lip, forcing the vision from his mind. Dot and Charlie were his world, and he didn't need anything—or anyone else—in it.

10

*A*shleigh rubbed the crème through her hair before scrunching the thick locks into a bun on the top of her head. She'd given up on the straightener in the first week of school and had slowly adjusted to accepting her curls, even with their inclination to frizz at the slightest hint of rain. It had been the perfectly groomed Emma who had suggested using a hair product. She had picked this crème up on one of her trips to town for Ashleigh to try.

Her thoughts drifted to the kind teacher's aide for a moment. An enigma, Emma shared very little of her life with her workmates. Ashleigh shrugged. Everyone had their reasons.

She shoved her feet into sneakers and bent to lace them, a little surprised to find she needed to hitch up her jeans when she straightened again. A wave of pleasure washed over her. She didn't have any scales but the loose-fitting clothing was giving her a heads-up— her goals were in sight. Daily walks, running up and down the school steps, and the regular games of tennis must have been helping.

This morning, Claire was collecting her for a day out. The plan was to head to Girraween National Park first to explore The Pyramid. Claire had assured Ashleigh she could not consider herself a resident of the Granite Belt before exploring a few of its icons. After their hike, they planned to visit the cheese factory for lunch before calling in to Stanthorpe for a quick look at the shops. In a week's time, the Easter holidays would bring crowds of tourists to the area— something neither she nor Claire particularly enjoyed.

A horn sounded, and she glanced through the window at Claire's blue Subaru in the parking area. After throwing her front door open, she waved before grabbing her hat and backpack and locking the tiny house behind her.

She jogged across the grass, grinning at her friend standing by the car.

'Ready for a big day?' Claire asked.

'Yep. Looking forward to it.' She pointed to the clouds building in the west. 'Let's hope they stay away —at least until this evening, anyway.'

Claire grimaced. 'We'll be right. Girraween, here we come.'

DESPITE THE COOLER weather and her increased fitness, Ashleigh was still puffing when they reached the top of The Pyramid. A visible track in the stone led to the iconic boulder teetering on a massive granite hill, an indication of the vast number of walkers who had ventured to its summit.

After taking an obligatory photo of Ashleigh pretending to hold the balancing rock in place to show her family, Claire led the return walk while they discussed the possible homecoming of Claire's sister, Briony.

'She's been in Yamba for ages now, helping her friend at her café. I reckon she's probably about ready to head back to Scotland.' Claire sighed. 'I know she and Alex have really missed each other. To be honest, I thought their separation might mean the end of their relationship, but apparently not. I was hoping she would hang around for a while. It feels like years since we spent time together,' she finished wistfully.

Ashleigh shot her a questioning glance. 'You sound as bad as Netty and me. When we were little, we fought like crazy, but as adults, she's the best sister ever— except for being "Miss Goody-Two-Shoes" in Mum and Dad's eyes.'

'Do you resent her for that?' Claire asked.

'I think I did for a while. But now ... well, she's too

nice a person to resent. I think I'm finally accepting we're just different—and with our parents' standing in the community being what it is, Netty's personality fits their brief better.'

She chuckled, and Claire joined in with a burst of laughter.

HAVING WORKED up an appetite by the time they'd reached the cheese factory, they tasted an array of gourmet cheeses before devouring lunch in the Jersey Girls Cafe. Then, satiated, they cruised into the town of Stanthorpe.

They had barely made it from the car park to the main street when the skies opened and a deluge forced them into a run. Keeping as close to the shops as they could without touching the glass, they laughed, shivering as they made their way along the footpath and turned into the wide-opened doors of the sports store.

Claire grabbed Ashleigh's arm. 'Over there.' She pointed to racks of jackets and outdoor wear, behind which a vast array of boots and shoes filled a section of the wall.

'Wow. I didn't realise there'd be so much choice here. I was waiting until I go home for Easter.' Ashleigh arched an eyebrow at Claire. 'Looks like we might find something?'

Half an hour later, Ashleigh was sitting on a seat, her chosen boots beside her. Walking shoes were more difficult. As she thrust her feet into her third choice, a familiar voice called.

'Ms Ashleigh!'

A mixture of surprise and delight surged through her as Charlie ran the remaining few metres and stood facing her with a wide beam on his face.

Heat burned her cheeks as she stood. Behind the rack of jackets only steps away, Charlie's father stared at her, a twitch of his mouth drawing her gaze to his.

'Hello, Charlie.' She smiled down at the child before returning to meet Damian's eyes. 'Hi, Damian.'

Claire subtly touched her elbow against Ashleigh, catching her attention. *Sorry*, Ashleigh mouthed. Facing Damian again, she said, 'I guess you know Claire—my friend.'

Damian smiled. 'Hi, Claire. We've never actually met, but Rhys has mentioned you once or twice.'

'I hope whatever he's said is good,' Claire laughed. 'The bush telegraph works well in small towns.'

'True.' He inclined his head. 'In places like Feather-wood Falls, it's hard not to hear what goes on—even when you're not in the tennis or gardening group.'

'Oh!' Ashleigh turned her gaze from Damian to Claire. 'Claire, Charlie is one of my pupils—and this is his father.' She added sharply, 'Who apparently has no interest in playing tennis.'

'I didn't say that.' Damian glared at Ashleigh, his green eyes flashing. 'I said I'm not in the tennis or garden group. That doesn't mean I have no interest.' He clamped his mouth shut and turned to Claire. 'I think your friend has formed her opinion of me—and it's not a good one.'

'Now who's jumping to conclusions?' Ashleigh snapped. Aware of her nostrils flaring, she concentrated on deep breathing to quell her rising temper.

'Woah.' Claire rested a hand on each of their arms. 'I appear to be in the middle of this ... difference of opinion. How about we calm down?' She gave Ashleigh a little shove. 'Sit down and decide which shoes you're buying while I say hello to this charming young man.' She squatted in front of Charlie. 'And what brings you and your dad to town, Charlie?'

'We're going camping in the holidays,' he announced, his voice high with excitement.

'Lovely!' Claire chatted with him for a few moments, asking about their plans and listening while Charlie told her about the new tent they were buying.

Ashleigh ignored Claire's order and remained standing. Electricity pulsed between her and Damian as they faced each other, with Claire and Charlie between them.

Ashleigh let out a slow breath, feeling calmer now —although her heart still pounded. Swallowing her indignation and ignoring his father, she asked Charlie, 'Which shoes do you like best?'

He held his finger to his lips as he studied the three different shoes on the floor. 'Those.' He pointed to the blue walking shoes with black-and-blue striped laces. 'They're a pretty colour—like the male wrens.'

Claire's glance swung between the boy and Ashleigh. 'Good choice, Charlie. I agree with you. Wrens are lovely little birds, aren't they? And these shoes remind me of them too.'

'Right then. Come on, Charlie. We need to get a couple more things, and I'm sure these ladies have other places they want to be,' Damian said curtly.

You're not wrong there.

'Okay. Bye, Ms Ashleigh. Bye ...' Charlie trailed off as though unsure what to call Claire.

'You can call me Claire.'

He nodded and took his father's outstretched hand.

As they walked away, Claire bent and repacked the unwanted shoes into their boxes. 'Wow. What's going on between you two? That was awkward.'

Ashleigh sighed, her hands resting on the chosen footwear. 'Nothing's going on. He's just an obnoxious parent who seems to enjoy rubbing me up the wrong way.'

Claire tittered. 'Really? You could have fooled me.'

11

*T*he last day of term arrived in a rush. After waving the bus passengers goodbye, Ashleigh remained where she stood for several minutes while the old Toyota Coaster disappeared into the distance.

The children living in town had headed home long ago and the school grounds suddenly felt eerily quiet, as though life had been drained from their core.

Emma had wished her a happy holiday as she left, and now only Quinn remained—supposedly tidying up final paperwork before he and Joanne drove to the coast.

Despite looking forward to seeing her family again, Ashleigh revelled in the peace and late-afternoon sunshine. A breeze suddenly whipped up a pile of leaves from under the ancient oak tree that stood near the school entrance, strewing them across the car park. The reminder that autumn was arriving encouraged her to turn and trudge toward her little house. Like her comrades, she needed a trip home to Wellington Point. To smell the sea air, pay the obligatory visit to her parents, and enjoy the remnants of summer.

To avoid the mass exodus of traffic on the roads, she would have a quiet evening and leave the following morning before the first birdsong.

For tonight, though, she would do something she'd been meaning to since her arrival—have a meal and a drink at the Featherwood Falls Hotel.

Pub life had never been her cup of tea, and the shabby building across the road held little appeal. But without patrons, it would only get worse, and she would do her bit to help prevent that.

THE SMELL of beer hit her first, followed closely by the vague hint of roasting meat. A deep laugh filtered out from the bar. She glanced through the glass doors to where three men in high-vis shirts perched on stools. Hesitating, her gaze swung to the sign indicating a dining room. Was that where she should go? She wished Claire was with her.

A dark mop of hair capping a cheery face peered

around a door at the end of the corridor. 'Hi there. Can I help?'

Ashleigh stuttered, 'U-umm. Yes, please. I'd like to have a meal—if it's available?'

The woman stepped toward her and smiled. 'Sure. You're the new teacher, aren't you?'

Ashleigh nodded. 'Yes. Just finished my first term, so thought I'd celebrate with a meal and a drink before I nip off to the city for a few days.'

'Come on through.' The woman beckoned her, tucking a wayward strand of hair behind her ears. 'I'm Ann. I help old Ned out here now. Cook the meals and keep the place clean—well, as clean as I can, considering the age of the joint. My youngest headed off to high school this year—otherwise, I'm sure we would have met before now.'

Ashleigh glanced up at the elaborate, pressed-metal ceiling before resting her eyes on the exquisite fretwork panels above all the doorways.

'It must have been beautiful in years gone by,' she said as she followed Ann into a compact but gracious dining room. Threadbare patches showed through the floral carpet on which dark and heavy furniture stood, but the fresh white tablecloths and smells of wood polish and food cooking seemed to compensate.

'I've only lived here for a short while, but the locals say it was one of the busiest places around many years ago.' Ann hesitated for a moment. 'I've just gotta check the oven. Why don't you nip into the bar and grab a drink, then make yourself comfortable here. I'll be back in a tick to take your order.' She was gone before Ashleigh could answer.

As her initial discomfort eased, Ashleigh wandered around the room, studying the faded pictures hanging on the walls. The photos were mostly sepia or black and white, and most were dotted with age marks. Groups of thin men in ragged trousers and an assortment of hats, alternated between those of fine-looking horses and Merino rams. At each end of the room, a large oil painting dominated the tongue-and-groove-boarded walls. One was a landscape depicting hills, valleys, and the foliage of the area. It also featured a pretty, stony-bottomed creek indicating the artist had a thorough knowledge of the Featherwood Falls area. It wasn't a view she had been privy to, but with the shadows facing east and the direction of the water flow, the vista must be from somewhere in the hills behind Featherwood Station. She wandered to the painting at the other end of the dining room. It displayed a man standing beside a horse and buggy while, behind him, a sandstone building with a wide veranda running along the front stood out against the dark-green back-drop of bushland.

Ashleigh leaned forward for a better look. *That's Claire and Ginny's home!*

Ann returned at that moment and stood beside her.

'Admiring Featherwood Falls' history? There's plenty of it here.'

'Yes. Is that the homestead at Featherwood Station?' Ashleigh indicated the painting with a tilt of her head.

'I believe so. The bloke beside the horse is Angus Shepherd, Claire and Briony's great-grandfather. There are lots of stories going around that he was a greedy man. Thought he was a cut above everyone else in the district—"Lord of the Manor" type.' She grunted. 'Poor Ginny got a shock when the truth came out. He got friendly with an orphaned Chinese girl as well. The bloke who killed Ginny's husband was that woman's grandson.'

Ashleigh gazed at the woman with wide eyes. 'Really?' Studying the picture again, she recalled the conversation she and Claire had on Ashleigh's first visit to the property. Claire had mentioned her neighbour was responsible for her father's death but had said nothing about blood ties.

'This whole region contained dozens of mines generations ago.' Ann waved an arm toward the array of photos. 'A lot of these show that history—tin miners, gold fossickers, and everything in between.'

'I didn't realise that.' Ashleigh spoke softly. She'd been here for nine weeks, oblivious to the history of her new home. A wave of excitement surged through her, and she smiled at Ann. 'I'll have to read up on it.'

'You probably only have to ask Ned, or Lola and Frank, to get a good idea of the past.' Ann thrust a laminated sheet of paper at Ashleigh. 'Meanwhile, here's the menu.'

Hunger had left her while she absorbed Ann's information, but now her stomach rumbled and she ran her eyes over the choices. There were only three. Roast beef and vegetables, mushroom risotto, or battered fish and chips.

Ann screwed up her face. 'Not exactly a restaurant, but until a few months ago, you would have had only one choice.' Grinning, she leaned closer to Ashleigh. 'Ned wasn't big on cooking. Had a health scare a while back though and realised he needed help. In a past life, I was a shearer's cook, so he called me.' She shrugged. 'And here I am.'

'Good for you—and Ned. I'll have the roast, please.'

'Righto.' She pointed to the bar and glanced at her hand. 'You haven't got your drink yet. Do that while I get your meal.'

As Ann hurried toward the kitchen, a small smile hovered on Ashleigh's face.

The woman may not have the finesse of a well-trained waitress, but if she'd cooked for shearers, Ashleigh was certain the food would be good.

The sound of deep voices wafted toward her as she pushed the adjoining door open. The workmen were still leaning on the wooden counter, and one laughed at something another had said. A quiver of nerves gripped her. Swallowing, she approached the bar.

Wearing a checked shirt with a torn breast pocket, the bearded old man shuffled closer, his rheumy eyes squinting through dirty spectacles. 'What can I get you, girly?'

'Umm. I'll have a lemon, lime, and bitters, please.'

While she waited, watching the frail little barman prepare her drink at a snail's pace, a movement caught the corner of her eye. She swung around. Her breath stopped in her throat as the man strode across the room. Damian!

He nodded at the other patrons. 'Gidday, fellas.'

They responded with a grin and a friendly reply before his gaze fell on her.

'Won't be a tick,' Ned said, distracting them both for a second. 'The usual?'

'Yep. Thanks, Ned.' Damian pointed to the pink-tinted glass the old man was holding with a quivering hand. 'That for the lady?'

Ned nodded.

'I'll get that, too.'

Ashleigh froze. What? It was bad enough to be confronted with this infuriating man without being subjected to his condescending generosity in front of strangers.

Biting her lip, she met his gaze again and muttered, 'Thanks.' Then, after rescuing her drink from the puddle of condensation on the timber, she turned and hurried into the dining room, closing the door firmly behind her.

The breath whooshed out of her lungs as she plonked herself on a chair. What was it about Charlie's father that make her feel like an irresponsible child? Did he speak to others the same way?

Ann arrived with a ginormous plate full of steaming meat and vegetables in one hand and a jug of thick gravy in the other.

Ashleigh stifled a groan, her heart thumping and her thoughts still in the room next door. She shot Ann a polite smile. 'Thanks. It looks as though you're used to feeding an army.'

Ann shrugged. 'Yeah, well. The price is the same, so why shouldn't you have the same-sized meal?' She snatched the tea towel from her shoulder and wiped her hands on it. 'Sorry I can't chat. Gotta get the meals out for those fellas.' She flicked her index finger at the closed door between the bar and dining room and grinned. 'Nice meeting you.' As she leaned her back on the swinging kitchen door, she added, 'Let me know if you want dessert,' then disappeared.

Ashleigh stared at the mountain of food. Her stomach cramped at the thought of the men all piling into the room, accentuating her solitude. Her hunger faded.

I'll be lucky to get through this lot.

Ann elbowed her way through to the bar with a meal in each hand, while Ashleigh ate quickly, eager to dash back to the privacy of her little home. Pulling a couple of twenty dollar notes out of her pocket, she then handed them to Ann as the woman hurried past her again. Then, after Ann had rushed back with her change, she ate as much of the delicious meal as she could manage and walked quietly out of the hotel onto the footpath.

A quick glance in either direction confirmed there was no sign of Damian's ute. He must have left already. She released a slow breath and placed a hand on her full stomach as she scurried across the road to home.

Her suitcase lay on the bed, empty. While she waited for the kettle to boil, she hastily threw an assortment of clothes into it, gathered her toiletries and make-up from the bathroom drawer, and assembled the items on the bench top, ready to grab after her early morning shower. After filling her teacup and preparing for bed, she propped up her pillows and climbed under the doona.

While sipping the hot drink, she opened her laptop and searched *mining in the granite belt, Queensland.*

The more she read, the more her interest piqued. Fossicking had never featured in her life—and it was certainly not an activity her family had considered. However, an invisible thread anchoring her to this place provoked her interest. Further searches revealed snippets of farming history, tales of European arrivals —particularly the Italian and Greek communities, and the Chinese—who had all worked hard to establish the rich fruit-and-vegetable growing area of the plateau.

With her mind bursting with surprise and enthusiasm—particularly after reading about Stanthorpe having the third largest tin mine in the world during the late 1800s—her trip to see the family would be a fleeting one. Two days, three at the most, should appease her parents.

During Netty's last call, she had talked about nothing except the new man in her life, Jack. Ashleigh doubted there would be a lot of time for the two sisters to spend together, anyway. And with Maeve having headed to France with another friend, what else was there to keep her in Brisbane? No, she would ring Claire in the morning and return as soon as possible to Featherwood Falls. A couple of days hiking the tracks and trails of the region would prove much more interesting—of that, she was certain.

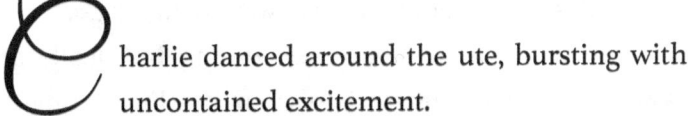 harlie danced around the ute, bursting with uncontained excitement.

'Come and help me with the food, Charlie,' Dot called from the veranda, her frail arms weighted down with a small but heavy wooden box.

The boy raced over to her and peered inside as she rested it on a chair.

'Did you put our biscuits in?' he piped.

The previous day, when Damian had been chopping enough firewood to keep Dot going for a month, Charlie had helped the old lady make a batch of plain biscuits. While Dot rolled and cut them in the shape of assorted animals, Charlie had pushed currants into place for eyes and trickled a thin line of chocolate icing across each face. Some of the doughy animals appeared to be smiling, while many wore a squiggly line that could have represented any emotion.

'Yes, Charlie. There's enough for you both, and I've kept some here to have with a cup of tea while I think of you and your dad having fun.'

Charlie jumped up and down on the spot, clapping his hands.

While Damian stacked additional chopped wood on the ute tray, Dot and Charlie assembled the bedding, bag of clothing, and one of the LED lamps in a pile on the veranda.

By nine in the morning, they were ready to go.

Damian grinned at his son waving frantically at Dot. His heart squeezed. It was such a little thing— taking his only child on a three-day camping trip. And yet to Charlie, it was as exciting and important as a beach holiday may be to another child. Had he been neglectful? He was sure Laura would have thought so. Born and raised in the city, beach life, movies, and eating in fancy restaurants had been of paramount importance to her. Having a child had not.

His stomach squirmed with the familiar ache of blame. It had been he who wanted a child, not her. Her pregnancy had surprised them both, and to her credit, she'd agreed to go through with it.

After a trouble-free pregnancy and birth, Laura had struggled. Following the diagnosis of post-natal depression, Damian had been certain her medication and the support of he and her girlfriends would pull her through.

But it hadn't been enough.

He'd come home one evening to find Charlie in his cot, screaming, and Laura dead on the floor of the bathroom. Every tablet prescribed to her was gone, the empty containers strewn across the tiles.

The following months had been a nightmare. While he'd prioritised Charlie, his position as arborist for the local council suffered. The inquiry, coroner's findings, and media invasion had added to the pressure.

He glanced over at his son, noting the smile fixed on his face, his eyes sparkling with anticipation. A pain gripped him, but it was a pain filled with love—enough to make his eyes prickle. The call from Dot's neighbour had turned out to be their saviour and, as they say, the rest was history.

The dirt lane petered out to two-wheel tracks as they climbed hills and bounced along basins—each rise taking them a little farther into the bush.

After almost an hour, Damian pulled up next to a set of cattle yards. 'Hop out, mate. We'll check the water before we go any farther.'

A mob of glossy, black cattle grazed nearby where the scrub was sparse and the grass plentiful. Tucked behind the yards, a trough shimmered, its contents lapping at the top of the concrete ring tank while a thick poly pipe ran down the vessel's side and into the earth below.

Damian marched into the bush, casting his eyes along the raised furrow showing the direction of the underground pipe while Charlie trotted along behind him. The land fell steeply to a gentle stream coursing its way to the valley beneath the lush undergrowth. In a clearing next to the creek, a pump—its solar panel perched high on a sturdy pole—forced the water from the narrow watercourse to the trough on a supply-and-demand system.

'That looks good, Dad.'

Damian smiled at his son and bent to check the connections. 'Yep. All okay here.' He straightened and gazed around the clearing. The cowpats dotted around and flattened patches of grass signalled the area as a popular resting place for the row of cattle who now stood in a line along the bank with curious stares.

Charlie pushed a tiny hand into his father's work-roughened one, waving a stick with the other. Despite the little boy's bold approach, he clung to his dad's side as they pushed through the herd and returned to the vehicle.

The land plateaued a few-hundred-metres farther on, opening to a wide expanse of grassland that was dotted with massive eucalypts and patches of smaller shrubs. A granite outcrop topped the rise and from beneath it, the tinkle of a spring echoed from the rocks.

'I thought we could camp here, Charlie. What do you think?' Damian grinned at his son and reached out to ruffle his hair.

'Great! Can we put the tent up now?'

'Righto, mate. Let's find a nice, flat spot with no rocks and get started.'

An hour later, with the camp set up and a fire laid within a ring of rocks ready to light, Damian poured himself a cup of coffee and a hot chocolate for Charlie. He screwed the lid back on the flask and sat on a log conveniently lying nearby. Next to his father, Charlie pressed his warm body against Damian's as the midday sun filtered across the paddock. A chilly breeze had sprung up, blowing from the south.

Welcoming the rays now warming their backs, Damian narrowed his eyes as he studied the sky. 'Not sure what the weather's going to do, Charlie. I reckon as soon as we've eaten, we put our packs on and go exploring, just in case this change brings heavy rain.'

Charlie met his father's suggestion with a feverish nod, shoved the sandwich he was holding into his mouth, and leapt to his feet.

∽

A SCUD of light rain struck as they reached the top of the east-facing ridge. Damian paused to draw breath, grinning at his enthusiastic son. Although his pace had slowed a little, Charlie had displayed more energy than Damian expected and all thoughts of potentially having to piggyback him to camp vanished.

Although slightly built, Charlie possessed a strength Damian hadn't recognised before. Not only physical strength, but a mental determination and desire to soak up every sight and sound.

'Why don't the birds sing when it's raining? Why are the clouds shaped like that? How do the lizards know where to find food when they hatch out of their eggs? What bird is making that call?'

The questions continued, challenging Damian's knowledge. With no mobile-phone reception up in the hills, there was no hope of searching for the answers he didn't know. So instead, he compromised, jotting down the questions with unknown answers in the notebook he carried in his top pocket. 'When the holidays are over, you can ask your teacher to help you find the answers. Okay?'

Under the broad-brimmed hat, Charlie's face lit up with joy. 'That's a good idea.' Dismissing the drizzle with a shrug, he said, 'Can we look for the plane now?'

Surprised at Charlie's vitality, Damian checked his watch and frowned. 'I'm sorry, mate. It's still a long way to go. We don't want to be caught out here in the dark when we've got our camp all ready, do we?'

Disappointment flashed across Charlie's face, the edges of his mouth drooping.

Damian sighed. 'Remember, we will not see an entire plane. It crashed ages ago and there's only a few pieces left now. How about we get up early in the morning, pack our lunch, and make finding it our project for tomorrow?'

Charlie brightened immediately. 'Can we cook the sausages on the fire? And have some of the biscuits Dotty and me made?'

'Yes, mate. I'm not sure that biscuits are okay for dinner—perhaps we'll just have one while we get the fire going. Then after we've eaten our meal, we'll toast the marshmallows over the coals.'

While he stared at Charlie's bright smile—a miniature version of Laura during their early days of marriage—guilt once again weighed heavy in his chest. If he hadn't assured her a child could enhance their troubled relationship, she would probably still be here. He chewed his lip. If she were still alive, there was no way she would have agreed to move to the bush— especially to keep an eccentric woman in her nineties company. The decision to care for Dot would have certainly been the catalyst that ended their marriage— baby or no baby.

The rain stopped, and the clouds lifted. Casting a

look over the stunning vista, Damian breathed in the clean air, smiling at the drips sliding down freshly washed leaves. Distant hills and peaks became visible again as the sky cleared, their hues of purple and grey contrasting with the brighter tones of the immediate surroundings. From somewhere close by, a koel called, signalling rain was still possible.

Charlie stood still, and distracted by his thoughts, Damian almost bumped into him. 'Sorry, mate. What are you looking at?'

'Nothing special. Just looking.' Charlie breathed out a contented sigh and turned, smiling, to his father. 'Isn't this the most beautiful place ever?'

Damian grinned, nodding. The last of his remorse melted away. 'Yep, sure is.'

They descended the peak, making their way back to camp—Charlie darting ahead while Damian trudged thoughtfully behind him.

Charlie was right. This was a beautiful place to live. Deep in his heart, Damian knew his marriage to Laura had been floundering almost since it began. Her battle with depression had clouded her whole adult life, and he had been wrong. Having a child had not helped her one bit.

He swallowed his regret. Dwelling on it was holding him back from making the most of being Charlie's dad. And that would be tragic. As Charlie trotted gaily ahead, his blue jacket almost covered by the red backpack firmly strapped to his back, Damian smiled. The boy filled his life with delight and purpose. He would continue to remind Charlie his mother had loved him, but otherwise, it was time to move on.

With every stride, Damian's face softened as the burden of guilt he'd held on to for so long lifted from his broad shoulders.

13

*G*rowing apprehension filled Ashleigh as she drove along the motorway. To distract herself, she increased the volume on her playlist.

A few short months ago, she would have been singing along with the music blasting from the car speakers as she wove in and out of the busy traffic. Ignoring the scowls from fellow motorists as she dropped into the lane in front of them, she would have grinned and perhaps given them a cheeky wave.

Now the noise, fumes, and aggression shown by other drivers unnerved her. She hadn't noticed it before. Had living in the country for just a few months made that much of a difference? Apparently, it had.

Forty minutes later, she turned into the driveway,

pushed the remote for the enormous garage door, and drove into the cavernous, four-vehicle parking area.

Netty met her on the stairs, throwing her arms around her with the ferocity of a long-lost lover and almost knocking Ashleigh backwards.

'It's sooo good to see you,' she enthused. After snatching the carryall from Ashleigh's hand, Netty turned and sprang back up the steps without waiting for Ashleigh to reply. 'I can't wait for you to meet Jack.'

Ashleigh rolled her eyes. Was that what the energetic welcome was all about? Meeting the boyfriend. The familiar affability of her sister's company washed over her as they entered the living area. Across the room, full-length glass doors opening onto a wide patio provided a view past the perfectly trimmed hedge at the bottom of the lawn and across the harbour to the Manly marina.

'Where are Mum and Dad?' Ashleigh dropped her shoulder bag on the cream-leather couch and cast a glance around the room.

'Dad's out jogging and Mum popped to the bakery to get fresh croissants for brunch.' Netty bounced behind the island bench, a wide smile on her pretty face. She was wearing a red bikini that accentuated her shapely figure under the see-through cotton dress. With her long, blonde hair scrunched into a messy bun on the top of her head and her clear, tanned skin, Netty bore little resemblance to Ashleigh. 'Coffee?'

'Love one, thanks. I'll put my gear in the bedroom while you make it.'

Ashleigh picked up the overnight bag from the middle of the floor where Netty had dropped it and trod along the polished boards to her bedroom. She stopped dead in the doorway, her eyes widening. Where was the pretty patchwork quilt her grandmother had lovingly pieced together for her eighteenth birthday? She absorbed the changes to what now appeared to be a hotel room in stunned silence. On her bed was a plain, white doona cover with cushions propped against the snowy pillows in deep shades of red. Her faded pink lamp had been replaced by an elegant, gold light stand with a white-satin shade. She dropped her gaze to the floor with a sinking feeling. The sheepskin mat she'd loved scrunching her toes through had gone, exposing bare, polished wood.

After pulling open the wardrobe door, she released a relieved breath. The clothes she'd left behind when she moved to Featherwood Falls were still there, including her favourite puffer jacket—purchased for the first of the family's many skiing holidays in Japan.

She dragged a box from the cupboard's depths and flipped open the lid. Ashleigh reached inside and carefully removed the Royal Albert tea mug that had been her grandmother's before running her eyes over the balance of the contents. Memories of love and contentment oozed from that box. Following her gran's death,

Ashleigh had moved into her small but homely town-house. She'd revelled in her solitude and it had allowed her space to grieve and reflect. While her parents' lives were filled with constant scrutiny under the public eye, the year of living alone had provided Ashleigh with a temporary understanding of what living a "normal life" might feel like.

Except for the occasional, cheery "Good morning" from a neighbour, and the few months Maeve had moved in with her before buying her own apartment, the home had been her refuge away from critical eyes. She'd bathed in the anonymity and had been devastated when the estate was concluded and the town-house sold.

The months leading to her move to Featherwood Falls had not been happy. Occasional boyfriends had come and gone over the years. She'd questioned her choice of career and then, following her outburst and subsequent resignation at school, her self-confidence had gradually faded.

'Coffee's ready, Ash!'

Jerking her attention from the box to her sister, she pushed herself to standing, plastered a smile on her face, and returned to the kitchen.

As though she'd only just noticed her, Netty gaped. 'Hey, you look different.'

Ashleigh shrugged and touched her hair. 'Oh, you mean I've stopped straightening my frizz.'

Netty shook her head and spoke slowly, gesticulating for Ashleigh to turn around. 'It's not only your hair. You've lost weight. And your face looks different. Kind of ... happy?'

Ashleigh roared with laughter as the front door slammed.

Their father thumped up the stairs two at a time before pausing at the top to smile at his daughters. Like Netty, Mark Paton was tall and slim. Despite working long hours and having celebrated a fiftieth birthday, he still ran every morning and worked out in the gym downstairs.

He strode across the room and hugged Ashleigh before stepping back, his hands resting on her shoulders. 'It's good to see you, love.'

'You too, Dad.'

'You look great. Does that mean you're happy?'

Ashleigh smiled into the dark-brown eyes that mirrored her own. The creases on his face had deepened while the fine remnants of his auburn hair had been shaved completely, leaving his head wearing only a hint of gold.

'I am, Dad. Best decision I've ever made.'

The squeak of a garage door sounded beneath them.

'Mum's home,' Netty announced, picking up two mugs of coffee and carrying them toward the patio.

Their father bounded ahead of her, opening the

door for Netty before returning to the steps and planting a kiss on the cheek of the woman appearing from below. 'Hello, love. Ash is home.'

After dropping the brown-paper bag on the counter, Julie Paton leaned forward and air-pecked her daughter's face briefly. No-nonsense but totally appropriate social greetings were in Julie's genes. She dished out affection in measured quantities and never included the all-encompassing hugs her husband shared with their daughters. Freshly styled blonde hair topped her perfect make-up, while smart white slacks and a bright-pink top covered her short, curvy body. 'Hello, dear. Did you have a pleasant trip home?'

Ashleigh gave her a wry smile. Her mother's greeting was such that an onlooker might have thought Ashleigh was a friend or relative, but certainly not a daughter. 'Yes, thanks.' She pointed to the bag of croissants. 'I'm looking forward to one of those. I'm peckish.'

'Of course.' Julie stretched her neck toward the patio. 'Netty! Have you prepared brunch?'

Netty wandered to the fridge and extracted a platter of sliced fruit and a bowl of yogurt. 'All done. You guys go outside. The table's set. I'll bring everything out and make a fresh pot of coffee.'

Feeling rather like a guest in a posh hotel, a sudden urge to giggle welled up in Ashleigh's throat. She gave a small cough to quell it. What on earth would her parents do when Netty moved out—eventually. Straightening her shoulders, she stepped onto the balcony.

FOR THE REST of that day and the next, the family spent time together, eating, swimming, walking and—for the first time in what felt like years—actually talking about a myriad of different subjects.

Jack duly arrived an hour before the scheduled evening meal. Netty had prepared a buffet fit for royalty and graciously removed the two bottles of expensive champagne from his hands before introducing him to her sister.

He was tall and strikingly good-looking with dark hair, a close-clipped beard, and a demeanour that oozed the solicitor he was—exactly as Ashleigh had expected.

His handshake was soft, his skin smooth, and his clean fingernails were neatly trimmed. As he released Ashleigh's fingers, she dropped her gaze to those that had just touched hers. Her glance triggered a sudden picture of another man's hand—these were large and work-roughened with dirt engrained in the lines and cracks around his nails. Her welcoming smile quavered for just a moment.

Grateful for the distraction, and the unexpected

attention, Ashleigh strove to be the person her parents wanted her to be for two whole days. She walked across to King Island at low tide each day while talking and sharing her life in Featherwood Falls with them. Taking care to leave out her encounters with Damian, she brushed over the daily teaching routine and dwelt on the friendliness of the town's residents and the beauty that surrounded the area. They dined at a popular restaurant on her second day before spending a cosy evening in the media room watching the latest James Bond movie, *No Time to Die.* The only time she was alone was when she nipped into the saddlery in a nearby suburb and purchased a pair of navy-blue jodhpurs.

It was with mixed feelings that Ashleigh repacked her bag on Sunday morning and said goodbye to the family.

Julie hugged her briefly, surprising Ashleigh, and whispered in her ear, 'You look wonderful, darling. Country life obviously suits you.'

With her mother's words silently repeating themselves in her head, Ashleigh returned to Featherwood Falls with her car full of winter clothes, her grandmother's treasures from the box in her wardrobe—including the wool and knitting needles she'd found right at the bottom—and a full heart.

14

A smile hovered on Ashleigh's face as she pulled up outside the Featherwood Falls store. After bending to pat the top of Boris's head—the ancient blue cattle dog she had come to know and trust—she pushed past him and opened the door.

'Hello, love.' Lola's round face greeted her—the friendly smile as welcome as the fragrance of fresh coffee that wafted through the shop. 'That was a short holiday. Couldn't stay away from us, eh?' she chortled.

Ashleigh returned the grin. 'Something like that. I've discovered I don't fit the "townie" brief anymore.'

'Well, there's nothing wrong with that. You've fitted into the community beautifully here. I hope the school continues to grow so you can stay as long as you like.'

'Thanks, Lola. Me too.' She turned toward the dairy

fridge, pulled out a carton of milk, and scuffled in her bag for her purse.

Placing the item on the counter, she explained, 'My sister has sent me home with a ton of food, but I need milk—and a cup of your delicious coffee, please.'

They chatted for a few minutes before Ashleigh returned to her car and drove on to the school. Although she'd been away for only two nights, it felt like weeks.

Inside her cosy home once more, she unpacked the leftover salads, thinly sliced roast beef, and almond biscuits Netty had insisted she take. As an urban dweller, Netty had seemed unable to accept that Lola's store provided everything Ashleigh needed, and more.

Glancing at her watch, she finished her coffee and made herself a sandwich. Then she dialled Claire's number.

'Hi.' Claire's cheerful voice brought a smile to Ashleigh's face.

'Hi, yourself. How's your break going?'

'Great. Not exactly a break, though. Rhys and I spent Friday helping Mum drench the sheep.'

They both laughed.

'What about yesterday?' Ashleigh asked.

'We went to Tenterfield. Had a look at the touristy things—the saddlery and railway station to begin with. Then visited a winery and had lunch. It's years since

I'd stopped to enjoy the town, and Rhys said he'd only ever driven through it.' She paused to draw breath, then added, 'How about you?'

'Okay. Mum and Dad were both home, so we spent time together—and of course I met Netty's main man, the famous Jack.' Ashleigh chuckled. 'It's good to be back here, though.'

Understanding filled Claire's soft laugh. 'What are you doing this afternoon?'

'Nothing planned. What about you? Is Rhys still there?'

'No, he's working again. Why don't you come over and we'll catch the horses? It's about time you started those riding lessons we've been talking about.'

Ashleigh swallowed. Each time Claire had mentioned a lesson, it had rained or Ashleigh had made the excuse of waiting until she'd bought a comfortable pair of pants. Now there was no excuse and her stomach fluttered as she replied slowly, 'O-kay. I'll see you in about an hour?'

'Super. The forecast is for a nice day tomorrow too, so we could go for a long hike. I'll take you up to see the mine and we can come home a different way.'

'Sounds great. See you soon.'

As she zipped up the slinky jodhpurs, trepidation wormed its way through her insides. While her visits to Featherwood Station had eased her initial fear of the gigantic creatures, the thought of having to sit on top of a horse, never mind a moving one, knotted her stomach.

Stop being a princess. If Claire can do it then so can I.

Throwing a light jacket onto the back seat, Ashleigh slid into the driver's seat and headed to Featherwood Station.

Clouds blanketed the top of the range and she recalled Charlie's announcement that he and his dad were going camping in the hills. She hoped the weather was kind. If showers drifted over the valley, they could cut the riding lesson short, which would not be ideal. But she imagined being stuck in a tent surrounded by rain would not be a pleasant experience. She smiled softly. Charlie would probably still enjoy it whatever the weather did. He was like that— he saw a positive side in everything.

AN HOUR LATER, Ashleigh's concern had all but evaporated. Astride the elderly gelding they called Flash, she relaxed as he ambled around the yard at a gentle walk. At a little over one and a half metres tall, Flash's pony build was the perfect size for Ashleigh. Despite the horse's sturdy appearance, she was relieved she was a few kilos lighter than she had been in January.

'Do you want to try a little trot?' Claire asked.

'I thought the poor thing was riddled with arthritis?'

Claire chuckled. 'He has some, but he's doing well since we found a new product to add to his gummy-nuts each night. As soon as he hears the rattle of the bucket, he can manage a swift canter to the stables, so I don't think he's going to have trouble carting you around the yard a couple of times.' Stepping closer to the pony, she clicked her tongue while reassuring Ashleigh. 'Trot on, Flash.' The horse broke into a slow jig-jog. 'Ash, relax into the saddle and let yourself feel the beat.'

Bouncing around in the comfortable stock saddle, Ashleigh forced herself to concentrate on Claire's instructions. Feeling as though her teeth would rattle at any minute, she was pleasantly surprised when Flash's trot suddenly became rhythmic.

'Great, Ash. I know I told you to keep your eyes up, but if you can, glance down at Flash's shoulders for a few seconds. When the outside one moves forward, grip with your lower leg and lift your bum off the saddle for a second then sit again. That way you'll avoid the bounce and find the rhythm.'

Claire jogged around and around the yard as Ashleigh struggled to follow her friend's guidance. About to give up as a stabbing pain began in her side, it came to her. Suddenly, the bounce became a regular up-down movement and, although she missed the beat a few times, elation spurred her on for a few more circles.

The pony dropped back to a walk, and Ashleigh faced Claire with a beam from ear to ear. 'I got it!'

'Awesome effort, Ash. We'll have you on Splash before long and able to ride out in the paddock.'

Ashleigh glanced at the three horses grazing nonchalantly in the adjacent field. One was small and stocky like the pony she was on while another was a glossy dark brown and medium-sized with an athletic appearance. The third horse was tall and rangy, its coat mostly brown with white splashes over its rump and around its belly. From her position, it looked huge and terrifying. 'How about you let me get used to this little fellow first?'

Claire laughed, steadying Ashleigh as she slid off the pony with shaking legs.

With the lesson finished, the girls groomed and fed the horses before heading to the house for a welcome cup of tea.

Bursting with delight at her achievement, Ashleigh leaned back on the veranda chair, barely able to keep the smile off her face.

Who knew? This born-and-bred city chick could learn much more than she'd ever dreamed of. And it was all because of her gran's favourite motto, "Escape to the country! A change is as good as a holiday".

LATE THAT NIGHT, rain lashed at the windows of the tiny home, stirring Ashleigh from a deep sleep. She rolled over and pulled the doona up to her chin as thunder rumbled. A flash of lightning lit up the room for a second, and she shot into a sitting position.

Was it a small, isolated storm—or was it widespread, its ferocity capable of ruining the camping trip that Charlie had been looking forward to so much?

Groaning, she rubbed her tightening leg muscles and lay down again. Trying to look at the experience through a young boy's eyes, she guessed that weathering an electric storm was probably just another event that made camping more exciting.

By morning, all signs of the storm were gone, and Ashleigh woke to sunshine streaming through her window. She stepped onto the floor and grabbed the windowsill as her legs threatened to collapse under her. Every muscle in her back and bottom screamed, including muscles she hadn't realised she owned. She staggered stiff-legged to the shower and stepped under the cascade of hot water.

With a day of hiking ahead of her, she massaged and stretched as much of her aching bits as she could before cooking herself a hearty omelette for breakfast. Filling it with mushrooms, tomatoes, and spinach leaves, she reasoned it would give her the energy to cope with a physical day. Next, she packed lunch, snacks, and two bottles of water before donning her new boots and stuffing a rain jacket in her backpack.

Bracing herself against the chilly wind that blew down the valley, she cast a glance at the endless blue sky and walked the few steps to her car.

A FEW MINUTES before nine o'clock, she and Claire climbed out of the farm ute, leaving it parked at the far corner of Featherwood Station where the rolling pastures met the vast expanse of native bushland.

For the first section of the walk, they talked, stopping occasionally to turn and enjoy the vista. The sun's rays were getting hotter and Ashleigh was grateful for the shade that thickened as they climbed higher.

'A couple of years ago, this track was a mess,' Claire announced. 'Kirk cleared the undergrowth so now we could almost drive the quad bike up here if we wanted to.'

'That would make it easier for him to get to his fossicking spot, wouldn't it?'

'Yes, although it gets pretty steep soon and I doubt anything except a horse would make it. Anyway, it's kind of our legacy to leave it as natural as we can, so we bring nothing except ourselves this way.' She waved her left hand. 'Over there, above Glenrowan, there's a firebreak the bushfire brigade keep slashed, and behind that is the forestry's pine plantation which is always kept in good shape.'

'Is that the only commercial forestry area around here?'

'Yeah. There's more up the back of Stanthorpe—and probably other places I don't know about, but that's the closest to us.'

I wonder if Damian and Charlie live somewhere close to the forestry block? Charlie had told her about the birds and other animals he watched while waiting for the bus, and he often spoke of the bush.

They continued trudging up the track, pausing on each peak before their route dropped away again or continued over vast sprawls of granite. With each pinnacle, the view grew wider and the air cooler. Exhilaration increased Ashleigh's energy levels as she drank in the land's vastness. In every direction, moody grey bush melted amongst the shades of green while in the far distance, deep purple shadowed the hills. 'I feel as though we're on the top of the world,' she said.

Claire smiled. 'I know. It's pretty awesome, isn't it? Not far to go now to where Kirk fell into the shaft and broke his ankle.'

Ashleigh had heard the tale of Kirk's unfortunate

accident that subsequently unearthed the skeleton of a long-forgotten miner.

Her interest piqued.

Taking a swig of water first, they then pushed on to the clearing Claire had referred to.

Ashleigh gasped. 'Wow. This is lovely!'

A circular area of grass covered the clearing. On one side, the ground dropped away—the area marked with a row of star pickets supporting a netted fence and dotted with flapping red flags. Directly opposite the girls, a small timber shelter provided protection from the south-west, and between that and where they now stood was a ring of smoke-blackened rocks surrounded by an assortment of seats fashioned from logs.

'This is it.' Claire pointed to the red flags. 'That's where the old mine shaft is. It's covered now, but Kirk put the fence up to help prevent wildlife from falling over the edge. He's spent a lot of time up here and knows where the danger spots are.'

'This is amazing. Is it kind of like a wildlife refuge?'

'Yes. That's exactly what it is. Years ago, Mum and Dad started putting exclusion fencing around the entire area. It was too dangerous for stock, and they wanted to protect the mines and give the wildlife somewhere to live without predators. Over the last couple of years, Kirk and Mum have finished the fencing and Kirk's been trapping pigs, wild cats, and foxes. There are still a few here I think, so it's a constant job, but hopefully one day it'll be free of introduced pests.'

'That's amazing, Claire. Are other neighbours doing the same?'

She shook her head. 'Maybe some are, but it's an expensive project and most of the properties around here are small and don't have the bushland we have.'

'One of my pupils lives somewhere in the bush. I don't know where, but it's his father who works for the forestry department.'

'Hmm. Not sure where that would be. But ... the next valley runs up into the bush too, and I know there are two or three extensive properties somewhere there.'

Ashleigh mulled over the information as Claire shared snippets of history. Remembering the painting of Claire's great-grandfather, she questioned her friend about the original division of land, the mining years, and the introduction of fruit-and-vegetable growing in the region.

Eventually, having divulged all she knew, Claire shot Ashleigh a sympathetic look. 'Why don't we eat lunch and, instead of hiking farther up the valley to inspect the mines, we head to the Glenrowan boundary and follow the road along to the next valley? It'll be easier on your sore legs. We can go to the mines next time.'

'Sounds good.' Ashleigh grinned wryly, drawing a long breath and wiggling her toes. The new boots were proving to be more comfortable than she'd imagined and, although having woken stiff and sore, her muscles had softened and she was no longer in pain—for now, anyway. 'I'm up for it if you are.'

15

*C*harlie snuggled against his father as the thunder crashed above them. 'Will the rain come in our tent?'

'No, mate. The storm will pass soon. Are you warm enough?'

'Hmm. I like my swag.'

Damian grinned into the dark. While he'd had to dust off his old canvas swag and dry-clean his sleeping bag before re-inserting it, Charlie's was brand new. Still smelling of waterproof dressing, the outer shell encased a down-filled bag that would keep Charlie warm and dry in even the harshest of winters. When they'd first crawled into bed, the air had been muggy and still, suggesting an impeding storm. They'd both lain on top of their swags for a few minutes. Then the rain had arrived and the temperature plummeted.

'I hope it stops soon. I really want to go exploring again.'

'I know. Don't worry. The rain will be gone by morning.' He stroked Charlie's soft, dark hair. 'Go to sleep now or you'll be too tired to do anything tomorrow.'

'Night-night, Dad.'

'Night, Charlie. I'm here for you.'

The little boy pressed against his father and closed his eyes.

Minutes later, certain Charlie was asleep, Damian unzipped the front flap a fraction and peered outside. Sheets of rain blew almost sideways while trees swayed and dipped under the pressure. He stuck his head out under the narrow awning and raked the skies with his eyes. To the east, a patch of stars suddenly appeared amongst the blackness. Damian released a breath, barely aware he had been holding it. Thank goodness. He had been right. It was only a minor storm and would be gone within minutes. At least he hoped so. Charlie asked for so little—expected nothing. If their camping weekend was ruined, he would be heartbroken.

BOTH HE AND Charlie woke as the sky turned from black to clean, golden hues of yellow, orange, and red.

Outside, the grass sparkled as early morning glistened on the leaves.

After inspecting the campsite for any signs of flooding or damage, Damian lifted the cover from the woodpile on the back of his ute. It wouldn't take long to get a fire going, and a hot drink was just what they both needed to start their day.

Charlie perched on the log seat with a folded towel underneath him for protection. He sipped his hot chocolate while he watched his father cook breakfast. After a hearty meal of leftover sausages, eggs, and tomatoes, they packed as much as possible into the ute in case of another storm, hoisted their backpacks on, and strode in the opposite direction to the previous afternoon's walk.

'Shall we have a look around the rocks first? See what lizards are hanging around,' Damian suggested.

Charlie nodded. 'And find the plane?'

'Yes. We'll search for the plane, too. Remember what I said though—we've got all day, so we don't have to rush.'

Within minutes, exploring the clump of boulders that clung to the side of a sharp rise had Charlie engrossed. While he poked around, Damian took time to assess jobs that would need doing before long. Although they were still on Dot's property, firebreaks and gazetted but undeveloped roads dotted the area. Despite being surveyed more than a century earlier, it was hard for Damian to comprehend the government considering breaking the swathes of native bush into small, unproductive farms. This bushland needed protection—but having cattle graze in the open areas helped enormously with fire control. It had been a long while since a slasher had been over the under-growth now covering the original firebreak. *I'll do them all in the next couple of months.*

'Dad!' Charlie's call interrupted Damian's thoughts, and he hurried over to him.

'What have you found?'

'Look.' Charlie's eyes were enormous and round as he pointed to a cleft in the rock.

Peering inside the deep, leaf-filled slot, Damian squinted. 'Can I borrow your torch, Charlie?'

After handing it to his father, Charlie returned his gaze to the space.

Damian held the torch steady, focusing on Char-lie's discovery. Nestled on a bed of crushed leaves lay a clutch of lizard eggs. There was no sign of a parent and he couldn't be sure how many there were, but he was pleased about evidence of wildlife reproduction, albeit small.

'Do you think they're bearded dragon eggs?'

'Not sure, Charlie. Blue-tongues and Cunningham's skinks give birth to live babies, so it wouldn't be them. You'll have to keep an eye on the area when we come to check the cattle next time.'

Satisfied with his discovery, Charlie willingly trotted ahead of his father as they continued their trek into the bush.

Hours later, the tired child and his dad plonked themselves on the grass next to a rusting sheet of steel nestled in the undergrowth. 'There's not much left, is there, Dad?'

'No. It was a long time ago, and when a plane crashes, the debris spreads for kilometres. And there's been a few fires through here over the years. Salvage teams would have removed what they could, but a bushfire would have melted any aluminium.'

'Oh.' Disappointment shadowed the boy's face.

'Never mind. You've seen it now. And maybe as you grow up, more rain and storms might wash the soil away and, one day, we could dig it up. Let's have lunch and then we'll take another route back to camp. Okay with you?' Damian said.

Charlie nodded tiredly.

After a rest and with full stomachs again, they rose to their feet and began the downhill hike. Damian carried both packs, having strapped Charlie's onto the top flap of his own so Charlie could walk more easily.

Stopping frequently, they followed a kangaroo trail to the edge of the bush where it opened to a wide but overgrown firebreak.

'Can you give me a piggyback, Dad?'

'Come here, mate. I can't fit you on my back as well

as what's already there, but I can carry you for a little while.' He leaned forward, picked his son up, and sat him on his shoulders. With the boy's legs hanging down Damian's chest, he could clasp them tightly, preventing Charlie from losing his balance.

Slowing his pace, they made their way silently, pushing the tangle of vines aside before crossing back into the bush and through to the other side where their tent remained, erect and untouched.

Hot and sweaty after his exertion, Damian unloaded the packs and pulled a towel from his clothing bag. 'I'm going to the creek to wash. Want to come for a paddle?'

Charlie leapt into life again, his previous energy now restored a little.

Damian stripped off and sluiced himself with the cold water while Charlie sat on a broken tree branch and dabbled his feet.

'That was a funny-looking tree we passed, wasn't it, Dad?'

'What tree?'

'The one shaped like a ... sort of vehicle. You know, square like one of those old-fashioned four-wheel-drive trucks I've seen in books.'

'Are you sure it was a tree?' Damian stared at his son, his eyes narrowing.

'I think so. It was the same colour as trees.' He

waved his arms about. 'Green and brown ... and like it's been in the mud.'

'Where was this tree?'

Charlie shrugged. 'Don't know exactly. Somewhere near the fire road. I could see it 'cause I was so high up —when you were carrying me.'

Damian frowned. Did Charlie really mean a tree shaped like a vehicle? Or a vehicle camouflaged to blend in with the bush? His veins turned icy, not only from the cold water. If there was someone hiding a vehicle up here in the bush, how did they get here without being noticed—and why?

16

_T_he girls reached a divide in the track and paused.

Claire pointed to the left fork. 'That's the way home, but if we take this trail, we'll find a back lane that runs parallel to the main road. It's only used by residents. You okay with that?'

'How far is it?'

Claire shrugged. 'Not exactly sure. Two k's? Maybe a bit more.'

Ashleigh nodded, reluctant to admit she was tiring. 'What about the exclusion fence you mentioned? I know we came through a complicated gate where we left the ute, but how do we get out this side?'

'Don't worry. After the trouble with the drug runners on Glenrowan, Kirk prioritised this side of the property and installed a gate in case of fire.' She slipped her hand into her jeans pocket and withdrew a key. 'This fits all the locks around the place. It was the most practical way to establish security without becoming too complicated.'

'Oh.'

Following Claire along the narrow pathway, Ashleigh drank the last of her water, tripping on a tree root as she swallowed. She tucked the empty vessel in the side pocket of her pack and focused on the ground instead of her surroundings.

The fence appeared and Claire let them through, ensuring they locked it behind them. With the dirt road providing easier walking, they tramped side-by-side, their conversation now minimal as their energy waned.

After a couple of kilometres, a dirt road branched up the hill and Claire pointed to the mailboxes on the roadside. 'Someone must live up here.'

'Have you been up?'

'Don't think so. If I have, it would have been with one of my parents years ago and I don't remember it. Shall we explore?'

Ashleigh's feet were sore now and her back aching. 'How about we walk for twenty minutes? If we don't find a water source or anything interesting, we turn around and go back.'

Claire looked at her watch. 'Okay. It's after four and

the sun will set in about two hours. We'd better step it out.'

Watching where she put her feet to so as not to twist an ankle in one of the deep ruts, Ashleigh drew a deep breath and trod alongside her friend.

Exactly twenty minutes later, Claire stopped, resting her hands on her hips. 'Well, this is it. A big, fat nothing.'

Ashleigh stared up ahead. 'It looks like a side track beside that big eucalypt tree. Let's just go that far, then turn around.'

'Okay. Sure you're not too tired?'

'I'm fine,' Ashleigh lied. She hadn't come all this way to ignore the only point of interest in kilometres. If it was a house, perhaps the owner would let them refill their empty water bottles. Flexing her shoulders, she led the way to where two narrow wheel tracks swung to the right while the wider section of road continued up the hill.

Stopping suddenly, she grabbed Claire's arm and pointed. 'See! There's a shed or something. Maybe there's a tank where we can get water.'

Forgetting their exhaustion, they increased their pace as they approached the small, timber shack. A border collie dog rushed at them, barking frantically. Ashleigh clutched Claire's arm again.

Claire ignored her and held her hand out toward

the dog. 'It's okay, little one. We're not here to hurt you. Just want a drink of water.'

Although it didn't come any closer, the dog wagged its tail.

'There you are. There's nothing to be afraid of.' Claire approached cautiously until the dog sniffed her then moved to smell Ashleigh.

Ashleigh stood perfectly still, allowing the dog to inspect her before she felt the warm lick of a doggy tongue on the back of her hand.

'Look at that,' Claire said. 'It thinks you're a friend.'

Ashleigh chuckled. 'Probably knows I'm as worried as it is. Shall I pat it?'

Before Claire could answer, the dog had nudged Ashleigh's hand as though asking for human contact. She reached down and stroked the soft black-and-white head as a thin, frail voice sounded.

'Lass! Who is it, girl?'

Staring for a moment, Ashleigh took a few steps toward the tiny person. Under a wide-brimmed hat, the person's face was almost invisible, while baggy trousers and an old felt jacket covered the small body. Ashleigh wasn't sure if it was a man or a woman. 'I'm sorry to bother you, but we've been hiking and have run out of water. We wondered if we could fill our canisters, please?' she called.

The person pointed toward a large tank attached to a steel shed on the far side of the shack. 'Over there.'

The girls thanked her and hurried past, filled their bottles, and returned to where the person remained fixed to the spot.

'Thanks again. We appreciate your help,' Ashleigh said, smiling. As she met the soft, grey eyes beneath the hat brim, she blanched, clamping her jaw shut to prevent her shock from being obvious.

At close quarters, the individual was an elderly woman, her long, white hair in a plait down her back. One side of her face—the side they had seen as they passed on the way to the tank—was clear with a plump, rosy cheek highlighting a myriad of age lines around her eye and mouth. On the other, the flesh was pale. Puckered. Knotted and twisted out of shape with the top part of her lip missing and the bottom a thickened lump. Ashleigh's heart somersaulted. She was facing someone who had survived a fire—or something even more horrendous.

Not wanting to display her horror, she gabbled. 'Thanks again. I'm Ashleigh Paton ... and my friend is Claire Shepherd.'

'The teacher.'

Ashleigh's jaw dropped at the woman's comment. 'Yes. I teach at Featherwood Falls.'

The old woman gave a small nod, signalled the dog with a slap against her leg, and walked back to the shack.

As the dog trotted to her owner, Ashleigh glanced

at Claire's mortified expression. She rushed toward her and whispered, 'Come on. Let's go.'

AFTER STRIDING down the lane in silence, her tiredness and aching feet now forgotten, Ashleigh paused at the mailboxes. 'Who is she?'

Claire shook her head. 'I've got no idea. Never seen her around town.'

Ashleigh huffed. 'Well, she knew who I was, so someone's keeping her informed.'

Claire frowned. 'Yeah. I wonder ...' She trailed off, and Ashleigh beckoned.

'Come on. We can talk and walk—and if we don't get a move on, we'll be walking back in the dark.' She took a few strides before turning to face Claire again. 'What do you wonder?'

'I vaguely remember stories of a reclusive woman living in the bush somewhere. I know nothing about her, but I seem to recollect an old fellow coming out of the post office when I was going in one day. He had a box full of groceries in his arms and must have just collected mail.' She paused for a moment. 'There were a couple of newspapers on the top of the box ... and a letter or two. The old man called something out to Frank inside. I can't remember the exact words, but I was puzzled about what he said—something about being a slave to a hermit who should do her own running around.'

'So, do you think the woman we just met could be the hermit he was referring to?'

'Maybe. Whoever she is, she's obviously been through a tough time in her life.' Claire fell silent as they plodded along the track toward Featherwood Station again.

They passed the tree-lined back boundary of Glenrowan and rounded the bend leading home. The taut, high fence surrounding the property appeared in the distance as the sun slid behind the ridge, leaving shadows in its wake. Ashleigh smiled at Claire, the relief on both their faces visible.

'Sorry, Ash. It was supposed to be a nice day of hiking today, checking out the mine and taking time to have a good look at my home farm.'

'Hey, don't apologise. We might need a rest tomorrow, but it's been an interesting day.'

'You're not wrong.'

17

———

*I*t was dark by the time they reached the farm ute, with only a few bright dots appearing in the sky and the temperature plummeting. After heaving their backpacks onto the tray, Claire unlocked the vehicle and rubbed her hands together. 'Hop in before we freeze.' She started the engine, switched on the lights, and glanced across at Ashleigh. 'You know who could tell us who the woman is ...? Lola.'

'Of course. Everyone says she's the town historian.'

Claire giggled. 'She certainly knows more than most people, but she's not a gossip. If the old girl we just met has secrets only Lola's heard, Lola might be reluctant to share them.'

'Well. I see that as a good quality. But ... if we explain that the old woman knows who I am, Lola might agree it's only fair that I know who the woman is.'

Claire switched on the cabin light and held her left arm to read her watch. 'Frank will lock up in a few minutes. Do you want to go straight to the store and ask?'

'Would that be okay? I mean ... you don't think it's rude?'

'Nah. It's the Browns we're talking about here. They're more like my grandparents than anything else. They'll be pleased to see us.'

'Great. Let's do it.'

AFTER A QUICK STOP at the homestead to let Ginny know they were safe and would be back for dinner within an hour, they continued into the village and parked beside the store.

'Hello!' Frank's cheery, weathered face greeted them as they stepped onto the roadside. 'What brings the two prettiest girls in town to see me?' he joked.

'Ha-ha, Frank. You're full of it as usual,' Claire quipped. 'We're hoping you and Lola can answer a question for us.'

His face crinkled in another smile, and he waved toward the small gate that led into the yard behind the shop. 'Head in there. Lola will be feeding the animals. I won't be a tick—just locking up.'

Ashleigh followed Claire through the wrought-iron gate and along the flagstone path leading to the back porch. A row of LED tubes lining the eaves of the building cast yellow light over the path and into the yard. Under their glow, a variety of sheds and coops could be seen leading into the dark while a neat vegetable garden, edged with violas, hugged the house wall.

Lola emerged from the henhouse, the hem of her apron held in one hand, forming a cotton basin filled with eggs. She latched the door behind her. 'Hello, girls. What a lovely surprise to see you both.'

'Hi, Lola,' Claire called. 'Have you got a few minutes to talk?'

'Of course, love. Always got time to talk. You should know that.' She threw her head back and laughed noisily. After toeing off her gumboots on the porch, Lola pushed the door open. 'Come in.'

Fragrant scents of herbs and tomatoes greeted them as they entered the living area. Ashleigh had never been through the solid door dividing the shop from the house but Lola's timber cabinets and stone-topped benches provided a second—and much cosier —environment than the commercial, stainless-steel worktops and ovens of the shop.

On either side of a combustion wood fire, two

chairs with antimacassars over the armrests faced a gigantic television screen. A long, squashy couch sat against one wall, and a bookcase filled to the top with a wide assortment of books—from classics to romance novels and children's nursery rhymes—on the other.

'Sit down. I'll just unload these eggs and give the casserole a stir. Then we can have a friendly talk.' Lola shuffled into the kitchen area, transferred the eggs into a carton, then removed a large pottery tureen from the oven. When she lifted the lid, Ashleigh almost swayed with ecstasy. Her stomach rumbled and for a few seconds, she could think of nothing but chomping into whatever the dish contained.

Lola returned to one armchair before plonking herself down with a sigh. 'Oh, it's good to sit.' She gave a wry grin, and both Claire and Ashleigh smiled sympathetically. She wasn't the only one glad to flop into a chair.

Lola appeared ageless with her brightly coloured clothes, vibrant earrings, and her ability to seem unfazed by anything that came her way. Ashleigh guessed her to be close to seventy, if not older. Working on her feet all day could not be easy—and yet, in the few months Ashleigh had been in Featherwood Falls, she had never once heard Lola complain.

'I won't muck about, Lola. I know you'll be eager to have dinner and hook into the next episode of whatever drama you're watching now,' Claire said, and they both laughed—the laughter of friends who knew each other's habits.

'It's *Vera* tonight. Don't you just love those British crime shows?' Lola replied.

Claire smiled. 'Okay. So, Ash and I have been hiking, and … long story short, we explored a bit of the back country behind Glenrowan where that dirt road leads up the valley and into the bush.' Claire paused as Frank entered the room.

After a few seconds, waiting for him to sit down, she repeated herself, pausing as though to check she had their full attention.

'Go on,' Lola said.

'We ran out of water, so thought we'd call into the property up that way and fill our bottles again. Anyway, a woman appeared out of a sort of timber shack. She was polite and let us get the water, but that was all. I mean, she didn't invite us in or anything … and she was so tiny, with dreadful scars on her face.'

'Well, she probably didn't know who you were,' Lola said tartly. 'These days you wouldn't know who is around or who you can trust.' She raised her eyebrows at Claire. 'Last year taught us all about that, didn't it?'

Ashleigh scrunched up her forehead. There was a reference to something she didn't understand there but she was too interested in Lola's information to stop her and question.

Claire nodded, scooping her pale-gold hair back and re-tying the band around her ponytail.

Ashleigh leaned forward. 'The funny thing was, she knew I was the new teacher and yet seemed … well, reclusive. We left quickly but almost felt afraid.'

Frank relaxed back in his chair, his kind face solemn now. 'No need to be afraid of Dot.' He glanced at Lola as though requesting unspoken permission to explain.

Ashleigh stiffened, realisation consuming her every cell. 'Damian? And Charlie?' She thought about Charlie's loving references to "Dotty". Could his Dotty and the strange old lady be one and the same?

Lola nodded, and Frank continued, 'Dot Collins has lived up the valley for donkey's years. She and her husband arrived around the time we did. But they minded their own business, and we rarely saw them in town. Got a big place—around two thousand hectares, I think. Anyway, back in the nineties, when the drought was biting hard, a big bushfire took hold in the hills. No one knows exactly what happened, but the two of them weren't in their house when the Rural Fire Service arrived to help. Fire and Rescue dropped water bombs on their property and got the fire under control, but when they found Dot and her husband, he was just charred remains and she'd been badly burned trying to get to him. Dot was whipped off to hospital, and months later, she turned up back here and has continued to manage as best she can.'

Ashleigh swallowed the lump in her throat, her eyes prickling with unshed tears. Unable to speak, she imagined the horror the poor woman must have experienced.

'So, since then, I guess she hasn't wanted to be seen in public,' Claire whispered.

Frank drew a deep breath and blew it out again. 'I reckon so. Bob, her neighbour, calls in every so often and takes a box of groceries and her mail up to her.' He paused, his face softening. 'Although now she's got family living with her, he doesn't do that as much.'

'Family?' Claire asked.

'Yeah. A nephew, I think. No, a great-nephew and his little boy.'

'Yeah,' Frank answered. 'I think that's him. Don't see him around much. Mostly goes to Stanthorpe or Warwick to shop, I think. Nice fella though. Quiet. Keeps to himself.'

'Huh. We all know the last couple of years haven't helped,' Lola added. 'Poor kid didn't have a chance to mix with anyone until this year.' She narrowed her eyes and stared at Ashleigh. 'Is he alright? The child, I mean.'

'Yes, he's delightful. A bit eccentric too, I guess. But … now we've put the pieces of the puzzle together, I understand why.' Ashleigh pressed her palms together, lacing her fingers then loosening them again. A hundred thoughts tumbled around in her head, and suddenly she wanted to return to her little home and curl up in bed.

After thanking Frank and Lola, the girls returned to Featherwood Station. It took every grain of Ashleigh's being to not excuse herself from Ginny's dinner invitation. Her appetite had vanished. Could she invent a headache—or declare she was too exhausted to eat? No, if she did, Ginny or Claire would accept her apology but insist on sending her home with a container filled with delicious home-cooked food. Or they might insist she stay the night at the farm. That would only enhance her guilt, and she couldn't do that to them.

She would join the family for dinner, thank them, and then excuse herself after the dishes had been done.

Then she would drive herself home, snuggle under the warm doona, and reflect on Lola and Frank's revelation in private. She craved the opportunity to revisit every scar on the old lady's face, every question Charlie had ever asked, and every conversation she had had with Damian.

Only then would she decide whether she should share the information with Quinn. After all, Dot had proven how fiercely private she was, and the last thing Ashleigh wanted to do was upset a woman who had endured so much.

18

*D*amian drove into the shed, switched off the engine, and turned to his passenger.

'We're home. So ... what did you think? Will we be going camping again?'

Charlie beamed at him and nodded fiercely. 'Yep. It was fun.' He unclipped his seatbelt and opened the door. 'I'm going to tell Dotty all about it.'

'Righto, mate. We've got some unpacking to do, but I suppose it can wait until we've had a cuppa.'

Charlie raced to the house while Damian collected the esky from the ute tray and followed him slowly, a soft smile on his face.

Despite the rain, he treasured the time they spent together. His plan had been to teach Charlie some skills his great-uncle Thomas, Dot's husband, had taught him at a similar age. But somehow, he had learned as much from Charlie as the reverse. The child had always loved animals, but his passion for wildlife and their habitats had surprised him. He chuckled to himself. A real little Steve Irwin. Except Charlie was quiet and seemed to enjoy his solitude—or was that only because he knew little else?

Damian sat on a veranda chair, pulling his boots off as Charlie's high-pitched voice drifted out of the open door.

A vision of Charlie's teacher invaded his thoughts, and he grunted as he stepped inside. Fiery young madam. Why the hell did she keep popping into his head when he least expected it?

'What's the matter with you?' Dot asked. 'You look like you want to yell at someone.'

Damian laughed, shrugging off his thoughts and giving the little woman a gentle hug. 'It's nothing. Must have been that bacon we ate for breakfast, giving me heartburn. Sorry.'

'That's alright then.' She pointed to the esky. 'Leave that to me to sort out later. Now sit down and tell me all about it.'

It took almost an hour to drink a pot of tea and demolish Dot's freshly baked scones, with Charlie chattering excitedly, pausing every so often to confirm details with his father.

Stuffing the last scone into his mouth, Charlie slipped off the chair. 'I'm going to check on my friends.'

He reached the door and turned to face Dot, his forehead creasing. 'Did you remember to feed the possums?'

'Yes, Charlie. Mummy possum was waiting each night for me, just as you said she would. I gave her a piece of apple and some orange. Her baby's getting big now ... nearly big enough to get off his mother's back.'

Charlie grinned and shot out the door, slamming it behind him.

In the kitchen's quiet, Dot narrowed her eyes at Damian. 'So how did it go—really?'

'We had a good time, actually.' Damian's face melted into a contented smile. 'He's a great kid. Got so much interest and enthusiasm for everything. I worry I'm not giving him the same opportunities as other kids have, but he doesn't seem interested in going anywhere.'

Aware of Dot's scrutiny, Damian met the poor, disfigured face. Her skin may have been scarred, but there was nothing wrong with her eyesight—even for a ninety-three-year-old.

Before she could say more, he changed the subject. 'How did things go here? Any problems?'

She shook her head. 'No. Lass and I did our usual chores, and I read the papers.' She paused for a few moments. 'Had a couple of visitors, though.'

Damian's eyes widened, and he pulled himself up in the chair. 'Who?'

'That new teacher from the school and another girl.'

'What the hell were they doing up here, nosing around?' His temper flared, his voice rising.

Dot's eyes narrowed. 'Said they were out hiking and ran out of water.'

'Oh.'

'I think they were telling the truth. They both looked hot and tired.' She screwed up her face for a second. 'The teacher said her friend was Claire Shepherd. I haven't set eyes on her before, but she's the dead spit of her father, Lyndon Shepherd.'

'Well. I hope that's all they were doing,' he grumbled. 'We don't want anyone's interference—especially not Charlie's teacher.'

Dot stared at him for a few moments, and a warm heat flushed up his neck.

He pushed his chair back and stood. 'I'm going to unpack the ute.'

Aware of the knowing eyes boring into his back, he marched out the door.

CHARLIE HAD DISAPPEARED FROM SIGHT, but Damian wasn't concerned. Lass had gone with him and, anyway, he was sensible and more aware of the environmental dangers than most adults. It was only after almost two hours had passed that he was worried.

The sun was sliding rapidly in the western sky, the curl of smoke from the wood stove drifting in the cooling air when Charlie burst from the bush a hundred metres from the shed, the dog hard on his heels.

'Dad!'

'Charlie. Where have you been? It's getting late.'

Damian pressed a hand against his forehead as he stared into Charlie's huge blue eyes.

A telltale tear had left a clean track down one cheek and his lip quivered. 'You know the rainbow lorikeets that were nesting in the tree beside the old pump?'

Damian narrowed his eyes. The pump Charlie referred to was more than a kilometre away. No wonder he had been gone so long. 'Yes, mate.'

Charlie upturned his hands. 'They're gone.'

'Flown away, you mean?'

'How could they? It's only two weeks since they laid their eggs and now everything's gone. They were there when I checked before we went camping.'

'Perhaps another bird destroyed their nest?'

Charlie shook his head firmly. 'No, Dad, the lorikeets wouldn't have let them. They were the boss of the area and didn't let other birds near. I know 'cause I've been watching them.'

'How do you know they had eggs then? Isn't their nest high in the tree?'

Charlie bowed his head sheepishly. 'Yes—but I can climb really well now and there's a tree close to the nest that's easy to climb. I've been watching them through those binoculars you gave me last Christmas.'

Damian raised his chin, his frown melting into a knowing smile. How could he chastise Charlie for doing the same thing he had as a young boy? 'You shouldn't be climbing trees without telling me, Charlie. What if you had slipped and fallen? I didn't know where you'd gone and if you hurt yourself, it could have been hours before I found you.'

Charlie stared up at his father before glancing at the dog at his feet. 'No, Dad, I was very careful. But if I had a fall, Lass would have come and got you, wouldn't she?' he finished matter-of-factly.

Damian clamped his lips together. Charlie's explanation was probably true—but after hearing his observation of what Damian was now certain was a camouflage-painted vehicle, an uneasiness wormed its way through his gut. What was this vehicle and who had been driving it? The thought of the missing birds flew from his mind. Charlie being in danger of abduction, or worse, was a much more serious issue.

He resolved there and then that he would make enquiries. Talk to Rhys at the police station—and in the meantime, he would ensure Charlie was with either him or Dot at all times.

19

With only two days left of the school holidays, Ashleigh was determined to grasp the basics of riding before the new term began.

For the past few days, the weather had been kind and her confidence had grown with each day's lesson. Today, though, clouds had built in the east, and she hoped she would get to experience the ride around the farm as Claire had promised.

Dressed in jodhpurs and a flannelette shirt, she slid the zucchini slice out of the oven and sat it on a towel on the bench top. It looked perfect. Every bit as mouth-watering as Netty's version. A grin spread across her face. It had taken a while, but at last she had mastered the tiny gas oven. The oven was big enough to hold a medium-sized baking dish, and Ashleigh had deter-mined that during these holidays it would be one challenge she would meet. The bag of vegetables she'd purchased from a road-side stall earlier in the week was all but depleted now—and she was looking forward to a change of diet from the "practise" zucchini slices to a decent piece of steak. Today was the day to share her creation with the Shepherd family.

While the slice cooled a little, she plastered a second layer of sunscreen on her face and gathered the various essentials for the day—a warm jacket and rain-coat, a pair of clean jeans and shirt, and a bag containing hair-taming mousse and ties. Finally, she wrapped the dish in foil and then wound the towel around it and carried it carefully to her car, where she sat it on the floor. She'd learned the hard way that sitting items on the seat while driving in the country was fraught with unexpected problems. It wasn't only the wildlife hopping across the road, but the potholes and wandering cattle that required sudden braking—often with unfortunate results.

At eight-thirty, she pulled up outside the Feather-wood Station homestead, a smile on her face and the contents of the baking dish intact.

'Hi there!' Claire's welcoming call sounded from the dog kennels, and Ashleigh waved and walked over.

The five kelpies were milling around, sniffing the ground with one eye on Claire as though waiting for her instruction.

'I thought we'd take Drum and Flute with us today

for a good run. How do you feel about shifting a mob of sheep?'

Ashleigh raised her eyebrows. 'Wow. Do you trust me to help?'

Claire laughed. 'You'll be fine. The dogs do the shifting. We just park ourselves in the right spot so the sheep go the way we want them to.'

'Okay. If you say so.' Her stomach fluttered and she bit back the wave of anxiety. Despite the imposing height of Splash, she had allowed Claire to talk her into riding him on two occasions and had been relieved to discover he was the gentle and obedient horse Claire had assured her of, in the yard at least. In the wide-open space of a large paddock, she wasn't so confident.

'Shall we have a quick coffee before we leave?' Claire shut the gates behind three of the dogs, leaving two black and tan kelpies loose.

Ashleigh had visited enough times to familiarise herself with the dogs and was a little disappointed at not having Chime accompany them. She reached into her pen and gently rubbed Chime under the ears.

As though reading her mind, Claire said, 'Chime is close to her whelping date now, so we'll give Drum and Flute a run.'

'Gosh, I didn't realise puppies were imminent. Who's the father?'

'Banjo. He's sired a couple of litters now—but this

will be Chime's last. She's had enough pups and although they're a significant source of extra income for the family, we don't let any of our girls have more than four pregnancies.'

As Claire shared information about breeding dogs, they returned to Ashleigh's car, extracted the zucchini slice, and meandered along the path to the homestead.

A deep rumble sounded behind them, and Ashleigh turned. 'Looks like you've got a visitor.'

Claire scowled as she glanced at the burgundy-coloured LandCruiser trailing a cloud of dust behind it as it skidded to a halt beside Ashleigh's car. 'Just what we don't need. A visit from Uncle Donald.'

Ashleigh's jaw dropped at Claire's outburst. She was such a family-orientated person, her response to the impending visitor came as a shock. 'Not the favourite uncle, then?'

'Far from it,' Claire spat. 'I'll get Mum.'

As she spoke, Ginny emerged from behind the house with an empty washing basket tucked under one arm. 'I'm here, Claire,' she said in a low voice. 'You put the kettle on, and I'll deal with him.'

Ashleigh scurried up the steps after Claire, throwing a quick glance over her shoulder at the figure stepping out of the four-wheel drive.

Voices drifted inside while Claire made coffee and Ashleigh rearranged the fridge in order to fit her slice in. While she didn't shout, there was an agitated edge to Ginny's tone.

'Is Kirk around?' Ashleigh whispered.

'No, he left early this morning. He's fencing somewhere over Pikedale way and won't be home until late.' Claire glanced through the kitchen window and wrinkled her nose. 'I hope the rain holds off for a while. Mum might need us here for a bit.'

A quiver of alarm shot through Ashleigh. Who was this uncle? And why did he cause so much angst for Ginny and Claire?

It didn't take long for Ashleigh to understand her friend's reluctance to host the man sitting opposite her as she sipped her coffee.

'What brings a pretty young thing like you to a backward place like Featherwood Falls, Ashleigh?' His condescending tone rankled, generating an unexpected flare of annoyance within her.

She gritted her teeth, swallowing her irritation in an effort to remain polite. 'Work. I'm a teacher at the school.'

'Wow. So, Quinn needed help to control the ferals, did he?' He leaned forward, his pudgy belly squashing against the table while piggy eyes blinked at her from the folds of a weathered and overweight face. 'Have you got a boyfriend? I bet the young fellas around here are pleased to have fresh meat in town.'

Ashleigh's temper flared.

'How dare you speak to Ashleigh like that!' Ginny snapped. 'I'd thank you for remembering your manners in this house. Why are you here anyway?' She leaned her elbows on the table, her back stiff, her glare meeting his.

Ashleigh touched her cheek, willing the heat to dissipate while she gritted her teeth and watched the silent hostility unfold. *I know why this relative isn't the flavour of the month.*

'Thought I'd let you know I've employed another manager for Glenrowan.' A smirk widened his thick lips. Ashleigh swallowed her revulsion as he continued. 'We've had a bit of a revolving door lately. Not my fault. Just a sign of how hard it is to get good staff these days.'

Ginny grunted. 'So, who've you got this time?'

'An older couple. They're doing the lap of Aussie— you know, the grey-nomad thing. Looking for a place to stop a while though, so I've signed them up for a six-month contract. That should get us through the harvest and hopefully get next season's tomatoes planted.'

'Righto,' Ginny responded before bending to pick up the black cat that had been rubbing against the table leg.

Ashleigh waited, quietly observing Ginny's disinterest while confusion bubbled inside her. From her conversation at the falls with Claire she understood

the tale of the drug cartel and the owner's imprison-
ment. But what did Donald have to do with staffing the
property?

The minutes dragged as Donald polished off the
last of the peanut brownies.

Claire tapped her fingers on the table and cleared
her throat. 'What are the new employees' names?'

'Lee and Eileen Dawson. You'll probably see them
around a bit. Drive a Land Rover.'

'So, are you expecting two elderly people to harvest
everything on their own?' Claire's voice rose with
incredulity.

'Of course not,' Donald snapped, his lip curling
into a sneer. 'I've found a few backpackers who're
staying in the house. They reckon they'll keep it clean
and work in the fields. Suits the Dawsons because
they've got their caravan and like to get away exploring
the area when they're not busy.'

'And how often do you expect to come over to
check on things?' Ginny asked, her chin raised. 'After
all, as the property manager in the owner's absence,
you're responsible for the farm's well-being—especially after last year's debacle.'

Donald honked and coughed up phlegm, hauling a
freshly ironed handkerchief from his pocket and
wiping his mouth. Ashleigh gagged.

'I'll be calling in every couple of weeks. Sarah's in
control of finances, so will do the workers' wages. I'll

deliver them and cast an eye over the progress each time I visit.'

After what felt like hours, Donald finally pushed his chair back and ambled to the veranda, where he slowly pulled on his boots. 'By the way, how's Kirk getting on? Still keeping his end up?'

Ginny's face froze and in icy silence, she followed him to his car, casting a glance toward the girls as if to say, *I'll see him off the premises.*

'Gosh. Now I know why he's not your favourite uncle,' Ashleigh said softly.

Claire nodded and collected the empty mugs. While they stacked the dishwasher and headed out to the paddock to catch the horses, questions swirled in Ashleigh's head. Claire's strides were quicker and more purposeful than usual, as though determined to increase the distance between her uncle and herself. Ashleigh struggled with the temptation to question her friend further.

They collected the bridles, slung the saddles over the yard rail, and were donning their safety helmets when Ashleigh couldn't contain herself any longer. 'Who's Sarah?'

'Donald's wife.' Claire rolled her eyes. 'God knows what she ever saw in him, but, to her credit, she's stuck around. They've got a son, Andrew, who's at uni at the moment. He's lovely and used to spend most of his holidays here with us when he was younger—you can probably guess why. Donald and Sarah own a farm close to Warwick, but Sarah's an accountant so works in town. Poor Andrew used to be left to do a lot of the farm work while his father swanned around the countryside looking important. Now both he and Sarah have stood up to him and we haven't seen her for years. She lives her own life, according to Andrew. I have to admit, I wonder what Donald has over her. He's such a sleaze, and she's so nice. I've never understood what she sees in him or why she stays around. Fortunately, Andrew takes after her and, with her financial help, is enjoying uni.'

Ashleigh chuckled. 'It's interesting how colourful people's lives are. Mine's boring by comparison. Although Dad's been through a few things in the political minefield.'

'I can imagine. Living under the spotlight wouldn't suit me. I hate the way the media seem to dig up stuff that bears no relevance to a person's current life.'

The horses galloped toward them, Akela leading with Splash close on her heels and the two ponies making their way up the slope, stiff-legged and with necks stretched and noses in the air.

Ashleigh lowered her shoulders, refusing to

acknowledge the familiar bolt of intimidation that shot through her as she faced the oncoming charge.

An hour later, Ashleigh sat deep in her saddle, metres to the side of the open gate, the gentle gelding watching the sheep rush in front of him with pricked ears. Their brisk trot to the paddock had heated her inside and out as her fear eased and exhilaration blossomed. A wide smile spread over her face. In a little more than a week, it astonished her to discover not only did she love being around the horses and dogs, but she was actually enjoying riding. Although, she still likened it to sitting on a potential time bomb a metre and a half from the safety of the ground. Today was her biggest test. Until now, circles of trotting and the occasional canter in the big yard had expanded to a gentle trot in the paddock beside the house. Today they were covering kilometres of farmland—and Claire had promised a steady canter along the flat after they'd shifted the flock.

While the midday sun warmed her shirt-clad shoulders, her mind wandered back to the conversation held at the homestead table earlier. She drew herself up, her breath catching in her throat. Donald had said the new workers at Glenrowan drove a Land Rover. Was that the same vehicle that had roared out of a side lane, almost wiping her off the side of the road weeks earlier? No one in town drove one—country folk out here mostly drove a Toyota of some sort.

She frowned. Should she mention it to Rhys or Claire? It definitely wouldn't hurt to share it with Claire as they rode back. Perhaps Damian might run into the grey-nomad speedsters on a dirt track somewhere and give them an earful. Grinning at the thought, she waited until Claire had closed the gate, picked up her reins, and urged Splash forward to join his friend.

20

'I'll mention the vehicle to Rhys tonight. He's taking me somewhere special for dinner.' Claire shot Ashleigh a wry grin. 'Probably the pub for his favourite chicken parmie.'

They both laughed. A flash of envy momentarily consumed Ashleigh. Somewhere deep inside, she yearned to be in a relationship like Rhys and Claire's. At the tennis evenings and when she and Rhys had been at Featherwood Station for a barbeque, Ashleigh couldn't help but notice the easy way the two of them sparred, laughed, and seemed to understand each other without words—not to mention the deep, meaningful glances they gave each other at random moments.

'Thanks. The couple I saw are most likely genuine retirees.' Ashleigh grimaced. 'I hope I'm not making something out of nothing. Only they looked a bit ... surprised, I guess. Maybe because they didn't expect anyone to be out and about that early in the morning.'

'Yeah. Possibly. Still—anyone Uncle Donald employs needs to be on Rhys's radar. He's not exactly an expert judge of character.'

A vision of the obnoxious man flashed through Ashleigh's mind. She glanced at her friend. Relaxed and at one with the vibrant bay mare, Claire displayed elegance and grace regardless of the dirt on her sleeve and her battered navy vest. Ashleigh struggled to comprehend the blood ties between Claire and her uncle until her thoughts swung to her own family. They were good people, kind and caring. But she understood the chasms that prevailed in even the closest of families.

'Ready for a canter?' Claire yelled, disrupting Ashleigh's thoughts.

'Okay.' She shortened her reins, her stomach fluttering as Splash jumped into a canter and followed at Akela's heels.

TIRED AND ELATED, Ashleigh waved goodbye to Claire late in the afternoon and drove home. It was the Saturday before school returned, so she planned to spend the following day preparing for the term.

As she drove through the gates beside the principal's house, Joanne waved frantically from the bottom step. Ashleigh braked and called out, 'Welcome back! How was the holiday?'

'Fabulous.'

Quinn appeared at the top of the house stairs and followed Joanne toward Ashleigh's car, hobbling across the loose gravel on his bare feet. Both he and Joanne wore shorts, their arms tanned and their faces wearing relaxed smiles.

Ashleigh met their greeting with a grin. 'Looks like it. Did you get the rain at the coast?'

They looked at each other for a moment, their mellow expressions soft and filled with love. 'A few showers and storms, but nothing that stopped us from doing what we wanted,' Joanne said. 'There's lots to do and see around the Noosa area and we made the most of it.'

'How about you?' Quinn leaned on Ashleigh's car, crossing his arms over his chest and rubbing his upper arms. 'Why don't you come in for a coffee? We can get out of this chilly wind and catch up.'

'Sure.' Ashleigh switched off the ignition and followed the pair inside.

A few minutes later, settled at the kitchen table, Ashleigh sipped her coffee. Joanne and Quinn downloaded the events and activities that had filled the previous few days. Jet skiing, fishing, swimming, alternated with drives to Maleny, Eumundi, and Nambour for shopping and a variety of meals at restaurants and cafes might have seemed idyllic to most, but they no longer held appeal to Ashleigh.

She smiled politely, delighted they had enjoyed their break away but not one bit envious. A lifetime of living by the sea and regularly dining out had well and truly filled her needs. Now she revelled in the peace—although her anonymity had not been quite what she imagined.

'What about you? Did you enjoy Brisbane? When did you get back?' Quinn's questions left no time to answer the first before he fired off the next.

'I had a lovely couple of days with the family, thanks. Then I came back here. I've been spending a bit of time at Featherwood Station learning to ride.'

'Oh. How lovely for you,' Joanne enthused. 'We were worried you would be lonely.'

Ashleigh shook her head. 'Nope. Just a lot of quiet time in between the physical activities with Claire.' She met Joanne's eyes and grinned. 'And I've been knitting.'

'Knitting?' Quinn raised his eyebrows.

'Yes. When I went home, I cleared my wardrobe and found the wool and knitting I'd started years ago when my grandmother was alive.' She chuckled. 'It's so hot in Brisbane, I didn't finish anything and lost interest. But now my life is different—and it's so much colder here—I've resurrected my original project and will finish the cowl scarf I was making.'

'Good for you.' Joanne's interest appeared to wane as she glanced through the window. 'The grass needs mowing and look at the weeds coming through amongst the vegetables. I've got to get into the gardens tomorrow.'

Quinn gathered the empty coffee mugs and pushed his chair back. 'And we'd better plan the term curriculum, Ashleigh.' He turned to the sink and rinsed the cups as he continued, 'Have any of the kids been hanging around the school over the holidays?'

'Not that I've noticed. Some of the older boys have ridden their bikes around the tennis court a few times, but I didn't intervene. They're nice kids and at least they're safe here. I think a lot of families took advantage of the last of the summer too. The pool near the bridge has been popular.'

He nodded with approval. Although Featherwood Falls wasn't big enough to sport a community swimming pool, the natural creek that flowed through the town was crystal clear and, over many years, the community had dammed it on the bottom side of the bridge to form a large pond. Above it, hanging from an ancient river gum, a thick rope swing provided hours of fun and laughter for the local children and adults alike.

'Have you seen young Charlie at all?'

She shook her head. 'Why do you ask?'

He shrugged and followed her out the door and back to her car. 'Just hopeful, I guess. You mentioned his father was taking him camping, but I thought he might have brought him in to town to play with Tom or Jessie—or anyone, really.' Rubbing his forefinger over his chin, he frowned. 'It's hard to improve a child's social behaviour if he doesn't get to mix with other children.'

'Perhaps. But the thing with Charlie is that he doesn't seem to mind. He talks about his father, and of course the person he refers to as Dotty. Who, by the way, is the enigma I got to meet earlier in the week, even though it was by mistake.'

'Really? And who is Dotty? A pretty, young hippy type who spends her days grinding her own grain and growing organic vegetables?'

His disapproving comment provoked a flash of annoyance from Ashleigh, sending pink heat to her cheeks. She threw him a withering stare. 'No. Dotty is a woman in her nineties who has had a tragic life. It turns out she's a reclusive relation of Damian who, after some sort of accident, needed temporary care. Damian and Charlie moved in to help and—well, they're still around.'

Quinn had the grace to look guilty as he asked gently, 'How do you know all this? Did she tell you?'

Shaking her head, Ashleigh elaborated. 'No. Claire

and I happened upon her ... dwelling.' Something inside told her to tread carefully. The last thing she wanted was for Dotty—and Damian—to be ridiculed, and she wasn't sure that she approved of Quinn's inquisitive tone. 'She let us refill our water bottles and we continued on our way. We asked Frank and Lola about her though as the encounter was kind of sad.'

'Interesting. So ... tell me more.'

Ashleigh shrugged. 'She's badly scarred and I guess she chose to hide herself away—and I don't think we should interfere with Charlie's home life.' She drew herself up, as though half expecting more questions, but continued, 'Charlie's doing exceptionally well in every academic way and has more knowledge of his environment than most of the older children in the school. He's courteous and well-mannered. A model student, really.'

'Fair enough. Sorry I spoke out of turn.' He gave her a rueful grin. 'I like to know and understand as much about our students as possible. Together with their parents, it helps us provide what they need, that's all.' His voice softened. 'You're doing a great job with the kids, Ashleigh. I'm not trying to undermine you, just reassuring myself you're not getting too tied up in the personal lives of your pupils.'

Ashleigh stared at him for a moment, biting her tongue as the familiar flame of rebellion rose inside her. How could she not take an interest in her students' personal lives? Didn't that help *her* understand them and provide the support they needed? Forming connections wasn't unique to the role of principal. It was reciprocal—that close contact and understanding helped her feel part of the community.

A wave of disappointment washed over her. She'd thought Quinn felt the same way as she did but suddenly realised that, no matter how much he said he loved Featherwood Falls, it was probably only a stepping stone in his career. 'Okay. Thanks for the chat, Quinn. See you tomorrow at nine.' She plastered a smile on her face, slid into the driver's seat, and drove over the thick kikuyu grass to her little home.

She felt flat, as though the carpet had been pulled from beneath her feet. Forcing herself to think of the positives, she kicked off her boots and threw herself on her bed.

At least I didn't lose my temper. She grinned.

Contentment had helped dampen her outspoken impulses. She loved her job and her life in Featherwood Falls.

21

*E*xcited chatter filled the room the following week as children caught up with their friends and shared events from their holidays.

After closely watching her thirteen pupils, Ashleigh was relieved to note how well-developed friendships had become, regardless of gender. While there were a few squabbles and disagreements, most of the time the children displayed a unity and comradeship that she had not witnessed when teaching in the huge Brisbane school.

And then there was Charlie.

After his initial excitement at returning to school and sharing snippets of his camping trip in the bush, he retreated into his shell, becoming quiet and contemplative for long periods. Eventually, during lunch break on Friday, Ashleigh followed him to the far corner of the sports field where a pair of little friar birds had been nesting.

He stood silently peering up into the foliage of the tree, and she stopped beside him.

She spoke softly so as not to disturb the birds. 'Is anything bothering you, Charlie? Would you like to talk to me about it?'

'Something's not right.' His words were matter of fact, but his lip quivered with barely contained emotion.

'Shall we sit down?' Ashleigh bent and ran her hand over the grass. 'It's dry.'

He lowered his tiny frame next to hers, hugging his knees to his chest and resting his chin on them.

'What makes you think something's not right?'

He turned an earnest gaze to meet hers, his vivid blue eyes flashing. 'I enjoy watching the birds and lizards making their nests, sitting on the eggs, and then seeing babies being born. Not only birds hatching, but insects and lizards … and everything.'

'I know you do, Charlie. Aren't we watching the little friar birds do just that now?'

'Yes. But in the bush, it's not happening.'

Ashleigh was confused. Did he mean in a particular bush? Or was he speaking about something she did not understand? 'Tell me more, Charlie.'

'There's favourite places I've been watching for a long time. I know where birds nested last year. And where they built another nest this year. I know they laid eggs, 'cause I saw them. But ... now the eggs are gone and so are lots of the birds. Dad and me saw a lizard's nest when we were camping. I want him to take me back to see the eggs this weekend—to make sure they're still there. But he says nothing's wrong. It's just nature and I'm worrying too much.'

She stared at his face, creased with concern. 'And you're sure you not? Worrying, I mean?'

'W-w-would you help me please?' he stuttered.

'How?'

'Would you talk to my dad? Make him see something's not right.'

'Oh, Charlie. I doubt your dad will listen to me. He knows I didn't grow up in the bush like you did.' The crestfallen look on Charlie's face tore at her heart. 'But I can try. Perhaps I could send a note home with you today and ask if we can have a talk. Would that be okay?'

Charlie leapt to his feet, a smile widening on his face. He wrapped his skinny arms around her. 'Thank you, Ms Ashleigh. I knew you were special.'

A lump stuck in her throat, preventing another word from escaping. Instead, she took the boy's hand, and they ambled back to the playground.

Not as special as you are, Charlie.

～

CLAIRE'S PHONE call the following morning blew all thoughts of Charlie and his father out of Ashleigh's mind. 'He asked me to marry him! We're getting married.'

'Congratulations.'

Claire's delight was infectious, and Ashleigh's smile widened. It had been such a busy week that she hadn't spoken to her friend to see how their dinner date had gone. A prick of guilt stabbed her, quickly squashed by the realisation that Claire must have been just as busy —or perhaps otherwise occupied.

'We've spent half the week talking things over with Mum and Rhys's parents. Not sure when the wedding will be, but we've decided it will be quite small. But ... we'll have a community-style engagement party soon and that will be a big one.'

'That's fantastic news, Claire. I'm thrilled for you.'

They chatted for a few minutes before Claire ended the conversation. 'See you at tennis this afternoon. I can't wait to show you my ring.'

As she shoved her washing into the machine under Quinn and Joanne's house, Ashleigh couldn't explain the dull emptiness she'd born for so long. Delight for Claire and Rhys filled her. They were a great couple and clearly in love. She enjoyed the peace and freedom of living here in Featherwood Falls. But something had been missing and now she knew what it was, the weight was easing. The love of another human.

She huffed out a long breath, crossed her arms over her chest, and gave herself a squeeze. While the washing was tumbling around doing its own thing, she would walk to the store and buy a cup of Lola's freshly ground coffee. That would help—and so would a chat with her favourite storekeeper.

The bell dinged as she pushed the door open and immediately the fragrances of coffee and fresh pastries filled her senses.

'Hello, love. How was your first week of term?' Lola beamed over the customer's shoulder as she handed change to the elderly gentleman, a newspaper tucked firmly under his armpit. 'There you go. See you next week.'

Touching the brim of his hat, he thanked Lola and turned toward the exit, shooting Ashleigh a nod and a small smile as he shuffled by.

'Pretty good thanks, Lola. And you?'

'You know what it's like here. A permanently revolving door—and after the couple of years we've just had, I wouldn't want it any other way.'

Ashleigh shared an understanding smile.

'So ... have you heard the news?' Lola's eyes sparkled with excitement, her earrings swinging with more ferocity than usual.

'About Claire and Rhys, you mean?'

'Yes, of course. Isn't it wonderful? It's been a while since we've had a wedding here and I can't think of a more deserving or better-matched couple than those two.' She pointed to the coffee machine, then craned her neck to peer through the front windows. 'Let's have a coffee together while there are no other customers.'

A few minutes later, comfortably ensconced at the corner table, they chatted about the upcoming wedding, how Ashleigh was going with her riding lessons, and a raft of other subjects. Lola had just asked Ashleigh how her time with her parents had gone when the doorbell rang and a middle-aged couple walked in.

There was something familiar about them, something Ashleigh couldn't put her finger on. She sipped the last of her coffee while Lola served them. Where had seen them before? Perhaps they were Brisbane residents on holiday, constituents of her fathers. A small smile touched her lips at the thought. They were dressed in shabby clothing with sandals on their gnarled, dirt-encrusted feet. She put a hand to her mouth, hiding her grimace. The smell of unwashed human drifted up her nose, and she choked back a gag. Pleased she had finished her coffee, she turned away and stared out the window. *Strange there's no car outside.* She grinned. *Perhaps they are on bicycles—or they left their vehicle over at the park. That's what lots of people do.*

Across the road toward the pub, Rhys was charging around the police-station lawn, pushing a well-used red mower, his shirt-tail flapping and his lanky, muscled body leaning forward as he marched up and down the yard. Ashleigh grinned. Featherwood Falls was lucky to have him, and now, with his commitment to Claire declared to all and sundry, she hoped he would be here for a long time.

'Sorry about that,' Lola whispered as the customers clanged the door behind them and she resumed her previous seat. 'They're the new people at Glenrowan.'

Ashleigh raised her eyebrows. 'The couple Donald Shepherd has employed?'

'Yeah. Apparently. Can't see them staying long—but, who knows.'

'They could do with a bath.' Ashleigh wrinkled her nose, and Lola nodded.

'I reckon. Haven't seen them around much, so they must be going to one of the bigger towns to do their shopping.'

A vehicle pulled up outside and several children tumbled out, dressed in soccer gear.

'Uh-oh. Here comes the lolly brigade.' Lola pushed herself upright again. 'I'll be a while.'

'That's fine, Lola. Thanks for the chat. I'd better get back and hang my washing out, anyway. See you soon.'

'Sure will, love.'

Ashleigh waited until the family had entered the shop before slipping out the door behind them. She exchanged a wave with Rhys as she passed—the deep concentration on his boyish face changing rapidly to a grin under the wide-brimmed Akubra.

At home, she hauled the laundry out of the machine and carried the basket out to the clothesline.

With the last item pegged securely against the increasing wind, she was ambling back to her house when her phone danced in her jeans pocket. 'Hello?'

'Ashleigh.' The deep voice sent a shock wave through her, and she stopped mid-stride.

'Yes.'

'Damian Cartwright. I got your note. You want to talk to me about Charlie?'

'Umm. Yes, please.'

'Has he done something wrong?'

She shook her head while gathering her thoughts. 'No. Not at all. Most parents have been to see me about their children at some point, just to ask how they're settling in—although we will have parent-teacher interviews toward the end of this term. It's just ... well, Charlie thought we should have a talk.'

The line was silent for several moments.

'Are you still there?' Ashleigh asked.

'Of course. I can't think why he wants us to talk now. But, if that's what he wants, I'm agreeable. Would tomorrow afternoon suit? I know it's Sunday, but I've got a busy week coming up and won't have much spare time.'

'Yes. That's fine. We can make it at two o'clock if you like.'

'Right. I'll see you at the school.'

He was gone before she could thank him or say goodbye. Anxiety clawed at her gut. What was she going to say to him? She couldn't very well just launch into discussing the puzzling disappearance of the bird's eggs—could she?

She entered her little home before closing the door firmly behind her. Two o'clock tomorrow seemed like a long time to wait—and yet a flutter of panic bit into her. She needed to get her head around how to handle the situation without it escalating into another fiery exchange like their previous couple of meetings.

Groaning, she dragged her thoughts to the afternoon tennis session, her mood brightening. At least that—and catching up with Claire and Rhys—would help to distract her.

22

*D*amian rubbed his forehead and pursed his lips. She'd said Charlie had not misbehaved, and he was sure his academic results would be every bit as high as others of his age. So, what on earth did this teacher want to talk to him about?

Surprised at the butterflies doing acrobatics in his stomach, he strode along the path before treading noisily up the stairs.

Ashleigh met him at the door, a tentative smile touching her lips. 'Thanks for coming. I won't keep you long.'

He nodded and followed her into the classroom, noting the pint-sized desks and seats.

Jeez, I hope she doesn't expect me to sit in one of those.

She didn't, indicating two adult-sized chairs in one corner. 'Please have a seat.'

He lowered himself slowly. *This is ridiculous. I feel like a criminal about to be cross-questioned.*

'Would you like a cup of tea or coffee?'

Her offer surprised him, and he stuttered, 'Umm, y-yes, thank you. Black tea, no sugar.'

While she vanished into the small kitchen, he gazed around. Although not large, the room was well set out, with the desks and chairs dominating one half of the area and a soft floor rug and seat toward the rear —he presumed for storytelling as a well-stocked book-case ran alongside it. Bright, colourful charts of all sorts covered the walls—an alphabet, collages and paintings featuring swirling colours and a random assortment of glitter, streamers, and wool glued in patterns that made no sense but screamed the efforts of young students, and a section with photos of each pupil. He stood and inspected them more closely. Underneath each image, clear, bold print dictated the name and a couple of lines noting the child's interests.

He grinned as he read Charlie's. *Creatures of every sort. The bush. Hot chocolate. My dad and Dotty.* His chest squeezed.

Ashleigh returned with two mugs and handed him one with a smile. 'Please don't think I've asked you to come in because Charlie has a problem. He doesn't. In fact, he's one of the brightest children I've ever taught and is popular with the other students, despite being so young.'

Damian released the slow breath he hadn't realised he was holding. *How did she know what he'd been thinking.* Deciding not to mention her surprise visit to Dot's home, he asked, 'What's the problem?'

She sipped her drink, the mug shaking a little. He clearly wasn't the only nervous one. Damian's shoulders eased.

'I was hoping we could discuss Charlie's worries. As you know, he has a passion for birds and many little creatures and he has been wonderful in sharing his knowledge with the rest of us.'

Damian nodded and took a mouthful of tea.

'He's been anxious about changes he doesn't think should be happening in the local environment. In particular, eggs disappearing from nests before they're ready to hatch.'

Damian snorted, releasing a breath, relieved the issue wasn't more serious. 'Yes. I'm aware of the problem. But nature does its own thing and perhaps the birds know something that us humans don't.'

Silent seconds ticked by. Ashleigh leaned forward a little. 'You mean floods and bushfires?'

'Perhaps.' He shrugged. 'Who knows, but that's what I've been telling Charlie in the hope he moves on and thinks about other things.'

'I will not argue with you, but I've been doing a bit of research myself since Charlie first expressed his concerns. From what I read, eggs that go missing from nests are mostly because of predators such as goannas and snakes ... or a member of the cuckoo family destroying them while the parent birds are off gathering food. Apparently, they then lay their own egg or eggs and fly away, leaving the poor nest-builders to incubate and hatch the cuckoo babies instead of their own.'

'That's correct. Didn't you know that?'

Ashleigh's cheeks bloomed pink.

Apparently not. 'Sorry, that was rude of me. I guess I take these things for granted, having also had a bush upbringing.'

She nodded, swallowing hard. 'But if cuckoo are involved, there would still be an egg or two in the nest? So ... are you saying Charlie is making a minor issue into an unnecessarily large one?'

He shook his head, determined to keep the conversation calm. Drawing a deep breath, he muttered, 'Look, I don't want to upset either you or Charlie. But ... I admit, even I am concerned about the amount of eggs missing from nests this year. Charlie doesn't know it, but I have been doing my own monitoring since he first mentioned the problem, and I agree. Something is not right—and I have wracked my brains trying to work out what it is.'

'Do you think someone should mention it to the police?'

'Dunno. Seems trivial really—especially when

Rhys already has a full agenda, but probably not a bad idea. I need to talk to him about another matter, anyway, so will pop in before I go home.'

They stared at each other for a moment.

Dusted with freckles, her pale face contrasted with the mahogany-coloured plait hanging over one shoulder. Deep chocolate-coloured eyes edged with thick eyelashes mesmerised him. He tried to drag his gaze away but couldn't. He didn't remember meeting a dark-eyed redhead before. Didn't auburn-haired people usually have blue eyes? And Charlie raved about his teacher, his adoration for her obvious. Damian cleared his throat. The time had come to call a truce. He would do what he could to make amends for his part in their previously spasmodic and outspoken encounters.

'Okay. Well, I'm relieved that you're aware of Charlie's concerns, and if there's anything I can do to help discover the cause of the missing eggs, I'll let you know.' Ashleigh smiled and held out her hand. 'Deal?'

He took the small but firm grip in his calloused paw and grinned. 'Deal.'

With her strolling to the car park at his side, unexpected satisfaction flooded through him. It had been a long time since he'd been in female company, except for Dot, of course. Perhaps he'd been hasty in judging Ashleigh. Her concern for his son seemed genuine—and knowing that made him feel good—really good.

Rhys met him in the doorway, his hand outstretched and his eyes wide as though shocked at the door having magically opened before him.

'Gidday, mate,' Damian said. 'You on your way out?'

'Yeah. But no urgency. Come in.'

'Thanks. Thought we'd better think about fire permits and control some of this undergrowth now the weather's cooling off. Have you been up in the bush lately?'

Rhys shook his head, a lock of straight brown hair hanging over his youthful forehead. 'Been busy. These kids from the city coming up here and dumping stolen cars are a worry. Especially when they set fire to them.' He frowned. 'You're right. It's time we got on top of the excess grass and debris, or one of these young dick-heads is going to trigger a massive bushfire.'

'Great. We've been lucky having a couple of wet years to give the farms a chance to recover—but there's always a negative, isn't there?' Damian grinned ruefully.

'Righto.' Rhys twisted his mouth, his gaze thought-ful. 'I'll get onto emergency services if you wouldn't mind rounding up the Rural Fire volunteers. How about we set a meeting date for ...' He flicked the pages in the desk diary, pausing. 'Monday week—say seven-thirty at the pub?'

'Sounds good. Thanks.' Damian cleared his throat. 'There's something else I wanted to run by you too.'

Rhys raised an eyebrow. 'Sure, fire away.'

'Has anyone reported exceptional losses of bird's eggs or strange vehicles camped amongst the bush lately?'

Creases formed on Rhys's forehead, and he ran a finger over his chin. 'I haven't heard anything. Why?'

Damian shuffled his feet. 'My son has a passion for wildlife and although he's only five, ever since he could walk, wild birds, lizards and all sorts of creatures have fascinated him. I don't mean like wanting to play with them or put them in his mouth—I mean, he studies them and barely moves, so the birds trust him. He's been getting upset over the last few weeks, though. Reckons lots of eggs are disappearing from nests and, sometimes, the adult birds have also vanished. It's not only birds' eggs, but he found a bearded dragon's nest over the holidays filled with eggs. He doesn't know it yet, but I checked on them yesterday when I was fixing a fence and they're gone too.'

'Okay,' Rhys spoke slowly. 'What are you thinking? Potentially a rat outbreak?'

Damian shrugged. 'Not sure. I haven't noticed an increase in rat numbers—only the odd native bush rat. They don't multiply like the feral black rats. As for vehicles. Now that people are holidaying all over the place, there's no end to unknown cars travelling through this area. You've gotta admit, it's a nice place to stop. Lots of waterholes, creeks, and bush tracks to explore. And with the camping areas and national parks so close to us, day-trippers are everywhere.'

'True. I'll do a couple of random breath checks over the next few days and ask people what they're here for —in a nice, chatty way, of course.' He grinned. 'Meanwhile, I'll talk to Claire. Find out if she or Kirk have noticed anything up their way.' His smile widened and his eyes sparkled. 'Not sure if you've heard. Claire and I are engaged.'

'Congratulations, mate.' Damian reached out and shook Rhys's hand. 'When's the joyous occasion?'

'We're not sure yet. We're thinking of keeping the wedding kinda small and more for family but are planning a bit of a shindig next month to celebrate our engagement. It'll be in the Featherwood Station woolshed—and everyone is welcome.'

'Even me?' Damian laughed, and colour rose in Rhys's cheeks. He didn't have to be a mind-reader to know that most locals thought of him as reclusive and odd.

'Of course, you. Bring your family. Everyone is welcome. Ginny and Kirk will do a spit roast and guests will roll up with salads and desserts. You know what it's like out here—everyone pitches in and everything works out.'

'Thanks, Rhys.'

Damian slid into his ute, warmed by the invitation. Except for the occasional drink at the local pub with his work team, his social life was zilch.

He drove away, not before glancing at the school, hoping for another glimpse of Ashleigh. An unfamiliar flash of heat shot through him. Would she be at the engagement party? Perhaps he should go. Even some of his workmates had made jokes about his gruff manner. For more than two years, he'd relished the excuse of having to isolate, but it was time to re-emerge into real life—and that included attending community meetings and functions.

No point even suggesting to Dot that she might like to come. Still, it was a month away and anything could happen between now and then.

23

*A*shleigh was returning from her regular evening walk when the vehicles started rolling into town. The pub car park was full, and several utes, cars, and trucks were parked nose-to-the-footpath in front of the building.

Her breath hitched for a moment. Then Quinn emerged from their house, gave her a wave, and called out, 'Coming to the meeting, Ash?'

'What meeting?'

'The environmental get together—you know, where they're deciding when and where the slow burn-offs will take place and what each department's role will be.'

'Oh. I thought the leaflet said it was for Emergency and Rural Fire Service members.'

'Yeah, well. The school's an important part of this

town and we need to know what's going on. At least then, if a child gets upset about fires burning near their home, we know who to contact and what to say to them.'

'I never considered that. Do you think I should attend?' Silently, irritation built up inside her. If she was supposed to attend a community meeting, why hadn't Quinn said anything before now? His behaviour seemed to have changed over the past week. He was quick to flare and, unlike when she'd first met him, less compassionate. Was something wrong with him or Joanne?

'Your choice. I'll be there so can pass on anything we need to know.'

If she was to attend a meeting, a change of clothes would be the least she'd need—and she was hungry. The prospect of being in a pub full of men was the last thing she wanted. She nodded and walked past. 'Okay, thanks. I'll give it a miss and look forward to hearing your report tomorrow.'

They shared a smile, and she hurried to her house.

It was after ten o'clock before voices and the sound of vehicles starting filled the air. Ashleigh peeped through the blinds. Headlights swung across the road as cars did U-turns and accelerated away. She idly wondered what had kept them there for so long. Surely a plan to clear potential bushfire materials didn't take two and a half hours. Or did it?

Her thoughts shifted to Claire. With the excitement of her engagement, and a large order of graphics hanging over her friend's head, their bush walks and riding lessons would likely not be a high priority until after the engagement party.

Disappointment filled Ashleigh briefly before a vision of Claire's delighted face as she rode Akela flashed through her mind. Perhaps a short ride would be just what both she and Claire needed?

I'll send Claire a text in the morning and ask.

She switched off the bedside lamp and pulled the doona over her. Outside, silence once again blanketed the village until a boobook owl hooted. Ashleigh smiled. Being lulled to sleep by the sounds of wind, night birds, and possum calls was a far cry from the rush of traffic and screeching brakes.

Autumn had arrived, and she loved the cooler temperatures and clear air. In a few weeks, Ashleigh would be halfway through her contract. Panic gripped her for a second. What if Quinn didn't want her to stay on next year? What if a few families left the area and the school no longer required a second teacher? She didn't want to think about it—and certainly didn't want to leave. Sudden realisation of how much she had fallen in love with this place jolted her wide awake again and she lay on her back, staring at the ceiling.

'Don't be stupid,' she said aloud, Donald's comment ringing in her ear. 'This town is growing, not shrinking. Anyway, the parents seem happy with what I'm doing, and I haven't lost my temper with anyone —yet.'

THE FOLLOWING DAY, Quinn asked Ashleigh, Emma, and Maria to stay back after school so he could brief them all on the upcoming fire plan.

Intrigued by the importance Quinn placed on it, Ashleigh whispered to Emma while the children were eating their lunch. After all, he'd never called a meeting after school before—except for the regular weekly staff meetings, of course.

'How does a district fire control plan have anything to do with the school?'

Emma looked at her as though she had two heads. 'Didn't you know—we're the evacuation centre if anything gets out of hand. And ... the local families rely heavily on us to keep the children informed but not frightened.'

'Oh.' Ashleigh felt like a school child herself. She should have known that. It wasn't something she'd ever thought about in the beachside suburb of Brisbane—

but that was no excuse. 'Have there been a lot of bush-fires around here in the past?'

'No, but during the nineties, we had several out-of-control fires and a couple of our pupils lost their homes. It was a frightening time for them and one I will never forget. That's why now they do annual burn-offs and pay a lot more attention to firebreaks.' Emma sighed. 'It was a tough lesson, but as we know, Mother Nature can be a brutal teacher.'

Ashleigh nodded, her face soft with compassion.

Hours later, as they sat around the tiny table in the kitchen, Quinn outlined the upcoming plan. 'They'll be starting with burn-offs close to main roads to reduce the chance of fires caused from cigarettes and vehicles with hot exhausts stopping or parking in long, dry grass. Then they will work in the bush areas, closely liaising with National Parks and local farmers. Of course, all controlled burns depend on weather.' He smiled, his calm but authoritarian tone restored.

Ashleigh relaxed. Perhaps a crisis had arisen in one of his or Joanne's families that they didn't want to discuss. Whatever it was, she was relieved he seemed back to normal. Feeling her phone vibrate in her pocket, she glanced down.

'With fine, still weather predicted over the next couple of weeks, don't be surprised if you smell smoke in the air. They'll keep us informed.' He smiled at each of them before clipping the loose pages together and tapping them on the table. 'Thanks for staying back. See you tomorrow, Ash and Emma—and on Thursday, Maria.'

While Emma and Maria stood at the bottom of the stairs chatting, Ashleigh hurried back to her little house to return Claire's missed call.

'So, let's go for a hike up to the mines next weekend,' Claire said. 'Rhys has the day off on Sunday and Kirk and Mum want to come, too. We'll pack a picnic and leave home around nine. Okay with you?'

'Sounds great.' Ashleigh fiddled with her hair. Should she ask about another riding lesson? Or did Claire think that Ashleigh joining them for mustering events was enough? Disappointment silenced her for a few moments. 'Umm, are you going riding soon?'

'Not until the farrier has been. Both Akela and Splash badly need their feet trimmed and the poor guy's been so busy—it could be another week before he gets here. I hope it's not too long before he comes or we'll both have a job and a half.' She laughed.

'Oh?'

'Yep, it's crutching time. So, if you're up to it, you can give me a hand to get all the sheep in.'

Ashleigh screwed up her nose. She had no idea what crutching was, but the word suggested it might be something both essential and distasteful. 'Oka-ay.' She spoke slowly, pausing for a few seconds. 'Umm, more detail, please?'

'Like shearing, only this time we only remove the wool from around the sheep's backside and face. It means they can then go through winter with a thick coat, but the important bits of their body remain clean. You, me, and the dogs will muster each mob one at a time, the shearers will crutch them, then Mum and Kirk will drench them and trim their feet if needed. Then we'll take them to a fresh paddock for winter.'

'Wow. That sounds like a big job, especially so close to your party.'

'Not as big as shearing. You'll have fun. Trust me.'

Ashleigh raised an eyebrow. Was Claire being sarcastic? She shrugged. At least her friend wasn't fobbing her off because of Ashleigh's incompetence.

They talked about their work briefly before Ashleigh asked, 'Everything going okay with the party plans?'

They filled another fifteen minutes with ideas for what sounded like the biggest event the district would experience in years.

When they finally disconnected the call, Ashleigh laughed out loud. It was so good to have a friend who accepted her exactly as she was. Maeve was the same, but now she was travelling overseas. Their worlds seem to have drifted apart. Her friend's social media posts—like her photos from somewhere in Spain after she'd completed forty-eight days walking the Camino —had kept Ashleigh informed of Maeve's adventures.

Ashleigh looked around her tiny abode and glanced through the window. Once she would have been jealous of Maeve. But she had her own freedom, and the distance between now and her previous life was worlds apart.

24

*T*he weekend arrived in a flurry of dry autumn winds. When stocking her backpack, Ashleigh had slid an extra bar of chocolate and a bottle of water in. Sunrise was getting later, and today she was ready for their hike before the fingers of gold crawled over the valley.

Bathed in the eerie early morning light, Ashleigh slung her pack into the boot of her car and headed to Featherwood Station. The Sunday traditional cooked breakfast was one not to be missed, and Ashleigh's mouth watered at the thought.

Clearly in high spirits, Rhys and Claire were dancing around the veranda when she arrived, waving barbeque tools in the air and singing along to Keith Urban's "Some Days You Gotta Dance".

Ginny rolled her eyes at Ashleigh as she trudged

up the steps. 'Ignore those two. Rhys has been busy, so they haven't had much time together for a while.'

Ashleigh chuckled, blew them both a kiss, and followed Ginny inside.

Kirk strolled toward them from the depths of the house, his massive frame darkening the hallway. 'Gidday, Ash. Good to see you. Ready to come mining with us?'

She smiled, her eyebrows rising. 'I think so. I've never been in a mine before—and I'm assuming it's not quite the same as a railway tunnel or checking out glow-worm caves?'

Both Kirk and Ginny laughed. 'Not quite. You'll be fine, though. We won't let you come to any harm,' Ginny added.

An hour later, they loaded their backpacks onto the farm ute. With the sun on her back, exhilaration melted the earlier twinges of anxiety that had plagued Ashleigh.

RHYS AND CLAIRE led the hikers, Kirk having pronounced himself the tail-ender, and Ashleigh and Ginny were in single file between them. As they struck out on the now well-formed track, a family of blue fairy wrens darted back and forth around them.

'These little feathered friends are a good sign,'

Ginny announced. She glanced behind her and met Ashleigh's questioning gaze with a chuckle. 'No scientific reason for me saying that. But every time we've been back this way since Kirk's fall, it's as though they're welcoming us into their private lives. And we end up having a happy and trouble-free day.'

Ashleigh had no recollection of wrens the day she and Claire had got sidetracked and ended up at Dot's place. Perhaps Ginny's vibes were telling.

Good grief. I'm thinking like Charlie now. Maybe nature does have a lot to do with determining our happiness.

The autumn sun beat down with surprising strength while underfoot, twigs and leaves crackled. Warm air circulated under the canopy of eucalypts and casuarinas, and for the first time, Ashleigh inspected the undergrowth. Her forehead grew increasingly more tense. *No wonder the meeting was called about reducing the fuel load.* If a lightning strike should hit this rapidly drying bushland, fire would be inevitable—with disastrous consequences.

Their pace slowed as their walk was interspersed with breaks for a drink or to inspect the variety of flora and fungi that popped out of the most unlikely places. They reached the clearing where Kirk had fallen down the mine shaft and perched on the assortment of logs while they ate lunch. Then, conscious of the shortening days, they shouldered their packs and continued up the next rise, over the granite outcrop, and along the narrow track that skirted the trickling stream.

After arriving at the largest of the caves, Kirk ensured each of them donned a headlamp and, leaving their packs near the entrance, they followed him into the cavern. A bat flew past Ashleigh's head and she jumped, letting out a squeal.

Ginny grasped her arm. 'I'm with you, Ashleigh. I know they're important, but I can't say I'm a fan of the humble creature.'

Bending as the opening narrowed and the roof height decreased, Ashleigh was pleased she'd worn an old pair of leggings instead of her jeans. Within a few metres, they were crawling on hands and knees until, suddenly, the tunnel opened into a circular arena just big enough for the five of them to stand, huddling close. Above their heads, the rock ceiling gave way to a sliver of sunshine highlighting thin tree roots that reached along the walls as though searching for nourishment. Dust motes floated in the shaft of light.

Kirk shone his hand-held torch around the walls. 'See the streaks? They show the various minerals trapped in the rock.' He continued explaining in more detail and Ashleigh understood how the variety of colours glinting in narrow streams through the stone could have dazzled prospectors in the past.

They dutifully followed Kirk and Rhys deeper into the tunnel before Claire declared she had seen enough and needed fresh air. Ashleigh wanted to hug her. A little claustrophobic herself, a shiver ran down her back while visions came to her of thin, sweaty miners slogging for hours decades ago, desperate to find the "mother lode". How had they done it?

'I admire you, Kirk, but I don't think mining will ever become a hobby for me,' Ashleigh said dryly.

He laughed a deep, throaty laugh that encouraged the others to join in, and on that note, they turned and slowly made their way back outside.

After stripping off boots and socks, they dabbled their feet in the water and sat on warm rocks, sharing chocolate and a container of sliced rockmelon.

Claire and Rhys huddled against each other murmuring, their fingers trailing gently along each other's bare arms. Ashleigh swung her gaze away from the loving couple toward Ginny for a moment. She was leaning against Kirk's upright knees, the two of them exuding both love and unity.

A pain shot through Ashleigh—an ache of envy that crept from deep in her belly to the top of her head. Tears pricked the back of her eyes. She hardly ever felt lonely. But, here, with two couples clearly in love, the reminder of how it might feel to experience the emotion left her bereft. For her, love was yet to be found.

～

As DAYLIGHT SLIPPED AWAY, they reached the last section of the descent where the bush thinned and the Featherwood valley vista spread before them. Something glinted through the trees, and Ashleigh stopped suddenly. 'What's that?' She tapped Claire on the shoulder and pointed.

Narrowing her gaze, Claire craned her neck toward Ashleigh as if to ensure they were staring at the same thing. 'That's the shed on Glenrowan where they were making the crystal meth last year. Not sure what it's used for now, though. Probably hay.' She shrugged. 'I'm pleased the trees have grown around it. At least we're not reminded of a period in the district's history that most would prefer to forget.'

Ashleigh nodded, and they tramped the final few metres to the gate. They slipped backpacks off and loaded them onto the ute, She hadn't even noticed the shed only fifty metres away the last time she had been in the area, and yet they must have walked right past it. Her feet ached at the memory of it. She'd been wearing her new boots and the little woman and dog named Lass had provided them with so many distractions. It was no wonder she'd missed a boring, corrugated iron shed tucked amongst rows of thick trees.

Eager to get home and into a hot shower, Ashleigh declined the invitation to stay for dinner and made her way slowly down the hill into the village.

As she turned through the gate facing her tiny home, the headlights caught Quinn standing in the driveway. Like a deer in the spotlight, he held an arm over his eyes before hurrying toward her.

She lowered her window. 'Is everything alright, Quinn?'

His face creased with concern. He leaned against the car, his hands clinging to the roof sill as though needing it for support. 'No ... well, not really.'

She switched off the ignition and began opening the door. 'Can I help? What's the problem?'

'It's Joanne.' He released his grip on the car and ran his hands through his dark curls. 'Oh, I don't know where to start. She didn't want anyone to know.'

In an instant, Ashleigh forgot her weariness and took his arm. 'Would you like me to come inside with you? Talk to Joanne?' She cast a glance at the school, now a large, square shadow behind security beams that cast an eerie light over the concrete and gardens. 'Or would you rather we talked in the school?'

He nodded toward the school, and she trod beside him as they made their way across the lawn and up the stairs. Once inside the kitchen, he slumped onto a chair and dropped his face into his hands.

Ashleigh's chest tightened. She'd never seen him

like this—not even close. 'Tell me about it, Quinn,' she breathed.

'When we got home from our Easter holiday, a letter had arrived for Joanne. One of those letters you dread. It was a recall to the breast clinic because something showed up in her last mammogram. Anyway, she went to see a specialist last week—you know, have all the tests, and ... well, the news wasn't good, and she has to have a mastectomy.'

'Oh no. Poor Joanne.' Ashleigh lay her hand on his arm. 'How soon?'

'We thought it would be weeks. But she got a phone call from the surgeon's team only half an hour ago to say they've had a cancellation for tomorrow and want her to go to Brisbane. I've been trying to get hold of Lyle to see if he can come for a few days, but he's not answering.' He raised his palms in a helpless gesture.

It took Ashleigh a few seconds to digest the information. 'Okay, so why aren't you over there packing? Your families live in Brisbane, don't they? Just go, Quinn. I can keep trying to get hold of Lyle—and if I can't, I'm sure we can get a supply teacher for a couple of days. If that doesn't work, Emma and I will manage.'

The relief on the man's face was palpable, and she smiled gently. 'Don't worry about the school or the children. They're good kids and it'll be okay.' She took him by the arm and led him toward the door as though he were a child. 'You nip home now. Pack bags for you both and get on the road to Brisbane. You've got my phone number. Let me know when you arrive, and we'll talk again.'

He nodded and shot across the grass as though demons were chasing him.

Her heart ached for them both. No wonder he'd been tetchy lately. Since getting the recall, they must have both been sick with worry.

After locking the school door carefully behind her, she trooped back to her car and drove it to her usual parking spot at the end of the tiny house.

Inside, she dropped her pack on the floor and filled the kettle, her exhaustion forgotten as she thought of Joanne. At thirty-seven, Quinn's wife was only eleven years older than herself. She chided herself for her fleeting self-pity earlier in the day and silently prayed Joanne's treatment would be successful and her recovery quick. She drew a deep breath and poured the boiling water over the peppermint tea bag.

If a touch of loneliness is the only problem I have, I'm a good deal better off than millions of others.

25

*I*t was almost ten o'clock before the call came from Quinn. Without preamble, he launched straight in, his voice filled with obvious relief. 'We're staying at a motel down the road from the hospital. Joanne's fine but worried, of course. And I've spoken to Lyle. He'll be there at eight in the morning. Joanne's mother will join us at the hospital tomorrow and once Jo's discharged, she'll stay with her parents for as long as required. Hopefully, I'll be back by Wednesday night so Lyle can do his usual Thursday at Wallangarra.'

Ashleigh slumped into her pillows. Although confident she and Emma would have coped, having the experienced, calm and humorous, semi-retired teacher for support would take a huge load off her shoulders. 'That's good to hear, Quinn. I hope you both get some sleep. Ring me tomorrow after school if you can for a progress report—and give Joanne my love. I'll be thinking of you both.'

They finished the call and Ashleigh lay back, staring through the window at the starlit sky, her hands clasped behind her head.

She held her breath for a few moments before puffing it out slowly as she processed the events of the day.

Glancing at the shelf above her bed, her mouth twisted. Folders and piles of teaching resources sat in neat heaps. Almost every Sunday evening, she spread them on her little table and planned the upcoming week's lessons. This weekend, she had done nothing— and she didn't care.

I'll have to wing it—and I bet the kids won't even notice.

AS THINGS TURNED OUT, Monday flowed easily once she had answered the questions of "Why isn't Mr Alderton here?" as subtly as possible. Lyle stepped into Quinn's position, and being familiar with the students, school life continued as though nothing out of the ordinary had happened.

The monthly parent and citizens' meeting was in full swing on Wednesday evening when Quinn returned. With the usual roll up of more than half the families represented, the committee had presented their reports—garden and lawn maintenance, tuck-shop earnings, and the treasurer's statement—when Quinn slipped through the door and sat at the back of the classroom. Despite his quiet entrance, heads swivelled and the murmur of voices filled the room.

'We heard you'd had to dash to Brisbane. Is everything alright?' one parent asked.

'Is your wife okay?' another said.

With a sigh of resignation, Quinn stood and plodded to the front before facing the curious group. 'Thank you for your concern. Yes, we have been to Brisbane. And to prevent incorrect rumours, Joanne has agreed you have a right to know. We appreciate the help and camaraderie we have experienced in this community and thank you all.' He paused for a few moments. The room was so quiet, they would have heard a pin drop. 'They diagnosed Jo with breast cancer. She has had a mastectomy and, although the doctors are sure they got it all, she will be on chemo for a few weeks to ensure they mop up every potential cancer cell.'

The second he stopped talking, the room erupted.

After many sympathetic comments, Michelle Marsh, Jessie's mother, stood. 'My sister has been through the same illness and needed a lot of support after she came home. I suggest we set up a roster to help Joanne—and Quinn—get through this. So ... to start off with, I'd like to take care of the laundry for you, Quinn. I can pop in two or three times a week and hang it out, then take a basket of ironing home. If that suits, of course.'

A flurry of approving nods and comments followed Michelle's offer, and several others took their turn to stand and reel off various responsibilities. 'I'll organise a cooking team and we'll provide meals for you,' one said. Another piped up with, 'Bess and I'll clean the house once a week.'

Ashleigh was gobsmacked—and from the look on Quinn's face, he was too. While she'd realised this was a community unlike any other, the depth of generosity shown tonight gave her goosebumps. The worried faces, compassionate comments, and incredible unity displayed made her heart sing.

Her thoughts flew to Damian. Would he have volunteered to assist if he had attended the meeting? She raised an eyebrow. Unless someone told him, he probably wouldn't find out his son's school 'family' were enduring problems. But, if he did know, she was sure the reliability and the tenderness toward Charlie that he'd shown would prevail. He would help out —somewhere.

With Quinn back at the helm, Joanne recovering well and buoyed by the news that the school community had been so kind and helpful, Ashleigh was delighted to receive Claire's call late on Friday afternoon. 'The shearers are coming next Tuesday and the farrier's been. How do you feel about giving us a hand getting the sheep in?'

'I'd love to.' Ashleigh hesitated for a few seconds. 'When?'

'Umm. We'll probably start tomorrow afternoon. Bring the wethers from the back of the farm closer. They'll be first in line, but we won't pen them until Monday night. Then we'll muster the ewes and stud sheep and organise them in the paddocks around the woolshed on Sunday, so they're handy to grab.'

'That's perfect. I'll do my lesson prep for the week

in the morning. That will free me up after bus duty each day if you need help with returning the sheep to their paddocks afterwards.'

'Fabulous. You'll get plenty of riding practise—and, you never know, you might end up loving the sheep as much as we do.' She laughed.

EAGER TO HAVE AS much time on Featherwood Station as possible, Ashleigh rose early on Saturday and spent the morning catching up with washing, ironing her clothes, and preparing lessons for the following week. Then, dressed in her riding gear, she headed to the station.

A cool breeze blew from the south-west. Pleased she had remembered her jacket, she pulled it on and entered the house garden where golden leaves were blowing in circles over the lawn.

'Hi there,' Claire called from the veranda, a mug in hand. 'You've timed it perfectly for a cuppa.'

Ashleigh grinned and followed her friend into the kitchen.

'Mum and Kirk are down at the woolshed, getting it ready for next week.'

'What do they have to do to get a shearing shed ready?' Ashleigh was genuinely interested. To her, a shed was a shed and didn't come under the same pressures as a home.

'Clean it for a start. Dust has a way of filtering through every crack and crevice, and the shearing shed is no different. They'll sweep it thoroughly, remove any cobwebs, do maintenance on gates and yards that need it, and of course, ensure the grinder is greased and ready for use.'

'Ouch. Grinder sounds serious.'

Claire chuckled. 'It's the machine the shearers use to sharpen the blades. If they're not precise, it would be just like a hairdresser trying to cut your hair with a blunt pair of scissors.'

'Okay. So, our job is to bring in the sheep—with the help of the dogs, obviously.'

'Yes. Mum's got Harp and Chime with her. Poor Chime is getting heavy in pup now, so we don't ask much of her. She just enjoys being part of the pack— and she loves Mum. We'll take Flute, Drum, and Banjo with us.'

They finished their drinks and walked to the stables with the dogs milling around their feet. Both Akela and Splash were in the big yard while the ponies grazed only metres away, as though pleased to continue eating while monitoring their friends. The wind had increased, and Ashleigh turned her collar up, shrugging deeper into her jacket.

'I hope this wind eases soon. It's not what we want

when the country is so dry.' Claire frowned as they saddled the horses.

After checking both horse's girths, Claire held Splash while Ashleigh mounted, then vaulted onto Akela and led the way to the next paddock. As they rode toward the back of the farm, the land rose and, above the cattle yards, a track wound its way through a gap between two massive granite boulders.

'This is the spot where Dad met the neighbour, Nigel, for the last time. It is where he died,' Claire said sadly.

'Oh no. How awful. Did you find out exactly what happened?'

'Nigel told the court he threw a rock at Dad after they had a row. He was in a rage but didn't mean for it to hit him, never mind kill him—so he said. It was a drawn-out process, and the coroner declared it was "Death by Accident". We'll never know, but assume he died instantly and rolled down the hill. The forensic team reckoned he didn't drown even though Mum found him face down in the creek. Apparently, no water in the lungs.' She heaved a noisy sigh.

'I'm so sorry, Claire.'

Ashleigh followed Claire's gaze to where Drum was trailing forlornly behind them, his tail between his legs.

'Drum's never forgotten. Of course, he likes to come with us, but there's something about this area that stresses him like the falls—which is why I always bring at least one other dog. Then, if he gets spooked and bolts home, I've got backup.'

Ashleigh ached with sympathy as she met Claire's dejected gaze.

They passed through the rock cutting in silence, consumed by their own thoughts. Along the track, approximately one hundred metres farther on, the land opened to a rolling spread of hills dotted with sheep.

'Gosh, it's pretty from up here, isn't it?' Ashleigh said.

'Yeah. It's a gorgeous view—and with the pest exclusion fence now in place to keep the feral animals out, you know, wild dogs, cats and pigs–it's safe to leave the sheep here.' She straightened and turned to Ashleigh, one hand resting on the back of the saddle. 'We're going to bring this mob back through the cutting. It's trickier than taking them to the bottom of the hills and along the flat, but it's much shorter.'

Ashleigh nodded silently, hoping she didn't have to follow Claire down the steep slope.

'If you and Splash could park yourselves over there ...' She pointed to a spot a few metres from the beginning of the track that led back the way they'd come. 'I'll head along the top fence line and send the dogs around the sheep. They'll bring them back this way, then keep them together until we get to the cattle-yard paddock. We'll leave them there until Monday. It won't take us long to get them in after you finish at school ... if that's okay?'

'Sure. Sounds good.' Ashleigh hoped she didn't sound too relieved. She was enjoying the ride—only slithering down a steep slope while clinging to the back of a live animal was not quite what she considered fun.

Her jaw dropped in awe as the three dogs circumnavigated the paddock before bringing the sheep together in a thick mob—their creamy coats appearing like the froth on top of a cappuccino from where she sat. Then, with Splash standing perfectly still and not even the flick of his tail disrupting the leader's concentration, the flock approached, some casting wary glances in her direction while hugging their comrades. In a flash, the river of woolly bodies rushed past and on to the cutting in the boulders.

Claire trotted up the hill, her face flushed and her mare scrambling on the shale. 'You go on. Follow at a walk while I close the gate.' She threw an arm toward the rapidly disappearing sheep and fired encouragement at the kelpies. 'Good dogs. Steady now!' And they fanned out around the flock, their ears pricked and their eyes glued to their charges.

The journey down the hill was steady and controlled. Ashleigh held her breath, expecting the stock to gallop toward greener pastures. But they didn't. With the dogs constantly circling them, containing them at a safe pace, they followed the track to where a gate stood wide open beside the cattle yards.

As they poured through the space, Claire called the dogs back to her and turned to Ashleigh with a smile. 'Phew. First lot done. Now we go over to the other side of the farm and bring the Merino ewes into the wool-shed paddock. Then we'll have a break before we fetch the stud sheep. They have to wait until last because they're Dorsets.'

Ashleigh raised an eyebrow. 'And that means …?'

'They have wool that's worth nothing compared to the Merinos. It's important that all the Merinos are cleaned up first, their wool packed into bales, and then we clean the shearing floor, ensuring every little lock of wool is removed. Then we bring in the Dorsets.'

'Hmm. Sounds like racism to me.' She grinned, and Claire responded with a laugh.

'You're doing really well, Ash—but you've still got a bit to learn before we can call you a farm hand.'

Ashleigh stood in her stirrups to stretch her legs and back. 'Hilarious. Come on then. I'm guessing lesson number two is about to begin.'

Claire shot her an encouraging smile. 'It certainly is. Actually, I was wondering if you'd do me a huge favour.'

Ashleigh stared at her friend, her insides tingling with wary anticipation. 'Sure. I think?'

'Rhys has got next weekend off and we want to go to Brisbane to get a few things for the engagement party—and have a look at wedding ideas and a dress for me to wear to our engagement party. A few people have asked me about the dress code, and I've told them they're welcome to wear whatever they prefer but Rhys and I will be dressing up a bit. It's not something we have many opportunities to do and we thought others would probably feel the same. So ... I guess I'd better ensure I set the standard.' She winked cheekily at Ashleigh.

Relieved she'd asked Netty to go through her Brisbane wardrobe and post up something appropriate when Claire had first mentioned her desire for a party, Ashleigh nodded. 'Sounds nice. How can I help?'

'I want Mum to come too—and I know Kirk will want to join in. He's been talking about having a weekend away with Mum for months. I thought you might like to stay overnight on Saturday—to feed the animals and keep an eye on Chime. She's still got a week to go, but I'd feel better if someone was checking on her regularly. It'll give you a break from being cooped up in your squashy quarters.' Her eyes glistened with hopefulness.

'Of course,' Ashleigh said. 'Not sure how good I'll be if something goes wrong, though.'

'You'd ring Frank and Lola. They used to look after the place for Mum and Dad when we were little and had a couple of days away, but they're slowing down now and ... you might enjoy it.'

Ashleigh nodded. The thought of spreading out on a comfy sofa in front of the enormous television, a cat or two on her lap and with a team of dogs outside to protect her, warmed her insides. After the shock of Joanne's diagnosis, perhaps a change of scenery for a couple of days was just what Ashleigh needed.

27

*D*amian wrestled with the dozer's gear box, pulled the lever to redirect the blade, and lifted his gaze to the jungle in front of him. How could this much vegetation grow in only two years? A stab of guilt whipped through him. He should have been more attentive. The forestry team took great care to maintain their tracks and firebreaks, so what had stopped him from prioritising Dot's property? It was his and Charlie's backyard, too. There was no excuse.

He grabbed the lever with both hands and grunted, pulling the rusty rod of steel toward him until he heard the clunk. The old yellow caterpillar had sat behind Dot's shack since before Thomas died and yet, with a bit of regular grease and oil, it fired up every time—even if a cloud of exhaust smoke almost choked him for the first few minutes. Now the bulldozer was idling nicely, the blade engaged and the throttle ready to boost. It lurched forward, the rattle of steel tracks almost deafening as they turned. He clamped his earmuffs on and directed the clumsy vehicle to the mass of vines, scrubby bushes, and fallen leaves.

He rubbed an elbow on the inefficient windscreen, catching a glance at his reflection in the slightly clearer Perspex. A thick film of dust covered his face, leaving patches around his eyes where his goggles sat. He'd been at it since daybreak, eager to protect their own property before the bush fire service needed his attention for the controlled burns.

Every time he turned the rust-bucket to face a new section of scrub, a vision of an auburn-haired, brown-eyed woman seemed to stand in the distance—watching, waiting, and taunting him, but then disappearing as he approached. He shook his head and rubbed a forearm over his sweaty forehead. Was he overtired? Had he inhaled too much dust, and it had addled his brain? At thirty-one, he was still a young man. But at the moment, he felt much older than his years.

Dragging his thoughts away from Ashleigh, he focused on his son, recalling the conversation they'd had before Charlie drifted off to sleep the previous evening.

'Remember to look out for the baby birds, Dad. If they fell out of their nests, they might be lying on the ground, and you mustn't run over them.'

His guts had churned at the thought, even though he was certain there would be no wildlife to worry about. At the sound of the dozer, the birds retreated to lofty positions, as if to keep watch, while smaller, ground-dwelling creatures scurried into the bush. He hoped if he could clear the worst of the debris while disturbing no trees, the little animals could seek refuge underground or in a high branch should a fire ever come this way.

He brushed the back of his wrist over the sweaty, dust-filled creases on his forehead and glanced at the thick glob of dirt that covered his cuff. *Huh. Lucky we've got plenty of water. It'll be needed tonight.*

Plunging the levers forward again, his mind wandered to his son. Although he had listened to Charlie's concerns, something much deeper gnawed at his gut. He and Rhys had touched on the possibility of rats, but he'd found no evidence of them. He didn't want to believe it, but acknowledged wildlife theft could be the issue. However—a much bigger worry left him uneasy, unable to sleep. Bushfires. With the air so dry and still, an ominous fear crawled over his skin. It was not unlike his feelings before a cyclone hit—an experience he'd had many times when working in north Queensland.

He shook his head and wrestled with the levers again, turning the caterpillar around one more time.

The sun slowly crept across the sky, surrounded by

clear blue with not a hint of moisture in the air. Clouds of dust surrounding Damian thickened, and by dusk, with most firebreaks now wide strips of clear, earthy land, he called it a day. His back ached and his eyes stung. Tomorrow they would begin slow burns on the other side of the valley while the days remained still and cloudless. He wasn't looking forward to it—but it was essential if the community and environment were to be kept safe.

After edging the machine back to the top of the clearing, he silenced it. Then he climbed down and trudged back to the cottage. As he drew near, Charlie ran toward him while his eccentric, loveable, and once beautiful little great-aunt waited on the veranda. His chest squeezed. Every single day, they were all reminded of the fierceness of fire and the need for prevention.

He would not let them down.

28

The following week flew for Ashleigh. With most of each day filled with school and children, she found she had only three hours of daylight at most to help on Featherwood Station. As soon as the bus disappeared, she raced home to change her clothes, then roared off in her car to the farm. The rest of the afternoon was spent yarding sheep before she and Claire saddled the horses and returned the freshly crutched, drenched, and pedicured animals to the paddocks.

After the shearers left on Wednesday evening, she stood by the stables, grooming Splash and Akela while Claire fed the dogs. Her mind wandered to her parents' home, their lifestyle, and her own upbringing. She couldn't stop the smile from spreading across her face. *I wonder what they'd think if they could see me now.*

It had been an exhausting and eye-opening few days—and she had loved every minute. After returning home each evening, she showered while the microwave heated her dinner, spent half an hour running over her preparation for the following day, and fell into bed. She didn't remember ever sleeping so well ... nor could she remember ever feeling so alive, fit, and healthy. Was she happy? She told herself she was—until she caught sight of a couple kissing or simply strolling arm in arm, talking and gazing at one another. Only then would she remember the hole in her life that, one day, she hoped and prayed would be filled.

EARLY ON SATURDAY MORNING, Ashleigh headed to Featherwood Station, her laptop and bag on the back seat. Her stomach fluttered, and she drummed her fingers on the steering wheel. Above, the autumn sun rose, its golden rays spreading over the hills, dissipating the mauve and pink tinges.

A family of magpies warbled as she pulled up outside the farm gate, as though to welcome her.

'Morning, maggies,' she replied before taking a deep breath of the still air and striding along the path.

'Hi, Ash. Thanks for getting here so early.'

Ashleigh blinked at her friend. With her strawberry-blonde hair hanging loose around her shoulders, her willowy figure clothed in a long, boho-style dress in shades of blue and aqua, Claire bore little resemblance to the woman in dirty farm clothes from only a day or two ago.

'Wow. You look amazing.'

Claire laughed. 'Do I look like I'll fit in amongst the city chicks?'

'Of course. Anything goes in Brisbane, but I'm sure you'll turn heads—in a good way.'

'Right. Come with me. I've got a list of instructions for you.'

Ashleigh followed Claire down the hall before pausing outside a light-filled bedroom with a Queen-sized bed and French doors that led onto the veranda.

'This is Briony's. I thought you might prefer it to the spare room because it's got such a lovely view.'

Ashleigh stepped inside and took stock of the panorama. Similar to the scene from the front veranda, the garden—filled with roses and edged with shrubs and hedges—led the eye beyond their beauty to a patchwork of fields, a tree-lined creek, and the tiny village of Featherwood Falls.

She breathed a contented sigh. 'I won't want to close the curtains tonight. It's just too beautiful.'

Claire chuckled. 'I reckon you will. Once darkness comes and you're on your own here, it's a big, lonely sky to look out on.'

'Sounds even better.' Despite her retort, her pulse quickened for a moment. She would be the only human in this rambling old homestead for one night and two whole days.

They continued down the passageway to the last room on the opposite side. Despite many visits to the farm, Ashleigh had not been in Claire's study. Now they walked through her bedroom and onto the side veranda. Enclosed to form a long, narrow, and delightful work room, the room had been furnished at one end with two comfy-looking cane chairs and a small table with a television fastened to the wall. At the other end, a wrap-around desk held a large computer screen and piles of notebooks and folders. Between the two spaces, a door led down solid stone steps, worn to shallow grooves in the middle by generations of feet.

Windows ran along the outside wall, allowing light to fill the room despite the massive row of trees only metres away.

'This is such a nice workspace, isn't it?' Ashleigh cast her gaze around, noting the photo on the wall of a younger Claire, another girl she knew to be Briony, and a tall, thin man who could only be their father—the likeness between him and Claire so strong.

'I love it. I've got my studio apartment, but with all the benefits of the family homestead under the same roof.' She shuffled some papers on the desk and thrust an A4 sheet at Ashleigh. 'I've written down all the animals, what and when they need feeding, and the phone numbers for Frank and Lola and the vet.'

Ashleigh scanned the page before following Claire back through her bedroom to the kitchen.

Opening the fridge door, Claire waved an arm at the contents. 'There's a lasagne for your dinner tonight and heaps of stuff to make yourself a salad or whatever you feel like. Plenty of eggs and fruit for breakfast. Oh, and there's fresh bread, peanut brownies, and a lemon cake in the pantry.'

'Wow. I certainly won't starve.' Ashleigh giggled, raising her gaze to Ginny and Kirk as they walked through the veranda doorway.

'Hi, Ash. Thanks, heaps, for minding everything for us. We hardly ever get away—so really appreciate your kindness,' Ginny said.

Ashleigh ducked her head. 'Don't even think about it. I'm sure all will be well. You enjoy your break away and leave the rest to me,' she finished with way more confidence than she felt, but she wasn't about to let anyone else know that.

Kirk picked up the two bags from the floor, turning to Ashleigh. 'If you need to check anything on the farm, Ash, the keys to the farm ute are hanging on a rack inside the study cupboard. Come on, Claire. If we're to collect Rhys at seven-thirty, we'd better get a wriggle on.'

Ashleigh walked out to the car with them, waited while they loaded up, and then waved goodbye.

She removed her bag and laptop from her car, then turned back to the house with mixed feelings. Excitement fluttered at the thought of spending time in this beautiful home and garden, but beneath the pleasure, a sense of trepidation lay dormant, as though waiting to pounce.

After unpacking her bag, she wandered into the kitchen and made herself a cup of coffee and a piece of toast. Then she sat on the veranda, watching the little friar birds flit in and out of the ornamental grapevine. A gust of wind suddenly whipped past, stripping leaves from the vine and swirling them over the veranda and lawn. Then there was silence again—complete peace with only the distant chirping of tiny birds in the hedgerow.

29

*S*he wasn't sure how long she sat, her mind drifting from school to Joanne and Quinn, her grandmother—and Charlie. Favourites were something she'd avoided in her career. Although there was always a child or two she found an easier rapport with than others. But Charlie tugged at her heart. His solitude reminded her of her younger self—only she hadn't had the passion for all the living creatures he did.

With the little boy clear in her mind, she rose and rinsed her mug and plate. Then she ran her finger down the list Claire had left her.

She ambled around the farmyard, emptied the scrap bucket from the corner of the kitchen into the fowl pen, checked the horse's water trough and threw them some hay, then headed to the kennels.

Following Claire's instructions, she let the dogs out and waited while they sniffed around and completed the call of nature. She straightened Chime's bed, surprised that, unlike the others, the kelpie seemed disinterested in having a run. She waddled about for a few minutes then reappeared at Ashleigh's feet as though asking to go back to bed.

Ashleigh smiled at her. 'I know how you feel. Some days a sleep-in starts the day off well.' She stepped back, holding the pen door open. 'Hop in then.'

Closing the gate behind her, she called the other dogs back, relieved they all leapt into their pens without fuss. Chime's pen was twice the size of the others, the "house" section roomy and insulated. On the floor, a large, squashy bed filled the space, topped with a folded wool blanket and a thick towel. Pleased the dog still had almost a week to go before her pups were due, Ashleigh presumed from the little she knew about birth that those last few days could be messy. Was that why the towel was there? Or was it simply that Chime liked lots of layers in her bed?

'Good dogs. I'll be back to see you all later.'

She glanced at her watch, surprised the morning was slipping away so quickly. Ready for another hot drink, Ashleigh returned to the house, opened her laptop, and spent the next two hours preparing notes for the upcoming week, emailing Maeve, and sipping tea.

After lunch, she grabbed her vest, noting the wind had picked up, although the temperature was still warm for April. She tucked a water bottle into her pocket and laced her hiking boots. Then after locking the door behind her as Ginny had instructed, she headed to the henhouse, opened the gate so the hens could free-range for the afternoon, and let the dogs out for another run. This time she wandered over the hill leading to the falls, allowing the kelpies to stretch their legs. On their return, she locked them up again and struck out in the opposite direction across the farm.

Her common sense and a lack of confidence prevented her from saddling Splash, even though she was sure she would be safe. Walking was even safer, and although slower, she had all afternoon to fill.

Deciding to brave the cutting where Claire's father had met his end, she strode up the hills, panting and resting as she reached the top. Pausing where she and Claire had stood on horseback only a few days earlier, her eyes narrowed, taking more notice of the steep slope than she had on her previous trip. Laced with narrow, horizontal tracks where the sheep followed in single file, the incline looked more like a rough sea turned on its side. Shuddering at the thought of falling and rolling all the way to the bottom, she swung her gaze away and continued striding along the track that traced the line of native bush.

At the peak of a ridge, she sat on a rock and took a

few mouthfuls of water. Once again, the view capti-
vated her. She could never imagine tiring of it. With
the seasons and big skies above, change would be slow
and mesmerising. Colours ranged from the purple of
the mountains to the glossy green crops. Golden wheat
looked ready for harvest while deep green orchards
coated in white netting to prevent hail and bird
damage dotted the valley. She breathed out slowly,
pushed herself to her feet, and continued on.

Descending the steep section of the farm, she was
disappointed to catch only the merest glint of the
Glenrowan shed roof but got a bird's-eye view of the
flat vegetable-growing fields. Igloos where apparently
tomatoes—and marijuana—had grown, stood at one
end. The ghostly-looking poly tunnels glistened in the
afternoon sun, and tiny figures buzzed in and out of
them. A small tractor towing a trailer of wooden crates
was parked in front of the entrance to the closest
tunnel, and the figures seemed to tip something into
the crates. Too far away to be sure, she could only
assume they were picking fruit or vegetables and
emptying them into the wooden boxes.

A noise distracted her, and she swung her gaze to
farther south, where a cloud of dust signalled a vehicle
approaching the shed. She paced along the top of the
ridge, keeping the vehicle in sight as she walked. It
turned off the dirt track and disappeared behind a row
of trees, but not before she got a good look at it. She

frowned, uncertain. From her viewing platform, it appeared remarkably like the old Land Rover that had roared out of a side track on her first week in the valley. Could that be the vehicle belonging to the couple now managing Glenrowan? If so, why were they driving around the countryside when they had a property to manage?

Donald had said they would be "exploring" when the farm wasn't busy.

Certain no one would notice her movements, she closed the distance between the boundary fence and her, then slowed her pace, peering through the thick forest of trees to catch glimpses of the shed.

Although it was still hours before sunset, light appeared to shine through the windows, illuminating the dark building in much the same way as one of the haunted houses she'd seen in movies. 'Weird,' she muttered. Why would someone leave lights on in a shed during the daytime? She took another drink from her water bottle.

Must be seeing things. Perhaps some fruit or vegetables need to be kept under lights?

Dismissing her ignorance with a shrug, she zipped her vest against the cooling breeze and continued her walk as the faint screech of a cockatoo reached her. Following the pretty stream to the wide, level paddock near the woolshed, she studied the stud sheep as they grazed—the Dorsets—and recalled the pointers Claire

had shared to enable Ashleigh to recognise the difference between breeds.

'Hi, girls.'

At her call, some of them lifted their heads and
stared at her while others kept eating. With a paddock
of Merinos next door, she could finally see the differences. *Kinda like not being able to see the wood for the
trees, I suppose.* She stopped, her head tilted to one side.
Ah-huh. The Merino's wool appeared darker because of
the excess grease in their wool, which attracted dust.
Their fleeces were dense and long, and they had deep
wrinkles under their necks and around their rear ends,
rather like a stack of tyres. The Dorset coats were short
and white, their long, smooth bodies wrinkle-free.
There were other traits Claire had pointed out, but she
couldn't remember them now.

Proud of herself for having recalled her "sheep"
lesson as well as she had, she trudged along the track
toward the homestead.

Light was fading, the sun having slid behind the
western range. She hurried to lock the chooks back in
their secure pen, away from the threat of foxes, before
feeding the kelpies and giving them a last run for the
day. This time, Chime refused to leave her kennel.
Ashleigh frowned. Should she be worried? She
contemplated sending Claire a text but decided against
it. After all, the family rarely got away, and this was a
special weekend for them.

With the heaviness of indecision weighing on her, she talked to Chime for a few more minutes, convincing herself the dog's behaviour was normal. Her own hunger gnawed, and she looked forward to the lasagne. Squaring her shoulders, she ambled back to the house.

30

*S*he shot up in bed. Had something woken her? Snatching her watch, she squinted and read three-fifteen. Laying back on her pillow again, she strained her ears listening for any unusual sounds. Staring through the cold, black glass, her pulse pounded. She focused on the stars above, following the Milky Way across the sky—its twinkling river of white was stark against the inky backdrop.

A cat jumped onto her bed, and she let out a noisy whoosh of breath. 'Oh, it's only you, Oscar.'

The black cat began purring loudly, and she reached out and stroked him. Of course. Claire had said he usually slept on her mother's bed. Once he'd realised Ginny wasn't coming home, it made sense that he'd sought out another warm body to cuddle against.

Now wide awake, she lay facing the window, the cat curled behind her knees. Eventually, her legs grew stiff, and she carefully rose so as to not disturb Oscar, closed the heavy curtains, and returned to bed. Minutes later, at exactly the same moment a boobook owl sounded his distinctively cheerful call, she knew what was bothering her.

The Land Rover painted in weird, camouflage colours. The couple managing Glenrowan. And the missing birds and eggs. Could there be a connection?

Something deep inside her said there was. Charlie had sensed it, and no one was listening. She glanced at her watch again. Four o'clock. Another two hours before daylight. There would be no more sleep for her.

A million thoughts ran through her head. Should she ring Claire and Rhys? No, it was Rhys's weekend off. Damian? No, he might think she'd gone bonkers. It was too early to contact Frank and Lola, even though they were early risers. However, they had their own menagerie to tend to before opening the shop at seven-thirty.

In the end, she switched the bedside light on, propped herself up on pillows, and pulled her laptop onto her knees.

For the next hour, she trawled through everything she could find about the smuggling of Australian wildlife. The more she read, the more certain she became. She had only one problem. How could she find the evidence to confirm her suspicions?

By FIVE-THIRTY, Ashleigh had dressed and held a mug of coffee in her hand. It wouldn't be long until daybreak. She'd feed the hens and let the dogs out for a run, then she'd drive the farm ute as close to the boundary fence as possible without alerting anyone who might be watching. The windmill. That would be the perfect place to park. In the event of someone seeing the ute, she could say she was checking the water. Not that it was likely she'd be spotted as there was a hill between the windmill and the Glenrowan shed. Perfect.

She finished her coffee and stepped out onto the veranda. Although the sun was still to rise, streaks of gold, pink, and purple hovered over the grey ranges. Leaves rustled as birds emerged from their resting place, their song and the bellow of a cow the only sounds welcoming Ashleigh to the new day.

Despite the early hour, the hens were awake and scratching in the dirt. Ashleigh filled the grain scoop from the sealed aluminium bin and tipped it into the feeder before checking the water. Then she moved to the kennels and opened the gates.

With no movement from Chime, she peered into the darkened sleeping quarters. Tiny squeaks greeted her. 'Chime. Are you okay, girl?'

In the dark, only the dog's eyes shimmered. Ashleigh hesitated, not wanting to crawl in and get bitten. She shook her head and chided herself. She and Chime knew each other now, and Ashleigh had never met a gentler dog. Thumping sounded, and she smiled as Chime's tail whacked the side of the kennel. She breathed a sigh of relief, pushed the gate wide open, and leaned in. Lifting each knee slowly, she whispered to the dog as she edged toward her. As the squeaking continued, she reached into her back pocket and pulled out her phone. After rapping the flashlight app, she shone the beam into the darkness. Chime bent her head, her pink tongue glistening as she licked the tiny balls lying in a row along her stomach.

Ashleigh's mouth dropped open, and she sat back, hitting her head on the roof of the pen. 'Oh, my goodness. Chime, you clever girl. You've had your puppies.' It took a few moments for her to register the event. 'You're not supposed to have them until next week!' She smiled at the dog and reached to stroke her gently on the head. Without touching the squirming pups, she flicked the beam of light over them and counted. 'Four black and two red. Wow. Ginny and Claire will be so excited.'

After backing out of the pen, Ashleigh topped up all the water containers and emptied a dipper of kibble into Chime's bowl. 'I reckon you deserve extra today. I bet you're hungry after all that work.'

She murmured to the dog for a few more minutes, then called the others back, locked them in their pens, and hurried to feed the horses.

By the time she returned to the house, the temperature was rising as the morning sun soaked the veranda. Itching to ring Claire, she forced herself to eat breakfast and waited until the hands of the kitchen clock crept around to seven-thirty. 'I'm not waiting any longer.' Snatching up her phone, she tapped Claire's number and waited.

'Is everything alright?' At Claire's anxious tone, Ashleigh instantly reassured her.

'Absolutely. Not only is it alright, but you and your mum are now the proud dog-grandparents, or whatever you call it, of six gorgeous, little puppies.'

Claire squealed with delight. 'Really! Is Chime okay? She wasn't supposed to go into labour until later in the week.'

'I know. You said. But ... we've all heard these things often forget to follow the rule book.' Ashleigh waited for a moment, reassuring herself Claire was listening before she continued, 'Chime seems fine, although she wouldn't come out of her bedroom. The pups were all feeding—four little black ones and two red. I'll check her regularly throughout the day and send you photos and messages.'

'Thanks, Ash. That'll be fabulous. I can't wait to tell Mum.'

Ashleigh opened her mouth to ask how the shopping and wedding planning was going, but Claire got in first. 'Thanks for ringing, Ash. Talk later, hey?'

'Okay.' And the line went dead.

Her mouth quirked with the hint of a smile. Claire hadn't asked about anything else and she'd sounded happy, so Ashleigh presumed the weekend was going well.

With the excitement of the puppies' arrival having consumed the past hour or more, her purpose for getting up so early had completely faded. It surged again with a vengeance, and her stomach did a somersault.

The last thing she wanted was for her friends to come home early—and her not be here. She opened the cupboard above the study desk and reached for the keys to the ute. On the hook next to them, three brass keys hung, the label above marking them as *Boundary Gates*. With only a second's consideration, Ashleigh carefully removed one of them and thrust it into her jeans pocket. Then she searched the linen cupboard for two old towels, darted outside, and hurried to the kennels.

Some of the food had already disappeared and Chime's water bowl was half empty.

'Good girl. You've already been up and about. Would you like to come out to stretch your legs?' She continued chatting to the dog as though she were human, opening the gate wide and doing her best to encourage her outside. Chime obliged, stepping past Ashleigh and heading straight to a clump of grass where she proceeded to toilet.

With one eye on her, Ashleigh quickly climbed inside the pen, replaced the soiled towel with the two fresh ones, and snapped a barrage of photos of the puppies—now quiet and curled together in a sleepy pile.

Chime bounced back into the pen, licked Ashleigh's hand as though to thank her, and snuggled back into bed with her babies.

A lump formed in the back of Ashleigh's throat. She had never witnessed a birth of any sort—and she hadn't witnessed this one either. However, an invisible, emotional thread seemed to connect woman and dog —a rapport that united them in wonder and joy. She ruffled Chime's ears gently. 'Have a pleasant sleep now. I'll be back soon.'

After refilling the water bowl, she bundled the stained towel under her arm and nipped back to the homestead. The laundry was old-fashioned—a sepa-rate room at ground level attached to the rear of the house. A double concrete tub ran along one wall, reminding her of her grandmother's old cottage—the one she'd lived in before Ashleigh's parents decided she must move to a townhouse with all the modern conveniences and a view out to sea. Ashleigh picked up a red bucket from the floor, filled it with cold water, and dumped the towel into it.

31

---

*A*fter sending the photos to Claire, Ashleigh pulled the bunch of keys from her vest pocket, locked the house, and hurried to the ute.

Although it had taken her hours to walk around the farm the previous day, this morning she arrived at the windmill in twenty-five minutes. It would have been quicker if she hadn't had to open and shut gates as she drove through paddocks, but she reasoned at least the stops gave her a chance to check the stock.

The air was warm with only the merest breeze bringing with it the smell of smoke from burn-offs across the valley. She wrinkled her nose and sneezed.

After stepping out of the ute, she closed the door firmly behind her then climbed the adjoining hill between the two properties. By the time she reached the top, she was panting with exertion, and she paused, hands on hips as her breath steadied. Then slumping to the ground, she leaned against a clump of small trees from where snippets of the massive shed were visible and waited.

By ten o'clock, with no sign of human or vehicle, and only the sounds of birds calling in the distance, she approached the boundary fence where she and Claire had crossed onto the gazetted but unformed road behind Glenrowan.

The key slipped easily into the lock. Leaving the open padlock hanging on the wire to enable a quick retreat if she needed one, she worked her way along the belt of trees in intermittent bursts of running and silent creeping until she was only metres from the building. Plaintive screeches leached from the shed— not those of a human but resembling the stressed or warning calls of the corellas she'd become familiar with since arriving in Featherwood Falls.

Wide, sliding windows placed at regular intervals ran along each of the long walls of the shed while one end was solid corrugated iron and the other filled with enormous doors. She stretched to peer through the windows, but they were too high for her. Casting a glance around, she spotted a half-buried rock resting along the track. She scratched away the dirt, cursing her short fingernails, and with a barely suppressed grunt, carried it over to one window. It wasn't big enough to stand on with two feet, so she gripped the window ledge with her fingertips and carefully placed one boot sole on the centre of the granite. It rocked, and she tightened her grip, terrified she'd do something as silly as falling and breaking an ankle. Then she'd have to admit to trespassing, and she certainly did not want that.

Steadying herself, she took a deep breath and craned her neck to peer through the cobweb-clouded glass. At first, she registered only stacks of pallets and boxes—the sort that fruit-and-vegetable growers used to pack and stack their produce. But then a light caught her attention.

Narrowing her eyes, she moved her gaze steadily along the opposite wall. The glass container—similar to a fish tank—appeared empty. Until something inside it moved. Her jaw dropped in horror as a snake slithered around the edge as though searching for an exit. Gritting her teeth, she adjusted her position and stretched out farther, gasping at the row of assorted glass containers and bird cages filled with a variety of native parrots.

Ice filled her veins. She only registered the sound of a diesel engine as a vehicle roof flashed past the windows on the other side of the shed. Releasing her grip on the ledge, she leapt back, casting a desperate glance around her. Clearly, anyone visiting had reached their destination as there was no other property or gateway at this end of the dusty track. She prayed the vehicle would stop in front of the sliding doors and not nose forward far enough to see her. Pressed against the wall, she could barely breathe. Her heart thumped so loudly she was certain the driver would hear it. The engine died as a bull-bar drew level with the front corner of the shed. Seconds later, two doors slammed, followed by the distinctive clank of chain and squeal of a steel door on runners being opened.

Voices sounded—one of them the deep tones of a man, followed by a female voice, gruff with agitation and the rasping, fluid-filled cough of a smoker. Unable to make out their words, Ashleigh leaned against the wall as the sounds echoed inside the vast building. The conversation drew near then seemed to pass by the window, muffled and fading. Ashleigh didn't dare step back on the rock in case she fell. Instead, she stretched on her tiptoes, certain her backbone would dislocate with the effort, until her eyes drew level with the sill. Then she bounced with one almighty spring. She had only a split second to notice the back view of the people and the wire cages both carried.

And that was all she needed.

She shoved a fist against her mouth before bending over and creeping slowly, silently, toward their vehicle. In a flash, she whipped her phone out of her pocket, tapped the sound button to silence it, and snapped a series of photos, ensuring she got a close-up of the registration plate. Then she crouched again and, praying the couple were still at the far end of the shed by the bird cages, inched her way across the dirt to the cover of a thick, scruffy-looking shrub. Branches scratched her face and tickled her nose as she pressed deeper toward the trunk. She squeezed her nostrils together with her thumb and forefinger, desperate to contain the sneeze that threatened while melding herself tightly against the rear of the plant's sturdy core.

Through the leaves, visibility was minimal. She hoped the same would apply to anyone glancing her way. Pushing a branch away slightly gave her a clear view of the building's entrance. If she could remain still for long enough, she hoped to get photos of the occupants as they returned to the four-wheel drive without attracting attention to herself.

A drift of smoke filled the air. Choking back a cough, Ashleigh pulled the front of her shirt over her face, holding the fabric against her skin and mopping her watering eyes. Something tickled the back of her neck and her skin crawled. A spider? She hoped not but allowed a hand to creep up and swipe under her hair just in case.

The sound of voices drew near again.

The woman emerged first, raising a cigarette to her lips and extracting a yellow lighter from the pocket of her baggy jacket before lighting the end. She sucked hard, the tip glowing red, then removed it from her mouth and blew out a long puff as she turned toward the vehicle.

Ashleigh moved a branch a fraction and pressed the large, white spot on her phone screen as the man wandered outside, moved to the far end of the sliding door, and leaned his shoulder into it. With his head bowed, it was difficult to get a clear picture of his face, but Ashleigh hoped it would be enough.

Chain clanked against the iron as the man snapped an enormous padlock through the links. Then he marched to the driver's door and climbed in.

With her teeth clenched, Ashleigh froze, daring not to breathe until the vehicle completed a U-turn and drove away. As soon as it had disappeared behind the shed, she extracted herself from the clutches of the shrub's foliage and ran to the opposite end of the building. After pausing against the wall, she peeped around the corner until the cloud of dust mingled with the gloom of smoke hanging over the western side of the valley.

She dashed back to where her rock still lay beneath the window, stepped up on it, and took several photos of the cages and tanks. The pictures wouldn't be clear, but she dared not brush away the spiderwebs or rub a sleeve against the glass in case someone noticed on their next visit.

With a last glance around to ensure she was alone,

she rushed behind the row of trees and jogged up the rise to the boundary gate. Snapping the padlock shut after slipping through the gap, she then sprinted across the crest of the hill and almost fell down the other side in her hurry.

Every cell in her body shook with exertion and terror. She leaned against the ute. What were those people doing? Certain the couple were Donald's employees, Lee and Eileen Dawson, even though she'd never actually met them, she didn't understand why they were keeping birds and reptiles in the farm shed? It was possible they had a licence to rescue injured wildlife. The birds hadn't looked injured, though. In fact, except for noisily protesting their captivity, they'd appeared remarkably healthy—not that she was an expert.

She slid onto the seat and started the engine. Then she drove back to the homestead with a rolling stomach.

There was only one other reason for capturing and keeping native animals—they were smugglers.

With Glenrowan behind her, Ashleigh followed the ridge to where the track descended toward the cattle yards, her heart still pounding while the events of the past hour tumbled around her head. She drew to a halt and looked back, alarmed at the amount of smoke that now filled the valley.

Like every other member of the community, she'd been warned about the weekend's efforts to reduce the hazardous quantity of dry matter that had built up in the bush. She had also read about the method used—a *cool* burn that crept at a manageable pace in the under-growth, surrounded by equipment and people trained in the process. She'd always thought all fires were hot, so wasn't sure what the reference to "cool" meant. But whatever the meaning, she hadn't expected there to be so much smoke.

Although the homestead was north of the thicker smoke, it almost blanketed the village. Her mind distracted from the going's on at Glenrowan, she screwed up her nose at the possibility of her tiny home and the school smelling for the next week or more before her thoughts swung to the kelpies.

At least Chime and her puppies won't be affected.

She changed into low gear and chugged down the slope, past the yards, and on to the machinery shed beside the house, every nerve in her body screaming. After parking the ute, she hurried to the kennels and let the dogs out of their pens. Chime darted past her, relieved herself, then returned to the kennel within a minute while the others ventured farther, sniffing the air and cocking an ear toward the smoke as though questioning its presence.

Ashleigh crawled into Chime's pen and, with growing confidence and determined to fulfil her role of responsibility, she picked up each pup, checked to see if it was a boy or girl, and ran her finger over each head with a feather-like touch. 'Three girls and three boys. Wow. Claire and Ginny will be thrilled.' One pup cried and Chime pressed against Ashleigh, licking the little creature with a long, pink tongue. 'Okay, back to bed now. Your mum's not really sure about me yet.'

She shut the gate behind Chime before striding

across the lawn to where the track to the falls began. Ensuring she had four kelpies milling around her, she marched briskly for several minutes while they stretched their legs, unable to quell her anxiety as the usually stunning view of the valley was masked in a blanket of smoke. After hurrying back to the kennels, she gave each dog a pat and shut them in their pens.

Her eyes watered again, and she strode around the side of the house and climbed the steps to the veranda. The breeze had strengthened, whipping clouds of smoke into ribbons and sending them scurrying toward the west.

She squinted in the direction the smoke was travelling. For a moment, she thought she saw a splash of orange amongst the bush in the next valley. She shook her head. *It can't be.* The SES had been very specific about where the burn-offs would take place this weekend—and the more isolated, western valley near where Dot Collins lived had not been one of them.

Pushing her palms against the veranda railing, Ashleigh waited for the next glimpse through the smoke haze, uncertain of what she'd seen and determined to get a better look.

A few minutes later, a gap appeared in the drift, and Ashleigh gasped. She hadn't imagined it. Flames glowed, smoke spiralling toward the tree canopy—caught by the easterly wind and mingling to appear as though it was all one fire, not two. And—from what she'd seen on television during previous bushfires around the country—it looked far from being under control.

Uncertain of the exact locality of Dot's shack when approached from the main road, she knew only that it was isolated and could be in the direct line of fire if the wind should change. Would Damian be there? Probably not. It was likely he would be part of the organised team on the eastern side of the valley—conducting the duties of a well-planned and equipped bushfire brigade. The thought of an elderly woman and a five-year-old child being on their own was terrifying.

SNATCHING UP THE KITCHEN PHONE, she dialled Lola's number. *Blast, it's engaged.* Without wasting another minute, she ran inside and collected the keys to her car, locked the house, and raced outside.

Roaring down the road at a greater speed than was safe, she briefly remembered Damian's angry spiel on speeding. She lifted her foot off the accelerator a touch, her pulse pounding as she flew past the paddocks, screeched to a halt at the T-intersection and, with a quick glance either way, shot out onto the main road.

Outside the store, she braked hard, switched off the

engine, and ran to the door.

Lola looked up from the kitchen bench at the racket the bell and Ashleigh's boots made upon her entry. 'Someone's in a hurry.' Lola raised her eyebrows, her earrings swinging as she tilted her head slightly.

'Lola. Is Frank here?'

'No. He's out with the fire brigade. They're burning off this weekend. I thought you knew that?'

'Yes, I do.' She stared at her friend and breathed out before continuing. 'I've been watching the smoke, and I'm sure there's a fire raging on the other side of the valley—where there's not supposed to be one!' Her voice rose in pitch more than she'd intended.

Lola lifted the hinged section of the counter and pushed past Ashleigh, hurrying to the door. They both stepped outside, peered through the thickening smoke, and stared at each other.

'I can't see a thing.' Lola spoke quickly.

Now that she had her friend's full attention, Ashleigh explained her concerns as briefly as possible. 'I'm worried about Dot and Charlie—and that other fellow living farther up their road. They could be in real danger, especially if the wind changes.'

'You don't have to worry about Bob. He called in earlier this morning. Said he was going to town for the Sunday markets. He always drops in on his way home and he hasn't yet—so he and his dog will be safe.'

'Well, I'm going to make sure Dot and Charlie are, too.'

Lola nodded, turned, and hurried back toward the kitchen. 'I'll see if I can get hold of Frank. If I can't, I'll ring the fire brigade. They all have radios so should be able to send a truck over that way to check.'

Ashleigh didn't waste time in replying. Instead, she hurtled back to her car, started the engine, and switched on the headlights as she proceeded cautiously through town. Blanketed by swirling, ash-filled smoke, she struggled to make out even the well-known landmarks. Somehow, she passed out of the village without running off the road and continued across the bridge and up the rise on the other side.

Farther along, the smoke billowed and lifted momentarily, exposing a dirt road leading off to the right. Praying she was heading in the right direction, she drove steadily, peering through the windscreen with watering eyes. It felt as though she had travelled kilometres when the road forked. Instinctively, she followed the right-hand track, sensing it led in the general direction of the fire.

Suddenly, out of the gloom, she spotted two mail-boxes on the side of the road.

'Yes! That's where Claire and I turned off.'

She spun the steering wheel and planted her foot. Too late, she remembered the deep gouges in the road a few hundred metres in as her little, low-bodied car fell into a huge rut. She accelerated hard, stopping as the wheels spun fruitlessly. 'Blast!' She threw open the door, grabbed her vest off the passenger seat, and ran up the track.

Coughing, she cursed the smoke and flakes of black soot that filled the air. Visibility was almost non-existent, but the grass on the roadsides had been mown. The fire hadn't yet reached here. She pulled her shirt front up and breathed through the fabric as she jogged. Every so often, she stopped and bent over, catching her breath and turning back to check if she could see anything.

It seemed like forever before she reached the wheel tracks that led into Dot's place. Now she sprinted, yelling at the top of her voice, 'Mrs Collins! Charlie!'

A bark sounded, and Lass bounded toward her then raced back to the shack.

Following hard on the dog's heels, she called again. Relief flooded her whole being as both Charlie and Dot stepped onto the veranda.

'What do you want?' Dot said.

'Fire!' Ashleigh stopped and pointed. 'Over there.'

Dot stepped away from the house and followed Ashleigh's direction. 'That's just the smoke drifting from across the valley,' she said calmly. 'It often happens when they burn off. It depends on the direction of the breeze.'

Ashleigh shook her head. 'No. You don't understand. I saw it from Featherwood Station. There's another fire on this side. One with more than just smoke.'

This time, the tiny lady's face creased even more than normal, and she wrapped an arm around Charlie. 'I can't see how ... but I'll take your word for it.' She cast a glance around her. 'As you can see, Damian keeps everything well mowed, and he's recently dozed the fire trails again. I'm sure we'll be alright.'

Desperation filled Ashleigh. She had to convince Dot it could be serious without frightening Charlie. 'You might be alright for the moment, Mrs Collins, but if that wind turns, the fire will be here in a matter of minutes. You can see for yourself how much smoke there is already. That's not what they predicted according to the information we were all given.'

As though the reality suddenly dawned on her, Dot put a hand to her mouth and her body crumpled.

Ashleigh leapt forward, catching her before she fell. 'Here, sit down for a moment while we decide what to do.'

'I'm scared, Dotty.' Charlie's whimper nearly broke Ashleigh's heart.

Having ensured Dot was sitting, she reached out an arm and enfolded the little boy against her. 'It's okay, Charlie. We need to be brave. Is there a car here? Or a truck—or anything?'

He shook his head. 'No. Dad took the ute, and we only have a tractor and the dozer.'

Ashleigh's stomach plummeted. She did not know how to drive a tractor, never mind a bulldozer. Even if she worked out how to start one of them, she'd be more likely to drive it through the shed. There was nothing else for it. 'Right, this is what we'll do. My car is stuck in a hole in the road—and we need help to get it out. So, either we find a nice, cool place somewhere by the creek or a waterhole we can get into—or ...' She cast a glance toward the wood-filled wheelbarrow standing at the end of the veranda. 'We empty that and make a little seat for Dotty, then we'll walk back to the road with me pushing the barrow and hope someone comes to look for us.'

'But how will they know there's a fire coming?' Charlie hiccupped. Ashleigh met his wide blue eyes and her heart squeezed.

She had to protect this little guy—and his elderly carer. Without realising it, the barrier she'd kept around herself for years began to crack and fall away. Perhaps trying to be as good as her sister, conforming to her parents' expectations, and fitting into a lifestyle she disliked had always been wrong. Her quick temper and dislike of the limelight had driven friends away, and now reality sank deep into her soul. It was time to let go of old habits and ways of responding to people and events. Life was important. Not only hers, but the lives of this dear little boy, his aged great-great-aunt, and their dog.

33

'We should go to the soak.'

Ashleigh startled at the thin, frail voice.

'What's a soak?'

'Tell her, Charlie.' The old lady flapped a hand toward Ashleigh.

'It's a sort of waterhole where a spring comes out of the ground. I could take you there if you like. It's got lots of moss and ferns around it and we can sit on the rocks and paddle our feet.'

Ashleigh glanced toward the woman. 'Is it far—and would we be safe there?'

Her nod was brief before her gaze went cloudy and she whispered, 'Yes. If we'd stayed there years ago, we would have both been safe.'

Ashleigh frowned, confused by Dot's response. Did

she mean she and her husband? With no time to question, she turned to the boy. 'Charlie, how about you and I grab a torch, some water, and a couple of blankets? Is there anything else we need?'

'Can I take my koala?'

'Of course. Come on. We need to hurry.'

It took only moments to collect the blankets, an enamel mug from the sink, and an insulated water bottle from the end of the bench. While Ashleigh draped the blankets around her shoulders, Charlie joined her, a threadbare toy koala tucked under his arm.

Together, they helped Dot to her feet and turned away from the house, shuffling across the mowed grass and down a gentle rise into the bush.

Dot appeared to have retreated within her battle-scarred shell—or was she always like that? Ashleigh suspected not from the way Charlie had talked about her at school. Desperate to keep them moving but calm, Ashleigh urged her charges along. Charlie led the way while Ashleigh had her arm around the old lady, supporting her frail body. Although slight, Ashleigh staggered under her weight, stumbling and grasping Dot tightly with one arm while grabbing branches with the other.

The wind strengthened, whipping swirls of ash, twigs, and smoke through the air in sudden bursts. Ashleigh's throat burned, her eyes streaming as they pushed through the trees until they parted, revealing what could only be described as a grotto. Not unlike the Featherwood Station falls and swimming hole, granite boulders, green with moss and dripping with rivulets of clear water, surrounded the pond. Small ferns poked out of cracks in the stone. While it was much smaller than the one Ashleigh and Claire frequented, it was large enough for the three of them to sit around the edges, huddled together in the cool dampness. Leaves rustled above them, the wind gaining strength, but the smell of smoke was less noticeable here.

They sat for more than an hour, Ashleigh checking her watch every few minutes as time seemed to stand still. With her concern growing as Dot's frailty appeared to intensify, she wrapped the blanket around the old woman.

When Dot spoke, Ashleigh had to lean toward her, straining to hear the words as boughs creaked and the wind howled.

'We should have been here when the big fire came years ago. My husband insisted we try to get to town. We had a row, and I refused to follow because I thought it was safer for us to come to the grotto. But he felt useless—claimed he needed to help the fire-fighters. He hadn't been gone long when I changed my mind and ran after him.' She stopped and her rheumy eyes gained clarity as she stared into

Ashleigh's. 'But I couldn't find him ... and the fire got me just as the men came. The worst part was never saying goodbye.' Her voice faded away as a tear slid down her cheek.

'Oh, God. You poor woman.' Pain constricted Ashleigh's whole being—as if she was amongst the flames. 'You must have been terrified.'

'It was strange. I wasn't scared by then. I thought it was God's will. My time was up.' Her eyes roved over Charlie, and a small smile crept into her misshapen mouth. 'But God must have had other ideas ... and now I have Damian and Charlie.'

Biting back her own tears, Ashleigh could barely breathe.

Charlie jumped to his feet, turning his head to face the path to the house. 'Dad!' Charlie's shriek blew away in the wind.

Ashleigh grasped his hand. 'We'll call together. It'll be louder—and you flash the torch around. If someone's looking for us, they might see the light in the smoke.'

He nodded fiercely and opened his mouth to yell.

While Ashleigh yelled, 'Here!', Charlie repeatedly shouted, 'Dad!' Even Dot seemed to rally and joined in with a rasping call.

Crashing sounds reached them, drawing closer as they kept up a constant barrage of shouts.

'We're here!' Ashleigh gave the last yell before

breaking into a coughing fit as three men charged out of the bush in front of them.

After falling on his knees beside his son, Damian cradled Charlie in his arms, his face streaked with soot and his hands and protective clothing stained black. 'Are you all okay?' He lifted his gaze to Dot and then Ashleigh.

Her chin quivered, and she clamped her lips together. 'Thank you for coming' was all she could say.

Huffing out a grunt, he shook his head slowly. 'Thank you for getting here first—and bringing Dot and Charlie to safety.' He reached out and squeezed Dot's hand. 'Are you alright, Aunty?'

The old lady lifted her head and gave him a small smile. 'I'm fine, thanks to Ashleigh. Charlie and I were inside cooking, and you know what that old stove is like sometimes—it smokes when the wind's in the wrong direction. I thought that—and you fellas burning off—was the problem. Never realised there was a fire near us ...' She pointed at Ashleigh. '... until she came.'

Uneasy at being under the spotlight and unable to meet Damian's eyes, Ashleigh focused her attention on a small frog crouched under a moist leaf.

'Thanks, Ashleigh. We owe you.'

Lifting her stare to meet his, she gave him the merest nod. *You owe me nothing. I came to check because I care about Charlie and Dot.*

They held each other's gazes for a few long moments, his green eyes deep pools of emotion in the bearded, soot-covered face. 'You're very brave. And I misjudged you. I'm sorry,' he murmured, his voice shaky with passion.

Slowly, like a butterfly emerging from a cocoon, a strange warmth rose within her. Beginning at her feet, it climbed into her chest and continued to her face, deepening the heat in her cheeks. She smiled. It was the first time since before her grandmother died that anyone had made her feel so important—so revered.

Their eyes met for just a moment longer. She believed him. He returned her smile, and for a minute, she thought her heart would burst.

34

'Come on.' Frank leaned toward Ashleigh, his hand extended, while Damian and the other man, who Damian had introduced as Steve, helped Dot to her feet.

Charlie clutched Ashleigh's spare hand, and he and Frank hauled her up.

She glanced down, wondering why her legs refused to move. Her energy was gone. Completely shattered, she stared at Frank.

He wrapped an arm around her, his face soft. 'It's alright. You're suffering shock and that's to be expected.' He hugged her to his skinny, aged body. 'We'll look after you—and Damian's not the only one who's proud. Lola got me on the two-way. Lucky, because we'd just returned to the truck to move to the next section. Anyway, she said you were coming here to check on Dot and Charlie and that you were in your own car.'

'I couldn't get it up the road.' Even her voice had lost its strength.

Frank chuckled. 'We could see that. Don't worry. We'll give her a tow and you'll be back in business. For now, though, we're taking you all to the school. There's a few locals there setting up food and drinks, and a couple of the women are nurses, so you'll be in expert hands.'

As she leaned on Frank, her strength returned slowly. By the time they got back to the shack, she breathed a sigh of relief despite her mind being filled with a dozen questions. 'Where is the fire? Is it under control? How would it have started?'

Damian lowered his aunt onto the veranda chair before answering. 'When we came here, two of the other trucks headed up the back road to deal with it. I guess we'll know more when we get to town, but I reckon they would have located it by now and have probably called for backup if they need it.'

Refusing to come to town with them, it took a few minutes for Damian to settle Dot on the couch inside her house, make her a cup of tea, and promise to return as soon as possible. Then he picked up Charlie and carried him to his ute.

Frank and Steve helped Ashleigh into the fire truck, and they drove back to the village.

'I really need to get to Featherwood Station,' she said. 'I'm looking after the animals while they're in Brisbane for the weekend.'

'Don't you worry, love.' Frank squeezed her hand. 'We'll get you checked over at the school, then I'll run you there myself. Damian and I can go and get your car out and deliver it to you.'

Before they reached the town, the two-way crackled and Ashleigh jumped at the sound of Damian's voice.

'Thought I'd let you know the guys used one of the bush tracks to create a backburn. The fire has now burnt itself out, but they'll hang around to mop up any spot fires. We got to it just in time. Dot's house is safe and so is Ashleigh's car.'

Frank snatched up the handpiece with a smile. 'Good to hear. Thanks, mate.'

'Don't thank me. Thank Ashleigh. See you soon.'

Ashleigh's lungs expanded as she drew herself up and released a long, shaky breath.

AN HOUR LATER, sustained by a cup of tea and a sandwich, Ashleigh shot Maria a grateful smile. Despite the older woman having portrayed a stern and private, almost secretive front for the entire first term, Maria's warm and caring attention astounded

Ashleigh, triggering an unfamiliar prickle in her eyes. After receiving a final hug from Maria, Ashleigh received the all-clear to return to Featherwood Station from an efficient, friendly nurse, who Ashleigh vaguely recognised from one of the tennis afternoons.

With her energy partially restored, Ashleigh searched for Damian amongst the growing crowd. It appeared the community's appreciation for keeping their district safe included a social gathering of massive proportions—especially with an unexpected emergency added to the mix. Having pushed the morning's discovery at Glenrowan to the back of her mind, she was desperate to share the information— and photos—with Damian. Of course, Rhys should be the first to know, but that was out of the question until he returned later that evening. Until then, Damian would be the one person who would understand.

Despite several children running around, Ashleigh couldn't spot either Charlie or his father. Perhaps they'd already returned to Dot. Her shoulders slumped and her heart felt heavy.

Frank appeared beside her. 'Ready? Come on. I'll run you up to the station so you can be there when Ginny, Claire, and the fellas get home.'

'Thanks, Frank.' She dragged her exhausted body to standing and took one last look around in the hope that Damian would walk through the door. He didn't, and she trudged silently behind Frank to the car park.

As they approached the homestead, she cast her gaze wide, relieved much of the smoke had subsided, leaving only blackened portions of bushland and a heavy haze hanging over the valley. 'It's so sad, isn't it? All those birds and koalas ... and everything else. They must be terrified when they smell smoke.'

'You're not wrong, love. I'm sure they are. But that's why it's so important we care for the bush. Why we have to conduct these slow burns. After all, it's what our indigenous ancestors have done for thousands of years.' Frank paused for a moment, his eyes narrowing. 'I'll be interested to hear what the firies have to say about how this one started. It's not as though we've had any electrical storms—and the roads and tracks over this side of the village are not busy. Only locals, mostly.' He screwed up his face as though contemplating, and Ashleigh hesitated for a bare second before beginning.

'I had an interesting morning—before I noticed the fire, that is.'

They pulled up outside the homestead gate, and Frank switched off the engine. 'Sounds like you've got something to share. Go on.'

Beginning with the birth of the puppies, she continued with her discovery of the well-lit shed the previous day and her determination to find out what was in it. When she finished, she met his astonished gaze.

'Good grief. Don't tell me Donald's gone and employed another bloody idiot. Worse than useless by the sound of things. This pair sound downright evil.' He paused, chewing his lip for a moment. 'Which way did they go when they left?'

She shook her head. 'I don't really know because of the dust. But it seemed weird they didn't go back to the Glenrowan house via the farm track.'

He nodded. 'It does. Unless ... I wonder if they banned the shed from the other staff.'

Staring at him blankly, she shrugged.

'Perhaps the workers have been told to spend their time in and around the vegetable paddocks and the hothouses—and not wander around the farm,' he mused.

'Yesterday I saw a few people working around those tunnels. They were loading or unloading wooden crates being towed by a red tractor.'

'Hmm. Well, thanks for sharing that with me, Ashleigh. I reckon when Rhys gets home, he'll be interested in hearing what you've got to say—and inspecting those photos.' He glanced at his watch. 'Geez. It's after five already. I'd better get back to Lola. She'll be wondering what the hell has been happening.'

Ashleigh slipped out of the car and closed the door.

Leaning against the open window, she shot the old man a smile. 'Thank you for everything, Frank.'

He grinned, lifted a forefinger from the steering wheel in acknowledgement, and drove away.

BEFORE SHE HEADED INSIDE, Ashleigh wandered to the kennels to check on the puppies. After letting all the dogs out, she smiled as Chime trotted a few metres away, glanced back at her as if to say, "You're in charge", and then continued to sniff the ground.

Ashleigh crawled into the pen and lifted the pups onto her lap. They wriggled and squirmed before settling themselves in a heap on her legs. The smallest of them, a black female, snuggled against Ashleigh's tummy and she stroked it softly with one finger.

A dog barked suddenly, quickly joined by the others as they rushed toward the house gate.

Ashleigh hadn't heard the car arrive. She quickly placed the puppies back in their bed and followed Chime, the last to reach her beloved owner.

'Hi, Ash.' Claire waved as she called out. 'We're home.'

Ashleigh's legs almost buckled with relief.

Within seconds, they enveloped her in a hug, first Claire and then Ginny.

'How's the midwife?' Ginny asked. 'I'm dying to see

them.' She stepped back and studied Ashleigh's dishevelled hair and dirty clothes. 'You look as though you've been through the bush in a hurry.'

A small grin touched Ashleigh's mouth and she raised her eyebrows. 'Something like that. I'll tell you all about it after you've seen the pups.'

Ginny's eyes narrowed but she said nothing as Claire grabbed her arm. 'Come on.'

'We'll unpack the car while you girls check out the new arrivals,' Kirk said.

Retreating to the kennels, Claire scrunched up her skirt in one hand and crawled into the pen. Then she passed each pup out to her mother and Ashleigh before extracting herself and holding a tiny, auburn-coloured pup against her cheek. 'Look, this little fellow is the same colour as your hair, Ash.' She laughed. 'Perhaps you should have one of these to keep.'

Ashleigh's heart leaped. She would love nothing more—and if she had to choose, it would be the smallest black girl, the one who had snuggled up to her only minutes earlier.

What was she thinking?

She was living in a tiny house in the schoolyard's corner. Her contract ended in December, and she had no idea what the following year would bring. Not only that, but she was also at work all day, and even she knew how much care and attention a young dog needed, especially a kelpie.

She smiled and said nothing.

After a thorough inspection of each pup, they returned all dogs to their kennels, and the women ambled toward the homestead.

Shadows filled the yard as the sun sank behind the hills and a misty haze hovered in the valley.

Ashleigh trekked up the steps beside Ginny, smiling wanly at the older woman's concerned frown. She had so much to tell them and yet, after her friend's excitement at greeting the new offspring, she wasn't sure where or how to begin.

35

'Sit down while Claire and I grab us all some cold drinks and nibbles.' Ginny faced Ashleigh with a soft, caring smile.

Kirk passed a beer to Rhys and turned to Ashleigh. 'Been an exciting weekend for you by the look of things?' His statement was more of a question as he waved toward the patches of blackened bushland with narrowed eyes. 'They weren't supposed to burn this side of the valley.'

'They didn't,' she began. 'At least not deliberately. Frank said they're investigating how it started because it certainly wasn't the burn-off crew.'

Both men looked at her, their frowns deepening as though suddenly noticing her filthy clothing and tired, hollow eyes.

Kirk sat next to her on the veranda as the women

appeared carrying a tray each—one loaded with glasses, a jug of lemon squash, and a bottle of wine, and the other a variety of small dishes filled with cheese, crackers, and other snacks. He waited until she had drunk half a glass of squash before he spoke. 'Tell us what's happened, Ashleigh?'

She drew a deep, quavering breath and began. 'I-it's not only the fire. That was awful enough. But ...' Her eyes met Rhys's. '... there's something bad going on at Glenrowan.'

Ginny groaned, and Rhys pulled his seat closer to her, his face taut with concern.

It was as though even the air stood still, so quiet was her audience. Without interruption, Ashleigh regaled the events of her trip to Glenrowan, ending with an exhausted shudder.

Ginny stepped forward and wrapped Ashleigh in a hug. Claire stared at her friend with her palms against her cheeks and a look of horror on her face.

Rhys pulled his phone out of his pocket, holding it for a moment while he spoke directly to Ashleigh. 'I need to ring James Avery. He's the local detective who's given us a lot of help over the past couple of years. Are you okay with that?'

'You don't think it could wait until tomorrow, Rhys?' Ginny asked.

Rhys glanced briefly at Ginny before returning his attention to Ashleigh. 'I know how tired you must be,

Ash. It's your call, but I think the sooner this gets reported, the better.'

She nodded earnestly. 'Absolutely. I don't think I'd be able to sleep anyway until I know something is being done.'

Ginny grasped her arm and removed the empty glass from her hand. 'Come on, my girl. What you need is a nice soak in a warm bath while Rhys takes things to the next level and Claire and I rattle up some dinner for us all.'

Ashleigh opened her mouth to object, but Ginny held her palm up. 'No more talk now. You're staying the night so we can look after you and I won't take no for an answer.'

Ashleigh smiled weakly and allowed herself to be thrust gently into the bathroom. The door closed behind her.

An hour later, the five of them sat around the table with, except for a few stray grains of rice, empty plates —evidence of a much-appreciated meal.

Her leisurely bath had revived Ashleigh and a thread of invisible steel seemed to have grown within her, enhancing her determination to share everything she had seen while it was fresh in her memory. James Avery was on his way to the property after his conversation with Rhys, and they expected him to arrive around eight.

The telephone rang, and Claire sprang to answer it.

'Hello.' She nodded and handed the receiver to Rhys. 'It's for you.'

Rhys pushed his chair back, took the handpiece from Claire, and retreated to the veranda. 'Senior Constable Rhys Morton.'

The others glanced at each other as he closed the door behind him, his voice fading. Claire rose to her feet and gathered the empty plates, the clattering a welcome distraction for Ashleigh.

'Tea? Coffee?' Claire asked.

'I think I'll have a coffee. Thanks, love. Not sure how long we'll need to stay awake tonight,' Ginny answered with a twist of her mouth.

'Yeah. Same for me, please, Claire,' Kirk said.

Claire looked at Ashleigh, her eyebrows raised in question.

'Camomile tea, please. The last thing I need is more stimulation.' They all shared Ashleigh's grin.

Rhys returned to the room as Claire was distributing the hot drinks and he reached for the mug of steaming coffee she handed him.

'That was Rob, the chief fire officer,' he murmured as though he did not believe what he was about to share. 'He and a couple of other fellas are still up in the bush, ensuring there are no sparks or hot spots ... and they've found some wire cage traps in what used to be a dense patch of eucalypts. Some trees have nest holes in the branches.' His gaze rested on Ashleigh. 'Looks like you're right. Someone's been trapping wildlife and, due to the number of cigarette butts strewn around in the dirt, I've a pretty good idea who it could be.'

'Geez, if it is the Dawsons, that's the third bad egg on Glenrowan. The place must be jinxed!' Kirk shook his head in disbelief.

'It doesn't exactly look great for my so-called brother-in-law either, does it?' Ginny folded her arms across her chest as she almost spat the words.

Ashleigh stared at Ginny, incredulous. 'Do you think he could be involved?'

'Huh. I wouldn't put it past him. But ... as we know, he's pretty good at keeping his nose clean and having others do the dirty work for him. We'll just have to see what James and Rhys come up with, I suppose.'

Car headlights shone through the kitchen window, and Rhys took a slug of his coffee before getting to his feet again. 'That'll be James.'

THE CLOCK STRUCK ten-thirty before James brought the discussion to an end and turned to Ashleigh. 'So, to summarise—I'll be back in the morning with a team and a search warrant. We'll split into groups and thoroughly search the entire property.'

'What if the Dawsons refuse to let you into the shed?' Ashleigh asked.

James grinned. 'We'll be equipped. Don't worry. A heavy-duty bolt cutter will solve that problem—if it arises.'

An icy shiver ran up Ashleigh's back. The following day was to be pupil-free for the staff to meet and collaborate for the upcoming term. But the anticipation of what the police may discover sent her nerves into a fizz, and she doubted she'd be able to concentrate.

Claire lay a hand on her arm and as though having read Ashleigh's mind. 'Don't worry, Ash. I'm sure Rhys will keep us informed—this isn't the first time we've been through something like this,' she finished with a wry grin as she met Rhys's gaze.

SLEEP CAME QUICKLY and more soundly than Ashleigh had expected, and she woke shocked and confused at the sound of her tuneful alarm.

After glancing at her watch, she threw back the doona and planted her feet on the cool, polished floor. *Cripes. It's six-thirty already.*

Sounds echoed along the hallway from the kitchen. After hurriedly dressing, she tidied her bed and brushed her hair, working a dollop of product through it before twisting the thick locks into a bun and pinning it to the top of her head. Then she shoved her belongings into her bag and hurried out to greet Ginny and Kirk, who were sitting at the table, sipping coffee.

'Morning, Ash. I've made a pot of tea—or I can make you a coffee?'

Ashleigh returned Ginny's serene smile. 'Thanks, Ginny. Claire still sleeping?'

'No. She's gone to check on Chime and the pups. She won't be long though if you can spare half an hour? I think she wants to show you the dress she bought for the engagement party.'

'Oh, of course.' With the excitement and exhaustion of the previous day, she had completely forgotten to ask Claire about it. She turned her gaze to the cat on the couch as her chest tightened. *How selfish of me. Poor Claire probably thinks I'm not interested.*

After dropping her bag near the veranda door, she retreated to the kitchen, took a mug from the cupboard shelf, and poured herself a cup of tea from the pot encased in a hand-knitted cosy.

'Do you feel like bacon and eggs for breakfast?' Ginny asked.

Ashleigh shook her head as her stomach roiled. 'Thank you, but no. I'm not hungry. I'll grab a piece of toast when I get home.' Wide awake now, her mind insisted on replaying the previous day's events. The smell of smoke still tickled her nose and the expression on Dot's face when she'd realised the severity of the fire returned to haunt her.

'Are you sure?' Ginny's forehead wore a frown, and Ashleigh touched the woman's shoulder.

'Thanks, Ginny. By lunchtime I'll probably be ravenous, but at the moment, I'm really not hungry. Maria will undoubtedly bring some of her home baking to share for morning tea, too, and I don't need two breakfasts.' Desperate to change the subject, she asked, 'How was the weekend in Brisbane? Did you go somewhere nice for dinner?'

'Oh yes, we wandered along the river and over the bridge to Southbank. There was no end of choices of places to eat and it was so warm, we sat outside a gorgeous Asian restaurant and watched the world go by while we ate.'

'Great. What about the stuff Claire wanted for the party?'

Ginny gave a dismissive flap of her hand. 'Oh that. We charged around that massive shop like a pair of vultures and came out with a full trolley-load.' She tipped her head back and laughed. 'You know Claire. She did all the research before we left and knew exactly what she needed and where we had to go.' She inclined her head toward Kirk. 'The fellas weren't interested, so they spent the time in the sports store next door.'

Before she could say any more, Claire opened the door, rubbing her hands together as she kicked it shut behind her. 'Brrr. It's nippy out there this morning.

Winter's not far away.' She smiled at them all. 'Morning, Ash. How did you sleep?'

'Like a log.' She raised one eyebrow. 'I didn't expect to, but I guess I must have been more tired than I thought.'

'Ash is waiting to see your dress, Claire.' Ginny got up from the table and crossed into the kitchen. 'I'll pour your tea while you show her.'

'Thanks, Mum.' She swung her arm in an arc toward the bedrooms. 'C'mon, Ash. You've got lots to see.'

Ashleigh gazed enviously at the silky, lilac sheath dress hanging from the wardrobe door. She reached for it and ran her hand over the soft fabric. On Claire's thin, muscly body, the style would accentuate every curve—in a good way. 'Wow. That's gorgeous,' she breathed. 'It's so simple and yet I bet it looks stunning on.'

'Yeah. Looks pretty good. Rhys hasn't seen it yet—but I reckon he'll approve.'

Ashleigh grunted. 'Huh! Of course he will. He won't be able to keep his eyes off you.'

As she studied the gown, a tiny smile hovered on Ashleigh's mouth. Confidence surged inside her. Claire would love the dress Ashleigh planned to wear.

Claire tipped a bag of decorations and boxes of fairy lights onto the bed. 'These are just what I was looking for. I reckon they'll brighten up the woolshed nicely.'

They sifted through them for a few minutes as Claire explained where she planned to use each item.

Ashleigh glanced at her watch. 'Sorry, Claire. I've got to go.' She gave her friend a hug. 'Let me know what happens next door, yeah?'

'Of course.' Claire squeezed her tight. 'Thanks to you, I hope these evil thieves will get their come-uppance.'

As they wandered out to the yard together, Ashleigh stopped suddenly. 'Oh, I forgot. I haven't got my car. Frank and Damian were going to deliver to me. They must have dropped it at school?'

'No worries. Hang on a tick and I'll grab my keys and drive you home.'

While she waited, her thoughts returned to Claire's comment about the thieves.

I hope for the animals, and for Charlie's sake, justice will be done.

36

The week seemed to progress ridiculously slowly. She and Claire texted back and forth several times, but even Claire hadn't heard a word—except to confirm they'd watched the police crawling all over Glenrowan for the past couple of days. While Ashleigh waited to hear more, her concentration vanished while she relived every minute of the previous weekend. Was that the effect delayed shock had on a person? Or was it because of the realisation she had become an integral part of the community—a completely new experience for her. She suspected the latter.

She reached into her pocket and withdrew the thank-you note she had found pinned under the windscreen wiper of her car when she returned on Monday morning. She studied it again, not recognising the writing. It had to be from either Frank or Damian as they were the ones who had rescued her car, and the words "Thanks will never be enough. Take care" matched Damian's circumstances more than Frank's. Certain he had written it, a warm glow burned within her. When would she see him again? How had he turned her from a responsible teacher into a blithering, lovesick teenager? Her eyes widened.

Oh my God. Is that it—love?

As THE SCHOOL day finished on Wednesday afternoon, Ashleigh was returning to her little house when her phone rang, distracting her from the jumble of emotions doing acrobatics inside her.

'Hi, Ash. Rhys here.'

'Hey. What's happening?'

He chortled. 'I thought you might be wondering. Have you got a spare ten minutes?'

'Absolutely.' She plonked herself on the step, her phone pressed hard against her ear as though to avoid a single word escaping her hearing.

'You were right—on every level. For a start, a search of the poly tunnels and staff accommodation confirmed there was no evidence of drugs or anything illegal—except for a couple of workers who had a bit of weed for personal use. That's a separate issue and is being taken care of.' He paused and Ashleigh waited. 'With the birds and animals, though, it turns out the Dawsons were working for a smuggling syndicate, which is now being investigated by the Federal Police. They'd stacked their car and the area under their caravan with traps and cages of all types—under covers, of course, and which have now been confiscated. Biosecurity and the RSPCA are also involved.'

'And the Dawsons?' she butted in. 'Where are they?'

'Oh, don't worry. It took a while, but eventually Eileen Dawson came clean.' He chuckled. 'Seems her heart wasn't really in it, and I don't think the marriage will be the everlasting type after this. She revealed where they'd trapped the animals and birds, so we've now conducted a thorough search, as some of her explanations were hazy. The fauna found in the shed is being checked and cared for before being released, and Damian and the rest of the emergency services team are helping us comb the area for traps or evidence of poaches. To be certain, we'll need a few more days. Probably wind it up after the weekend. In the meantime, we have charged the Dawsons with trespassing on private property, removal of protected fauna without licence, trafficking in protected fauna ... and potentially, there will be other charges as the Federal Police investigate the smuggling syndicate. They were refused bail while the investigation continues.'

Ashleigh released a long sigh. 'That's such a relief, Rhys.' She huffed a quiet chuckle. 'I've been so worried about being accused of interfering or trespassing myself ... but I'm glad they have found the real culprits.'

'Yeah. Me too. With our party happening in ten days' time, I didn't want all this hanging over the community.'

Ashleigh straightened and smiled. 'It'll be the perfect event to help us all put the drama behind us.'

'Sure will. I'll keep you posted.'

'Thanks, Rhys. Oh, and congratulations.'

'What for? If it hadn't been for young Charlie's knowledge of bush law and his trust in you to follow up his concerns, who knows where this would have ended. Not to mention the fire, of course. All I've done is my job. You're the brave one. That fire could have been catastrophic if the wind had changed. There's a lot of people who've got you to thank, not only Dot and Charlie.'

'That's kind of you, Rhys—but it really was a community effort.' She pressed her lips together as a wave of emotion engulfed her.

'Okay. Thanks again, anyway. Talk soon.' And he hung up.

Ashleigh dropped the phone in her lap and wrapped her arms around her knees. A bee flew past, resting briefly on the bright purple flowers of the duranta shrub nearby. She studied it for a moment, admiring its dedication. *I suppose we're the same, really. Most of us, anyway, want the best for those we love—and for all those creatures who deserve a good life.* A sudden gust of wind whipped around the side of her house, and she shivered, rose to her feet, and stepped inside.

DAMIAN SLUNG his pack on his back and trudged along the track amongst the trees. The grass-flattened trail was dotted with wallaby scat, evidence of the area's primary inhabitants. Above him, a pair of eastern rosellas shrieked, and he smiled.

'You're the lucky ones!' he called. 'Hopefully, you'll get your mates back soon.'

His shoulders ached with the weight of the timber and wire traps tied to his pack, but he ignored the pain and whistled softly as he trod along the fire trail. It had been an exhausting week, but a highly successful one. With the revelation from Eileen Dawson, he and his crew had located and removed more than twenty traps of all shapes and sizes. They had found only two with life inside—one, a beautiful blue tongue lizard and the other a black satin bower bird whose inquisitive nature appeared to have succumbed to the piece of blue tape fixed to the inside. He had released both, biting back the anger and gut-wrenching frustration that welled inside him at the thoughtless, greedy actions of the poachers.

But deeper still, a euphoria intensified as a vision of Charlie's worried face flashed across his mind. Damian's concern about Charlie fitting in at school, the boy's passionate devotion to wildlife and preference for the company of creatures over other children, had been for nothing. Since Charlie had revealed his worries to Ashleigh, and she had discussed the matter with Damian, her subsequent persistence had proved Charlie had been right all along. There had been changes occurring in the bush and it had taken a five-year-old to point them out. Damian's chest swelled with pride. Every person who had crossed his path since the vile discovery at Glenrowan had commended Damian on Charlie's ability to observe and *understand* nature to such a high degree.

His mouth twisted as he recalled the morning's conversation. Both Charlie and Ashleigh had risen in popularity with all and sundry in the little town, and he understood why. Now the fires had been doused and the Glenrowan excitement had died down, the upcoming engagement party at Featherwood Station woolshed was the most talked about event on the local calendar. Apparently, everyone at school was attending and for the first time in his life, Charlie had pleaded with his father to go. They both knew that Dot wouldn't join in. A thorough description of the event afterwards would be more than enough for her. But, for Charlie, Damian had simply replied, 'We'll see.'

Charlie's request had surprised him. Parties and crowded gatherings had never been his or Charlie's forte. Damian sensed a change—and not only in Charlie. His breath hitched as he pictured Claire and Rhys celebrating their joyful occasion, surrounded by family and friends, and Ashleigh hovering nearby in a pretty dress, perhaps with her hair loose and curly, cascading down her back. Should they go? Could he refuse Charlie's pleas and continue their reclusive lifestyle? He shook his head and drew a deep breath. Of course they would attend—and although he wouldn't admit it to Charlie, deep down he looked forward to seeing Ashleigh again.

Returning to Featherwood Falls had been the best decision he'd ever made, and it was time to put the past behind him and make a better life for them all. Humming to himself, he adjusted the load on his back, lengthened his stride, and grinned as he headed for home.

37

*A*shleigh stood by the fence, her face bathed in rapturous delight. Who could believe that only hours ago this building had clearly been a woolshed? With the doors flung wide, it twinkled with hundreds of lights. Tubs of flowers lined the entrance ramp, and excited locals packed the surrounding grassed areas. Music floated from inside, mixing with the babble of conversation.

'What do you think?' Claire stood at her elbow and handed her a glass of fruit punch.

'You guys certainly don't do things by halves, do you?' Ashleigh laughed, her attention caught momentarily by the Marsh family tumbling out of a dirt-covered four-wheel drive nearby.

Jessie came running toward her, barely recognisable in a pale-pink dress with a multi-layered tulle skirt and her hair tied in a wide ribbon on the top of her head. 'Ms Ashleigh. Do you like my dress?'

Ashleigh squatted and met the child eye-to-eye. 'I think you look like a princess.'

Jessie beamed. 'That's what my dad said.' Then she ran off to join a group of children swinging on the gate.

Ashleigh took a mouthful of punch and turned back to Claire. 'You look absolutely gorgeous.'

'So do you. Isn't Lola clever?'

Ashleigh glanced down at the soft chiffon dress. It was one her mother had bought for Ashleigh to wear to a family wedding the previous year. Only they had cancelled the wedding because of covid and the couple opted to have a small ceremony regardless—without guests. After receiving the dress in the post from Netty, she had tried it on, forgetting that due to her weight loss the pleated bodice and flowing skirt designed to hide her curves would hang on her like an old-fash-ioned nightgown.

After throwing it on the bed in despair and heading to the store for a cup of Lola's best coffee to cheer herself up, disappointment had remained.

'What's up, love. That's a face of distress you're wearing,' Lola had said.

Ashleigh had poured out her sorrows—not only about the ill-fitting dress, but of her historic inability to find suitable outfits for almost every occasion she'd attended. 'I guess I'm just a hopeless shopper with a hard-to-fit body—unless it's hideously expensive, or shirts and jeans,' she'd finished despondently.

'Rubbish.'

Ashleigh had blinked at Lola's sharp retort. 'Go home and get that dress. We'll see what we can do.'

She had ... and Lola's skilled sewing ability had, over three evenings, transformed the deep, plum-coloured fabric into a fitted bodice that flowed into a soft chiffon skirt, enhancing Ashleigh's toned curves. A pair of high-heeled but comfortable nude sandals boosted her height enough to confirm she was no longer a self-conscious teen pretending to be an adult, or the frumpy schoolteacher.

Tonight she felt beautiful.

'Come and see the cake—and meet Briony.' Claire's eyes sparkled as she spoke her sister's name. She turned and strode toward the shed, with Ashleigh trotting after her in the unfamiliar shoes.

A pretty, younger version of Ginny stood talking to a group from the tennis club, and she turned, her face lighting up as Claire and Ashleigh approached.

Where Claire was tall and thin, Ashleigh was delighted to note Briony was close to her own height and shape. She met her smile before being enveloped in a wild hug.

'Ashleigh! It's so good to meet you at last.'

Taking a step back in surprise, heat rose up

Ashleigh's neck. She hadn't expected such an effervescent greeting.

'I forgot to tell you about Briony,' Claire said. 'She's
the extravert in our family—and no doubt will be the
self-appointed MC for the evening.'

They laughed as the local women encompassed
Ashleigh effortlessly in the fold. After hearing Briony's
plans to return home to Featherwood Falls and help on
the farm while she waited for her boyfriend, Alex, to
arrive from Scotland, Claire excused herself and the
group broke up to wander toward other guests.
Ashleigh leaned against the yard railing, soaking up
the atmosphere, so different to anything she had ever
attended in her life before.

Evening sunset spread across the valley, the
shadows growing as the sky deepened from orange to
pink and then to a rich mix of lavender and purple.
Twinkling lights glowed brightly as the music grew
louder and guests drifted inside to dance.

Sensing a presence behind her, Ashleigh turned to
meet the youthful face of a man who could have been
mistaken for Claire's twin brother.

'Gidday.' He reached out a thin, bony hand and
squeezed Ashleigh's fingers gently. 'I'm Andrew, Briony
and Claire's cousin. Heard a lot about you.'

She returned his friendly smile while her mind
raced. *Donald's son?* A vision of the obnoxious, overweight man flashed through her head, and she fought

to keep her surprise in check. Bearing no resemblance to his father, Ashleigh acknowledged the genes must have been strong for him and Claire to appear so alike.

She raised an eyebrow. 'At least my reputation hasn't scared you off.'

He laughed. 'Not at all. Quite the contrary.'

A few awkward seconds ticked by before she asked, 'Are you on university holidays? I heard you were studying Ag Science or something like that.'

'Yeah. Agronomy. Vegetable growing, in particular.' He laughed again before adding, 'I'm a pea and bean man.'

Ashleigh grinned while he continued.

'I've only got a couple of subjects to go and ...' He waved an arm toward Glenrowan. '... it looks like I might move in next door to sort out the mess and give the poor workers a bit more support than they've had in the last few months.' He grunted, the corners of his mouth downturned. 'My stupid father couldn't run a chook raffle. He thinks he knows it all, but he's delusional.'

Frowning at his sudden outburst, Ashleigh hesitated before speaking. 'Do you want to move in next door? I've heard it's pretty rough and the house needs some work.'

He shrugged. 'Three of the workers have been living there and have kept it cleaner than it was when they moved in. Ginny said I can live here on Featherwood Station if I want to, and I reckon I'll take her up on the offer. Dad can do what he likes, but I don't think even Nigel will want him hanging around after his last choice of supervisors.'

'Are your parents here?'

'Nah. Away on a cruise.' He snorted. 'Perfect timing, huh? Conveniently absent when the cops want to interview him.'

Unable to keep the shock from her face, Ashleigh stuttered, 'D-Do you think your father knew? About the smuggling, I mean.'

He lifted a shoulder and dropped it again with a huff. 'Dunno. I'd like to think not ... but Dad's always tried to have one over everyone else—and mostly failed. Doesn't seem to stop him, though. I'm embarrassed to be his son, but I have to keep my nose clean and try to rectify any damage he's allowed to happen.'

A wave of pity engulfed Ashleigh. Although her own circumstances had been different, she understood how hard it must be for a son to cover for a parent. If she'd felt the spotlight on her over the years, she could only imagine what Andrew had been going through— and would continue to, it seemed.

They chatted for a few minutes before he waved a hand toward Kirk in the distance. 'See ya later. I promised Kirk I'd give him a hand with the spit roasts. I reckon most fellas around here would be sick of dealing with anything hot after all the bushfire trouble!' He chuckled and sloped off with the easy gait of youth.

Ashleigh scanned the increasing crowd. No sign of Damian or Charlie. She wasn't sure if she was relieved or disappointed. Allowing a small sigh to escape, she cast a last glance around and walked up the woolshed ramp.

At one end, food weighted down trestle tables while at the other a DJ was flipping buttons on a complicated-looking machine and leaning forward into the loud-speaker every few minutes to announce the next bracket of songs. In the corner nearest the back door, a queue had formed at the bar, briskly operated by a couple in white shirts and black vests—the friends Rhys had known since childhood who had willingly agreed to help.

Quinn and Joanne arrived, a peacock blue scarf around Joanne's head that matched her top and hid her baldness. Behind their bright, smiling faces, the stout figure of Maria, her arm hooked firmly into that of an equally stocky, kind-faced gentleman, entered the shed. Emma was close behind them. Emma caught Ashleigh's gaze and gave her a wave. Her neat school polo shirt had been replaced by an even neater white blouse and navy skirt and her usual low-heeled brogues for a pair of court shoes with just enough heel to be smart but practical.

They drew closer and Quinn called out, beckoning

to her with a wide smile lighting up his face. 'Hey, Ash!'

She grinned and wove her way through the crowd to greet them.

'I've got good news,' he said, grasping her elbow and steering her away from the music. 'I wanted you to know we've got two new families joining our community. I got a call yesterday afternoon from one of them. Apparently that big dairy farm on the road to town has been sold and two brothers and their families are moving in. And get this—they have seven children between them, all primary school age or younger!'

Ashleigh's smile wobbled. Did that mean what she hoped it might? More children for the school ... and younger ones coming on when the older children move to high school? 'Umm. Sounds good—I think?'

'It certainly does. It means a permanent second teacher is likely to be appointed—and that means you!'

'Oh!' The flutter of excitement grew in her belly. 'Really? You mean, I'll be staying here? I won't have to leave at the end of my contract?'

Quinn guffawed. 'Of course not, silly. Can't you see how much everyone loves you? Not only that, but you're also a brilliant teacher and you've fitted into the community so well. At the very worst, the department will be renewing your contract—this time for at least two years—if you want it, of course?'

She pressed her palms together as happiness bubbled through her. Suppressing an urge to leap up and down on the spot, she breathed, 'Of course I do. I can't think of anywhere else I'd rather be.'

'Great. Well then, let's make tonight one to celebrate—not only Claire and Rhys's engagement, but Joanne's positive report from the doctors and your opportunity to stay here for the foreseeable future.'

She beamed at him and nodded.

'Ms Ashleigh!' Jessie called from the group of children dancing wildly nearby. 'Come and dance with us?'

'Looks like I'm needed.' She shot Quinn a wry grin and stepped toward the cluster of writhing young bodies.

---

*a*fter dancing with her students for the next twenty minutes, she breathed a sigh of relief when the music stopped. Briony stood on a wooden box beside the DJ, overlooking the crowd, clearly preparing to make a speech. Ashleigh drifted toward the shed wall, raised her head to listen to Briony, and stared straight into Damian's gaze as he and Charlie entered the woolshed.

Heat burned through her.

Barely registering Briony's words, she clapped when those around her did. Claire and Rhys joined Briony together with Ginny and Kirk and, while cameras and smart phones clicked madly around her, she remained oblivious, a small smile fixed rigidly to her face.

They cut the engagement cake before announcing

dinner and, with a wave of enthusiasm, the crowd moved toward the trestle tables.

For the next hour, Ashleigh allowed her mind to drift as she picked at the food. Diversions by parents needing reassurance about their precious offspring, fellow tennis players, and a steady stream of locals who had suddenly developed an urge to encompass her as their friend filled the time—but not her thoughts. With a burning desire to turn and follow Damian's every move, she pinned a smile on her face and attempted to focus on the current conversation.

Her stomach turned somersaults as someone thrust a piece of rich mud cake into her hand. She stared at it for a moment before meeting Ginny's questioning gaze. Pushing crumbs of cake around her plate, she broke off tiny pieces to nibble before giving up and joining the women clearing the last of the meal away. Children drifted back to their friends and the music began again.

Ashleigh's face softened as the students in her class swarmed around Charlie. He beamed with delight, following his friend's uncoordinated dancing, joining hands, and swinging around the floor, oblivious to anyone watching.

'He looks to have settled in, doesn't he?'

She jumped at the sound of Damian's voice, relieved she no longer held a plate. It most certainly would have hit the floor as she did a double take.

Wearing a crisp pale-blue shirt, cream moleskin trousers, and polished R.M. Williams boots, Damian had also trimmed his hair and beard short, appearing much younger than the dishevelled, smoke-stained man whose stress had accentuated the dust-filled creases on his face less than two weeks earlier. 'I was wondering if you would dance with me?' he asked quietly.

She stared into his anxious eyes. Except for the colour, it was the same expression she'd witnessed in Charlie's so many times. Speechless, she nodded and let him take her hand.

He turned to face her, wrapping his right arm around her waist before stepping lightly forward and whisking her into the circle of dancers. Her veins fizzed, and, as he swung her around with expert steps, she silently thanked her parents for insisting on her and Netty taking dancing lessons as teenagers. After a set of old-time favourites—the Barn Dance, Pride of Erin, Gypsy Tap—and others Ashleigh couldn't remember the names of, her legs were tired and she was laughing and breathless with exhilaration.

He led her over to the drinks table and held up two glasses. 'Wine or beer?'

She inclined her head and pointed to the punch bowl. 'I don't mind a glass of wine, but just now I think I'd like something more thirst-quenching.'

The last thing I need tonight is to make a fool of myself.

He nodded, tipped a ladle of fruit punch into a glass, and passed it to her. Then, with a beer in his hand, he raised it. 'Cheers. Let's hope the second half of this year is better than the first.'

'I agree.' Her eyes sparkled at all his words suggested. 'Is that an apology for shouting at me the day we met?'

He flashed a smile, displaying a row of straight, white teeth. 'You will not let me live that one down, will you?'

'Nope. I'll always remember it as being my first impression of Featherwood Falls. Thank heavens that's changed.'

He tilted his head to the side, his eyes questioning.

'I got some good news tonight,' she continued. 'Looks like the numbers are increasing in our school.'

She wasn't sure if she imagined it, but his eyes appeared to brighten, lingering on her for a long minute before he spoke. 'And ...?'

'I get to stay. My position has only been temporary and if the numbers reduce, I'd be the first to leave.' She grimaced. 'And that, for me, would have been gut-wrenching.'

He nodded, his expression unmoving.

She dropped her gaze, but not before she caught sight of a bright shade of pink rising up his neck.

As though reading her mind, he rubbed it

awkwardly. 'Shall we go outside and get a breath of fresh air?' he said.

'Sure.' She floated down the ramp and across the grass to lean on the top yard rail in a haze of euphoria.

Groups of people stood around talking while the music inside struck up with Tina Turner's "Nutbush City Limits". Someone whooped and a rhythmic stomping began.

Tipping her head back, she stared into the inky sky. Dotted with stars and with the broad band of Milky Way drifting into the night, she nudged Damian, pointing. 'Did you see that shooting star?'

'Yeah. I did. Dot reckons it's a sign and you're supposed to make a wish.'

'A sign of what? Travelling space junk? A plane crashing?'

He laughed, a deep, smile-provoking laugh she couldn't help but join in with.

'And ... did you make a wish?' she asked.

'I did.' He paused, his index finger held to his lips. 'And it's my secret because I want it to come true.' They stood side by side for a long minute before he spoke again. 'Charlie and Dot would like you to come to our house for dinner. To thank you—and so Dot can get to know you better.'

She turned to face him. 'Really? And you? Do you want me to join you all?'

With his gaze resting on her face, her pulse thumped.

His voice was soft, and the breeze carried away his sigh. 'I can't think of anything nicer—except a cosy dinner for two?'

She took a deep breath to settle her thumping heart. 'Is that an invitation?'

'It certainly is.' He reached for her hand, a boyish smile hovering on his lips. 'Dance?'

With her fingers resting lightly in his warm, dry grip, they wandered toward the woolshed while she continued to suck gulps of air into her lungs.

Glimpsing Claire and Rhys spinning back and forth, jiving to Adele's "Rumour Has It", the tightness in Ashleigh's chest loosened and she released a long, happy sigh.

Charlie raced over and grabbed her other hand. 'Can we dance together, Ms Ashleigh?'

She turned her gaze to meet Damian's smile before answering, 'Of course, Charlie.'

Damian bent closer to his son. 'Tell you what. Let's both dance with Ms Ashleigh.'

After scooping up Charlie, he placed his left arm around her, and the three of them clung together, giggling as they negotiated their way into the crowd.

As they spun past the window, a flash of white shot across the sky, catching a second of Ashleigh's attention. If Damian was right, two shooting stars would have to be an even better omen than one. She hoped so —and made her wish.

What a night to remember. A chance to make a permanent home in Featherwood Falls. Good friends—and maybe, just maybe, there's more to look forward to.

His breath was warm against her neck, and she tilted her head back to meet his gentle smile, certain her wish would come true.

ACKNOWLEDGMENTS

Once again, I have loved spending time in Featherwood Falls with familiar friends and scenery.

No story evolves without help from at least a few people, and I have so many to thank for their generous time, advice and support as I continue to create my stories.

To Anna and Lauren at CREATINGink, thank you both for your wonderful editing and suggestions. I truly value your expert assistance and ongoing friendship.

Patti Roberts at Paradox Book Cover Designs— thank you so much for your gorgeous covers and so much more.

Getting the information correct in any story involving crime and the law is fraught with challenges. My eternal gratitude and love goes to Roger, my husband, not only for your knowledge and advice after a long career in the Queensland Police Service, but also for your passion for and understanding of Australian native animals, reptiles, insects and bugs.

Your help has been vital in creating both this story and my character, Charlie.

To my sisters, advanced readers, and much-valued proof-readers—thank you all so much for your patience, constructive critique, and professionalism.

I hope you have enjoyed getting to know Ashleigh, Damian and of course, Charlie. Featherwood Falls is looking forward to greeting you again!

ALSO BY HEATHER REYBURN

Tullagulla Series

The Cedar Tree

The English Oak

The Pepperina Grove

A Tullagulla Christmas

Fantail Ridge Series

Peninsula Promises

The Lupin Fields

The Scent of Promise

Featherwood Falls Series

A Stranger in Featherwood Falls

Secrets in Featherwood Falls

Sparks Fly in Featherwood Falls

Clouds over Featherwood Falls

Coming Home to Featherwood Falls

A Festive Featherwood Falls

A STRANGER IN FEATHERWOOD FALLS

To lose a loved one is tragic, but to lose a lifetime of dreams? Unthinkable.

Alone on a two thousand hectare sheep and cattle property, Ginny Shepherd questions her husband's sudden death, convinced it was no accident. As a series of farm related incidents unravel, heightening her suspicions, her livelihood is put under threat. Featherwood Station is Ginny's lifeblood—her passion, her home, and her haven and she is determined it will stay that way. But it seems someone else wants the property as much as she does and will stop at nothing to get it.

When a stranger finds a forgotten token gifted to him as a child, distant memories set him on a path to pursue his grandfather's dream. But, greeted with more questions than answers, he finds life in the heart of

Queensland's Granite Belt more difficult than expected.

A smouldering attraction forms between he and Ginny, alarm bells sound and frightening events escalate. Ginny's life is in danger.

Is the stranger who he says he is? Or could it be that someone has a grudge to settle?

SECRETS IN FEATHERWOOD FALLS

A small country town. A conscientious cop. And a whole lot of secrets.

Constable Rhys Morton is new to Featherwood Falls and knows one thing for certain—he wants to remain in this village as much as he wants to remain a cop. But just as he uncovers troubling historical information, an accusation threatens his security and he must weigh up his options. Should he pursue the cold case and risk ruffling powerful feathers, or protect his future and a budding romance?

Claire Shepherd is still reeling from her father's death and when fresh heartbreak strikes, she seeks peace in the haven of Featherwood Station, her childhood home. Sparks fly between Claire and the new cop in town and she is torn between her dream of managing her father's legacy or falling for a man whose position is only temporary.

Alarm bells chime when new neighbours move in. Is this little town the sleepy hollow Rhys believed it to be? Desperate to uncover local secrets, he seeks Claire's help. After all, she knows the area and he has nothing to lose—except his heart.

Secrets is Rhys and Claire's story and the second in the Featherwood Falls series.

CLOUDS OVER FEATHERWOOD FALLS

In a town teaming with secrets, three women find themselves inexplicably entwined.

At the edge of her future, sixteen-year-old **Zoe** teeters, uncertain. The vibrant city with its dazzling lights, familiar sounds and scents, exudes adventure and a dream career. But when unexpected tragedy strikes, she is left to navigate the world on her own, gripped by loneliness and fear.

Lola is feeling the weight of her years. Despite a loving husband, a flourishing business and a circle of faithful friends, something is missing. While she pours her soul into a menagerie of sick and abandoned animals, her heart aches for the return of her only child.

At forty-two and lonely, **Emma** is free at last. Lost love and an unwavering commitment to her late mother have confined her to the quiet charm of Featherwood Falls. And while her role as teacher's aide at the local school fills her days, she longs for something to happen—something that will transform her existence and redefine her life.

Can Featherwood Falls offer the key to uniting these women? Or will a dangerous voice from the past destroy family bonds, challenging the discovery of love and hope.

Clouds over Featherwood Falls is the fourth book in this series.

ABOUT THE AUTHOR

Heather Reyburn enjoyed an idyllic childhood in beautiful New Zealand, before settling on the Darling Downs in Queensland. With a passion for nature, animals, reading and all things farm related, it wasn't long before her rural lifestyle inspired dreams of writing stories of her own. She loves happy endings, history, suspense, and characters who remain with the reader long after "The End". When not writing, Heather is often found in the garden or spending time with her husband and family.

www.ingramcontent.com/pod-product-compliance
Lightning Source LLC
Chambersburg PA
CBHW030524120726
47904CB00005B/1614